A Self-Made Monster

Steven D. Vivian

Boson Books   Raleigh

2003

Published by **Boson Books**
An imprint of **C&M Online Media, Inc**

ISBN 1-932482-02-4

Design by Once Removed

www.bosonbooks.com

For Theresa
Without Whom
Nothing

Chapter One: A Monster, Half-Made

He lit his cigarette and tossed the spent match into his mouth, as a child tosses a peanut. The sulfur tasted good, and the Dunhill was a fine chaser.

The night was cold, but he did not button his jacket. He smiled as the students walked by in groups of two or three, their breath rising like puffs of steam. He suppressed a chuckle. He imagined the kids chancing to see him pressed against the cold brick of the library. They might be startled, might even drop their books and spiral notepads. But they did not see him, crouched ten feet away behind the shrubs. They hurried to their dorms and apartments. Tonight was Friday, and the parties had already started.

Above him, the library lights were being turned off. One by one, the windows went black. He greatly enjoyed the steadiness with which the windows blackened. In a few minutes, he would walk with the same steadiness as he followed his victim. His victim would not see him standing ten feet away behind the shrubs. The victim would not hear the steps ten yards behind, then five yards, then one.

The library parking lot was normally bright, but not tonight. The maintenance crew had not yet replaced the lamps. Still, Lori was not worried. Like other Tailor coeds, she had walked hundreds of times, day and night, across campus.

She opened the car door, tossed the books into the back, and dropped into the driver's seat. The car door resisted her pull.

He gripped the top of the door. "Move over."

"Where are you taking me?" She did not recognize the gravel road and flanking cornfields. Old houses and leaning barns were bluish-black silhouettes in the moonlight.

"Do you have any cigarettes?" he asked.

"I don't smoke."

He laughed. "They're bad for you, right?"

She nodded.

"They're good for me."

After ten minutes of silence and three more old barns, she gathered the nerve to study him. "I thought you were somebody I knew—" She cursed herself. If he thinks I know him, she thought, he might kill me.

"You probably do. I'm a professor at the college."

"You didn't tell me where we were going."

The dashboard lights rendered his face a faint sea green. "I didn't tell you because we aren't going anywhere. I am going home soon. You are not." He said something more, but she did not hear him. She heard only her heart, amplified to a deafening volume.

"It's surprising," he remarked, "how quiet my victims get. Must be disbelief, yes?"

She seized the wheel and yanked. The car swerved to the right. Professor Alex Resartus yanked the wheel to the left, but too late. The car careened into the ditch. The dashboard hurtled toward Lori's face and struck her.

"You shouldn't have done that," Alex accused. "Goddammit, the noise might have startled the farmers." He rolled down the car window, heard the hissing radiator and a distant bark.

"Let go of my hand," Lori pleaded. Alex had grabbed her left wrist when Lori seized the wheel, and he would not let go.

"You're bleeding... Goddammit it you're bleeding!"

He reached into his jacket jacket as if to give Lori a tissue, but instead revealed a carving knife.

"Don't cut me, don't cut me, don't—" She jerked her arm, trying to free herself from his grip. A second jerk propelled pain through her wrist and up her arm to her shoulder. But she was free.

Lori tried to open the door. It was locked. Her now free left arm reached for the door lock, but she could not grip it.

Her hand was gone.

"You cut me, you cut me, you—"

Alex gripped her neck and yanked. The dashboard hurtled forward again, striking her over and over. Each strike left more blood on the dashboard. Between my bloody nose and bloody wrist, she thought, I won't have any blood left. She wondered if she should ask the professor to stop hitting her with the dashboard, but she did not have time. Her neck was being twisted, and now the steering wheel column hurtled toward her.

He wiped blood from the steering wheel and dashboard; he licked all the blood off the latex gloves and stuffed the gloves into his jacket. He made a quick inventory: cigarettes, matches, knife. He had everything. He had to be careful because his memory was getting worse. But tonight had been easy.

He pulled a packet of cocaine from his pocket, opened it, and spilled the powder into the back seat. A nice little red herring. He walked into the cornfield, gathered himself, and began running.

Alex got home at 11:30. He had covered five miles in thirty minutes. He tuned his radio to the all-news station. No word of a tragic accident on county road 14.

The campus would be teeming with talk of the tragedy on Monday. A few friends would feel shock and grief; most of the victim's acquaintances would feign grief and revel in the exciting mystery: why was she murdered? Who killed her? A drug dealer? A drug crazed hitch hiker? Was she raped first? The autopsy would show that the victim had not snorted cocaine, but the cocaine in the back seat would inspire various drug theories. And the students would exchange gossip and theories ceaselessly between classes, during parties, and as foreplay.

Alex stood absolutely still in the middle of his living room, his senses on high alert. No discernible change. Satisfied, he walked to the living room window and pulled back the curtain. He could still clearly see his mailbox, twenty five feet away, at the end of his driveway under a street lamp. So far, so good. The student's blood had not harmed his vision or hearing.

Alex now walked to the bathroom, where he leaned forward and studied his reflection in the vanity mirror. His eyes were still blue, and his hair still nearly black. The darker hair was a relatively new feature. One night, Alex took a long drive and discovered a subdivision under development. Only the streets, sidewalks, and basements were completed. A jogger came loping down the street. The jogger was in his mid-twenties, six foot two, with his black hair in a virile ponytail.

As the jogger approached, Alex swung open his car door, and the jogger collided with the door. Alex stepped out of the car and told the jogger to be more careful. The jogger jumped to his feet and punched Alex five times. When the jogger paused, Alex slapped him. The jogger rolled like a felled bowling pin and struck a fire hydrant.

Alex dragged the jogger behind a house, cut his throat, and filled an empty water jug. When he was done, Alex used the jogger's shirt sleeve to wipe his bloody mouth and chin. Before leaving, he stuffed a newspaper clipping into the jogger's throat wound. The clipping described the satanic ritual slayings of cows, goats, and a tax attorney in Los Angeles.

In one sense, the jogger had the last laugh. Within two hours, Alex's light brown hair had turned nearly black. Fortunately, the change occurred during summer vacation. When fall classes started, Alex explained that a newly prescribed ulcer medicine had changed his hair color.

Such superficial changes were only an irritation. The internal changes were more serious. Alex sometimes wondered if a victim had suffered from Alzheimer's. His memory and his concentration, once useful for weeks at a time, had worsened.

7

Until tonight, Alex had avoided Tailor College students. But he reasoned that college students were usually healthy, which lessened the chance of bad blood. Tonight's blood seemed fine, and he celebrated with another Dunhill.

"Did you hear about the murder?" Jimmy Stubbs filled Holly Dish's glass with more beer.

"Something about it." She took a swig and licked away the foam mustache.

"It's intense," Jimmy promised. He scooted closer to Holly on the couch and shouted over the rock music. "Her feet and hands were cut off."

Bob Beck appeared. "Pretty great party for a Sunday." Bob was the fraternity president, and he gauged his fraternity's popularity by the size and racket of its parties. Tonight, about forty students lounged in the living room, enjoying the free beer and loud music. Bob now sat next to Holly and asked about Holly's roommate.

"Kris is kind of a bitch," Holly lied.

"Living with somebody," Bob cautioned, "you always see them at their worst." Bob hoped that Kris would show up tonight, but he was not optimistic, as the time was already 10:30.

"She is too a bitch," Jimmy agreed, though he barely knew her. His declaration made Holly smile. The smile encouraged him, so he repeated himself. I'm on a roll, Jimmy thought. Jimmy resumed his gossip about the murder.

As he talked, Holly paid reasonable attention, only occasionally looking away, waving at friends, or suddenly declaring, "God, I just love this song!" After praising a group–"The Hiss is so great!" or "Five Fingers On One Head is so great!" —Holly shut her eyes and gyrated to the beat. After thirty or forty seconds of gyrating, Holly swigged some beer and nodded for Jimmy to continue with the story.

Jimmy soon ran out of information about the murder, so he told the story again, but discretely exaggerated some details for dramatic effect.

"Her head was cut off?" Holly stuck her tongue out in disgust. "What an ordeal. You know that's wild. We read a story about a guy's head getting popped off in Resartus's class."

"What, you read horror stories in there?"

"No. It's Modern British lit. The story is *The Prussian Officer*, or maybe *The Russian Officer*. Something about, uh, about Russia."

"Sounds good." Jimmy knew nothing about literature, so he did not know what else to say.

"No, it was boring. But the guy's head did pop off. I think it was symbolism, or a symbolic head." She paused, waiting for the next song.

She frowned. "That song is boring. Hey, I'm out of beer."

Jimmy refilled her glass.

"Thanks," she smiled.

She smiled at me! Jimmy realized. And he felt that awkward lust, his penis swelling and his palms itching. She's perfect for me, Jimmy thought. At five feet five inches, she was only five inches taller than Jimmy.

Jimmy was summoning the courage to ask Holly for a date when she whistled across the room to a friend. "See ya, Jimmy. Thanks for the beer." She rose without looking at him.

Jimmy cursed under his breath. At least she had sat with him for half an hour. Jimmy watched her disappear into a circle of students passing around a joint.

He had to spool her.

That's it, Jimmy promised himself. Tomorrow he would transfer into Holly's literature class. He would be a week behind and he hated to read, but he would be able to see Holly every Monday, Wednesday, and Friday.

Professor Alex Resartus leaned against the lectern. "I forget. What was your homework for today?"

"Nothing," a couple students said.

"Not exactly. 'Nothing' is what you got out of your homework." He snapped his fingers. "I remember. More supposedly erotic fiction from our friend D. H. Lawrence." He glanced at his notes. "Now. What do you make of the gentleman in the wheel chair?"

Jimmy hid in a back corner. He did not speak or move. He hoped that by remaining still, like a hunted deer, the professor would not call on him.

Jimmy was the second student called upon. "I'm new in the class," he complained.

"Your excuse is old." Alex resented students who showed up a week late without announcement.

"And your name is Mr...?"

"Stubbs."

"Stubbs." Alex smiled. Perfect for the little smart ass, Alex thought. Sitting there in studied indifference, arms folded across his chest. "Stubbs," he repeated loudly.

Jimmy instantly hated the professor. The professor wore tinted glasses and battered cotton slacks. Maybe he's an old hippie, Jimmy guessed. Although he had never met a hippie, Jimmy hated them. Jimmy next noticed that the professor wore scuffed wingtips. Jimmy concluded that Resartus simply couldn't dress.

The professor also yawned, smoked, frowned, and forgot questions in mid-sentence. Worst of all, Jimmy could not understand a single thing the professor said. Metafiction? Mythic archetypes? Marxist subtext? For Christ's sake, Jimmy thought, he's just talking about a stupid story.

The class got worse. At one point, the professor forgot when the novel under discussion was published.

A student with a pasty complexion instantly raised his hand.

"Yes, Mr..." The professor shrugged amiably. "Your name...?"

"Edward Head." Edward enunciated each syllable precisely, hoping the professor would remember. Edward pushed a greasy bang of black hair from his forehead. "Lady Chatterley's made her appearance in 1928. A private edition."

Alex raised his eyebrows at this fact, one of many that he had forgotten. "That's right."

"An expurgated edition was put out in London in 1933. No, that's '32."

"That's very good."

"The complete edition," Edward continued, "wasn't brought out until 1960. That didn't do much good for Lawrence, 'cause he died in 1930."

The students shifted in their chairs, offended by Edward's knowledge. Several glanced at their watches. Jimmy cradled his chin in one palm and discreetly extended the hand's middle finger at the know it all.

After Alex dismissed class, Edward approached the professor's desk.

"Yes, Mr..."

"Mr. Head."

"Right."

"I wanted–I'd like to tell you that I really liked *The Best Year of His Life*."

Alex considered Edward anew. Not many students knew about his writing.

"I think it's really great. I took your class because of it." Edward's voice lowered, as if confiding a secret to a lover. "I found it in a book sale this summer — really, it's one of the best books I've ever read."

"Thanks." Alex lit a Dunhill, grinned through the smoke. He almost ate the match, then thought better of it. "That's quite a compliment. I do appreciate it," Alex lied. He was beyond caring.

"If you don't mind me asking — ?"

Alex smiled patiently.

"Well, why do you write? I mean, what's your motive?"

Nobody had asked that question in years. "I write for..." Alex gathered his thoughts. "...for the same reason I read. A desire to be elsewhere."

"Huh…you mean, someplace other from here? At Tailor?"

"No, not Tailor specifically. Just to be…elsewhere."

"What about your other novels?"

Alex removed his glasses and rubbed his hollowed, blood-shot eyes. "There are no others."

"But that one is worth ten bad ones, I mean ordinary ones."

"Thanks. Nice of you to remember."

Jimmy caught up with Holly in the hallway.

"I didn't know you were going to take this class," Holly said.

"My advisor told me I should take it for humanities credit. Is it tough?"

"I can't tell yet. What did you think?"

"I don't like the professor much."

"I've heard he's OK. Just all over the road. Did you know he's a writer?"

"Really?" Jimmy tried to sound interested. Before Holly had a chance to continue, Jimmy suggested they get a coffee at the student union. Holly agreed.

Jimmy discovered that besides talking about rock music and beer, Holly enjoyed talking about money. After graduation, she explained, she was moving to New York City to work in publishing. She hoped to be an agent. Agents, she said breathlessly, get up to fifteen percent of an author's earnings.

"That's why I'm in the class," she said. "He might have connections. If I do OK in his class, I hope he writes a recommendation."

"What kind of stuff does he write?"

"I don't know. Some sort of, of writing."

Talk turned to Resartus's assignments. Holly placed the class syllabus on the table. Jimmy pretended to study the syllabus and managed to move his chair closer to Holly's. Being short could be good sometimes, he told himself. From the corner of his eye, he could study the heft of Holly's breasts.

An erection forced him to reposition himself. He turned his head, pretended to cough, and repositioned himself a second time.

"This syllabus doesn't look too bad," he said casually. "I just think that—" He swore. Holly was three tables over, talking to Edward Know It All.

Chapter Three: The Dead Too Have Hopes

Alex worked in his office until the sun was safely in the distant west. He put on his sunglasses, got a cigarette, and walked to his car. Thank hobbled Jesus, Alex thought, it's only January.

He dreaded each spring because spring brought summer. Summer sun was the most dangerous. During the summer, he waited until dusk to come outside. He wore sunglasses, a hat, gloves, and a jacket with a full collar. Heavy clothing looked odd in July, so he said that he had suffered melanoma as a child. Winter sun was the least dangerous: he could go outside in the late afternoon if he wore sunglasses and dressed carefully.

But noon was always dangerous. Even the noon sun of January raised gelatinous blisters the size of fried eggs. And high noon in July! The thought appalled him. Alex would smoke and pop, like an insect trapped under a cruel child's magnifying glass.

At home, Alex searched through his dozens of bookcases and found a copy of *The Best Year of His Life*. The novel covered one year in the life of Eric, a surgeon. In the course of the year, Eric slips and falls on his wife while performing the Heimlich; her skull is split and she dies in the ambulance. Some months later, Eric's mother goes into insulin shock and dies on his operating table as he performs a biopsy. The mayor's daughter, awaiting a tracheotomy, dies of anaphylactic shock caused by anesthesia. Meanwhile, Eric's former girlfriend Happy threatens to sue for child support payments. Eric believes the child is his, but he is too distracted by his ruined career to communicate with her.

Eric's faith in medicine is ruined, and he even avoids seeing a dentist about a toothache. The toothache worsens. In drunken despair, Eric pulls the offending tooth, using only channel looks, oil of clove, and Old Bushmill's.

After pulling the tooth, Eric calls Happy and proposes a scheme. The scheme is complicated, Happy is not bright, and Eric must often pause to hold an ice bag to his mouth. But he finally manages to explain the scheme: Eric will perform needless exploratory heart surgery. Happy will file a malpractice suit, win, and the two will flee to Cancun.

The scheme succeeds, although Eric must bribe a colleague to testify against him in court. Eric and Happy flee with $2,000,000 to Cancun. Eric, Happy, and their child operate a hotel on the beach. Eric acts as the hotel's beachside bartender and off-hours dentist.

Several strips of transparent tape on the novel's dust jacket had turned yellow and brittle. Alex grinned at the reviews on the back:

"The finest example of black humor of the season. Horrific laughter, not mere bitterness!"-The New York Times

"Mr. Resartus's first novel blasts off and never falters. He is now the young member of that old fraternity of such writers as Heller, Donleavy, Stewart, and Southern, writers who kept black humor alive even as the uncertain new millennium waited patiently."-The Fresno Bee.

"No writer has of late combined a pessimistic outlook with comic technique."-The Chicago Tribune.

As he read the reviews, Alex tried to recall the promise his career once held. His family predicted fame and fortune. Alex fended off such talk, but hoped they were correct. The fact that Alex suffered from schizophrenia, the publisher hoped, might provide invaluable extra publicity. "You could be the next big thing, a real idiot savant!" his agent enthused. "Hard to buy that kind of publicity!" But *The Best Year of His Life* bombed. Alex's only royalty check, $788, mocked his hopes. He urged his publisher to promote the book more, but the publisher replied that the book was dead.

Dead, just like his brother David.

David, a physician, was murdered in an emergency room six months after Alex's novel was published. Alex happened to be with David that day, but he remembered only fleeting details: David yelling for help. Blood on the floor, on the ceiling, on hands and faces and white jackets. Somebody who was hurt or demented sitting beside Alex and laughing, blood spilling from his mouth.

Alex often tried to recall that day, but the details eluded him. Alex simply knew that he improved that day: no more anxieties, no more depression, no more David. And a new therapy, human blood, replaced David's drug therapy.

"Psychiatrists really are quacks," David often said while giving Alex another psychoactive cocktail: various mixtures of lithium, trazodone, and haloperidol. "Freud's primitive psychoanalysis is still polluting modern medicine. Analyzing dreams, for Christ's sake! But don't worry, Alex. Drugs will eradicate all mental illness in the 21st century."

Alex smiled weakly. "Well we're almost there."

"That's the spirit!" And so Alex's already brittle psyche was strained, whipped, and pureed by David's reckless drug therapy.

When David was murdered, Alex knew the novel was jinxed.

David's murder naturally dampened the family enthusiasm for Alex's writing. And besides, mom and dad confessed the day after the funeral that they did disliked *The Best Year of His Life*. "It's kind of depressing," his mom complained. When the novel died almost simultaneously with David, Alex hated David even more. At least he's dead now, Alex often told himself.

Alex used his novel's good reviews and the embers of his literary reputation to get a job at Tailor. Tailor was in the middle of Illinois, close enough for excursions into Chicago and St. Louis. And the surrounding dozing towns contained plenty of potential victims. The literary world forgot Alex. His schizophrenia, and his tendency to assume victims' traits, often left him severely disorganized. He could not develop his ideas. Now he sat at his kitchen table, staring at his copy of *The Best Year of His Life*.

If I could just concentrate, just remember things, Alex mused, I could write another novel.

Chapter Four: Plans

Edward Head lived two miles from campus in a bungalow that was converted into two apartments. Edward lived in the basement apartment and filled his time there studying, listening to CD's, and tinkering with videotape equipment and hidden microphones. Jill and Cheryl, two co-eds, lived in the apartment above him. On occasion, he used tiny microphones to spy on the coeds. Recently, the coeds had not provided much entertainment. They had stopped seeing their boyfriends and killed time with TV and arguments about bathroom rights.

Tonight, Edward enjoyed his latest hobby. He turned off the lights, drew the curtains, and spun his newest DVD: *Under the Big Top*. Light from the screen flickered across his face, and he smiled. The first image was promising:

A stained leather tarp. On the tarp, a nude woman with a green Mohawk is on her hands and knees. A male voice commands, "Turn around, Blinkey."

Blinkey faces the camera. She is in white face. Black greasepaint is smeared on her mouth, and red ovals highlight her cheekbones. A hand appears, places a cigarette in her mouth, lights the cigarette. Blinkey takes a long drag, then a second. Smoke rushes out of her flared nostrils. She nods.

The hand removes the cigarette. "Now it's Corkey's turn," a male voice announces.

The production quality of the movie is poor. When Blinkey looks up, the harsh lighting turns Blinkey's pockmarks into little craters.

Now a long shot of Blinkey, and the surroundings are clear: Blinkey is inside a circus tent. A male clown approaches from behind. He has a white face, fixed red smile, and maniacally raised eyebrows. He is removing his green suspenders. As he gets closer, he unzips his fly.

Now a close up. On the right of the screen, Blinkey's face in profile. On the left, an erect penis painted as a candy cane, white with red stripes. Blinkey closes her eyes and opens her mouth.

Edward was rubbing his crotch when the phone rang. He tried to ignore the interruption, but the mood was ruined and he turned off the DVD player.

"Hello?"

"Hi, Edward? This is Holly Dish. I'm in the lit class."

Well come on over, Edward thought to himself. He looked at his crotch. I've got a surprise for you.

Holly did not invite herself over. She simply asked if Edward had taken notes from the day's class. Edward said he did take notes, but he could recite Resartus's lecture without consulting them.

"We didn't get through much," Edward reminded her. He outlined the use of symbol in Lawrence's novel: the impotent husband in a wheelchair, the restless wife, the simple, passionate groundskeeper. Edward talked twenty minutes without stopping.

Holly's hand cramped from taking notes. "I need someone like you." A pause. "To take notes. Thanks again."

"Good night."

Edward did not bother to restart the movie. The sobering glare of the flickering fluorescent kitchen light made him feel foolish.

He wondered if Holly was actually interested in him, but skepticism chased the thought away. No, Edward decided, Holly Dish simply wanted notes. True, she had talked with him today in the cafeteria. She was friendly enough, but was simply killing time.

Edward imagined Holly starring in *Under The Big Top*. She sits on the tarp and pulls off a tee shirt. Next she lies back, pulls down her zipper, and shimmies out of her jeans. She pulls on yellow clown shoes; they are flat and wide, like the blade of an oar.

Her thighs squeeze and chafe Edward's face. The clown shoes oscillate, and—

--Edward's pants were already off. He flipped the light switch, sprinted into the living room, and restarted the movie.

Comfortable in a gray Tailor College sweat suit, Holly Dish lounged on her bed, reading the latest issue of *Me, Myself, and I*. The feature article exhorted her to "take charge of your own life and the lives of others!"

Holly accepted the article's thesis. As the article advised, Holly was planning her career and "taking the steps that make women winners!" Her phone call to Edward Head had been one such step. With careful teasing"—I need someone like you"—Edward would provide notes throughout the semester. Edward's notes greatly improved Resartus's lectures: they filled in the gaps, made transitions between points, and removed the tangents.

With such fine notes, Holly's chances of passing Resartus's class increased. True, she hated to read anything but magazines. But as the career articles declared, "You can't make it to the fast track with a short cut!" Holly resigned herself to try reading most of her homework.

If her plan worked, Resartus might reward her with a "B" (an "A" seemed impossible) along with a letter of recommendation. Resartus's would be the fourth such letter. The previous three had come from Holly's advisor, her gym teacher, and her freshman dorm director.

Holly's advisor, Dr. Blake, learned that Holly was in Alex Resartus's class.

"Professor Resartus is semi-known in the literary field," Dr. Blake told Holly. "I think that if you do well, a letter from him would help your career plans."

"What kind of stuff does he write?"

"I don't know. Some kind of writing."

Her advisor's ignorance did not concern Holly. A published writer was a published writer.

Holly finished the article and reluctantly turned to her homework. She was asleep in ten minutes, the book gently falling and rising on her stomach.

Chapter Five: No More Pulps?

Alex rarely received personal letters. His mail was typically bills and ads, and he waited until Saturday to unpack his mailbox. He dropped the mail onto the kitchen table. Electric bill. Numerous department store ads. Car insurance renewal form. Several credit card solicitations.

But underneath a pizzeria ad was a business envelope.

The envelope's upper left-hand corner featured the logo of *Guns, Blood, and Shovels*, and Alex laughed. *Guns, Blood, and Shovels* was a quarterly pulp of mystery, murder, and horror stories. *Guns* had published three of Alex's short stories over the last four years.

The note inside the envelope was from Tim Skillet, the editor.

Dear Mr. Resartus:

Our accountant—well, okay, we hire an accountant once a year to evaluate our health!—discovered an error in payment made for a story of yours, "Orville's Lesson in Love." Seems we underpaid you by twenty dollars. I've sent you a check, along with an extra fifteen. We at Guns hope that the extra money will inspire you to contribute more of your work. "Orville's Lesson in Love" was a hit with our readers. They'd like a follow up! Hope to hear from you.

Yours, Tim

"How kind of you, Mr. Skillet," Alex murmured, recalling the story. It was about Orville, a rapist. One night, Orville was working in his garage when a woman approached. She lived down the road, she said, and had lost her dog.

Orville raped her.

Afterward, he lay on his back smoking a cigarette. "You think that sex and violence are the same," the woman accused through bloody lips. Orville agreed. He stabbed her a hundred times then buried her in his back yard.

The next night, someone knocked on his front door. The murdered woman, her throat glazed with dried blood and moist viscera, stood under his porch light. She pleaded with Orville to let her in. When Orville refused, she threw herself through Orville's living room picture window.

She chased him through the house. She screamed repeatedly that

Orville equated sex with violence. Finally she cornered Orville in his kitchen. She grabbed a carving knife. He covered his face with his arms, weeping. "I'm sorry! Sex and violence are not the same! They're different!"

The woman laughed. Her upper lip was nearly sheared from her mouth, and it dangled over the side of her jaw. "Just so you won't forget." She drove the knife into his stomach.

As Orville died, the woman's voice deepened into that of a man's.

Orville awoke in prison. He had been convicted of murdering a woman while she searched for a lost dog. As Orville lay on his cot, sweat-soaked prison garb clinging to his skin, his cellmate slapped him. Orville's eyes widened. A six foot five con with watery blue eyes and a decorative nail through his earlobe stood over him. "Turn over. I'm gonna learn you the difference between rape and love."

"Orville's Lesson in Love" was published two years ago. The story was simple, yet Alex enjoyed the crude justice that the pulps demanded. And these days, Alex was grateful to see his name in print on more than bills and junk mail.

Alex wondered if he still had a readership, as the editor claimed. For macabre vignettes, yes. For a novel? Did the readers of *The Best Year His Life* ever wonder why Alex never wrote another book?

Alex walked down the hall to his study. He leaned against the doorframe, looked at his desk. On the desk was his computer. Next to the computer, a notebook with several ideas for a novel. The notebook was mostly scribbling and doodles.

The notebook beckoned. He flipped through it, pausing every few pages to review his notes. The notes were mostly character sketches, based on people he knew at the college. As he reviewed the sketches, Alex was angered for the thousandth time. He had written his first novel in three months, filling four yellow legal pads. He wrote standing up, fifteen hours a day, quitting at midnight to sleep on the floor. Alex had been afraid that if he quit writing, he would lose his train of thought.

Now, staring at his desk, Alex's anger soared. The anger demanded satisfaction, but the satisfaction had to be gained carefully, without mistakes.

He took highway 40 south, past Pine Lake. After a half hour on the highway, Alex turned left onto an unnamed gravel road. He cruised at 45, enjoying the soothing hum of tires against black road.

As he tossed his fifth cigarette butt out the window, the headlights revealed the blue windbreaker and red cap of a hitchhiker. Alex slowed, as if to pick up the hitchhiker; as the hitchhiker smiled, Alex stomped the accelerator.

Alex parked the car on the road's shoulder, and walked the twenty feet that separated the collision from the body. The hitchhiker was on his back, yet his face was flattened into the road.

After studying the body, Alex removed a notebook and pen from his jacket pocket. "This is probably a futile gesture, but the way you landed...Jesus!" In his notebook, Alex recorded the geometrical perfection and skeletal perversion with which the body rested.

Alex leaned on his lectern, trying to sound professorial. "Come on. We have to proceed. Come now. Review is important. Who can tell me what rank Mellors held in the army?"

The students shifted in their chairs. A few made no pretense of interest and slept. Holly Dish glanced at her watch, bored, but knew she had to make a good impression. She raised her hand.

Alex nodded.

"Indian," Holly announced.

"Indian?"

Holly repeated herself, then looked at her classmates. Several were laughing. Damn, she thought, he asked what rank, not what army.

"He was an officer," Holly nearly shouted.

"Good," Alex said. "As long as we're on it, what nation?"

More shifting in chairs.

Edward Head rolled his eyes. He waited for someone to answer. Finally, almost wearily, he spoke. "Mellors was an Officer in the Indian army. And as long as we're on it, his father was a miner, just like Lawrence's."

Deciding that only Edward had read the novel carefully, Alex continued with his lecture, often turning to his notes. Whenever he lectured, Alex was grateful that his secretary, Mrs. Mathews, was well organized. She kept all his notes on file. They were cross-indexed by title, genre, and author.

Alex wanted to discuss the novel's groundbreaking eroticism, but he ran out of time. "Let's break it off now. Next time, we'll talk about the real reason the book is famous."

A few students smiled.

As Jimmy Stubbs watched Holly walk out of the room, he stifled a lust driven groan. She was wearing a skirt today.

Jimmy's unabashed stare amused Alex. The little guy wants to wrestle her, Alex thought, and she'd pin him in ten seconds. Edward was watching Holly, too. But he was sly. He fumbled with his books and stole glances at Holly's buttocks, coiled under her skirt.

"Must be animal magnetism," Alex said as Edward passed the lectern.

Edward stopped. "I'm sorry?"

"Don't be sorry. I understand. How can I compete with her?"

"What–?"

Alex smiled, nodded at the departing Holly.

Edward looked toward the door, but Holly was gone. "Must be all that talk about Lady Chatterley and Mellors," he joked.

"We haven't talked about it yet."

"Anticipation," Edward conceded. He stood awkwardly, not knowing how to proceed. He wanted to build rapport with the professor. His attempt to talk about Resartus's novel had ended quickly. "I very much like Lawrence," he asserted, trying to sound scholarly.

Edward began rambling about D. H. Lawrence's home in Taos, New Mexico. Alex walked toward the door, but nodded, indicating that Edward should follow.

From the rear of the class, Jimmy Stubbs cursed. The know it all, he thought, is after Holly too.

Alex bided his time, waiting for the sun to ease. He swiveled around in his chair, rested his feet on a pile of books in the windowsill, and gazed out the window of his fourth floor office. The window offered a pleasant view of the court that separated Elmhurst Hall from the library entrance. The court featured concrete benches, scattered abstract sculptures, and a garden of perennials. A cluster of students stood chattering in the court, the breeze ruffling their hair and their jackets. The setting sun reddened the students' faces. In another thirty minutes, the court would be dark and safe.

Two hours earlier, Alex had bid Edward Head a good afternoon. Edward had even managed a joke: "I know it's goofy to say that you're a hero of mine, but I guess you are. But I'll try not to grovel in public."

Alex smiled, rubbed his eyes. "Public groveling is always good."

Talking nearly non-stop, Edward had offered a treatise on literature that spanned from the Ancient Greek to the Modern British, from Euripides to James Joyce.

"Quite a leap, Edward," Alex had noted.

"The connection," Edward explained, "is Euripides and Joyce were both iconoclasts. Euripides overturned the structure of tragedy in the fourth century B.C., and Joyce overturned the structure of the novel in the 20th century."

"And Joyce's use of the stream of consciousness!" Edward gasped. "What a breakthrough!" Then a minute later, "The phrase 'stream of consciousness' was coined by William James, which is cool because he made empiricism extreme. You know, that experience is the essence of the world." He caught himself. "I know you know all this stuff, Professor Resartus. But it's fun to find someone to talk about it with."

"Of course."

Edward was off to William's brother, Henry James. "Henry's concern with international themes is, it's neat. You know, when *in The Golden Bowl...*"

Now, peering at the rising dark in the courtyard, Alex was thrilled. Edward had a magnificent disciplined mind. And Alex was going to take it.

Chapter Six: A Dry Run

Alex studied Edward's habits for two weeks. Five nights a week, Edward studied into the early morning in the academic center. The college kept classrooms open all night for aspiring scholars, and Edward was certainly scholarly.

On the first floor, data processing students stared at computer screens and labored over programs. On the second floor, students worked in study groups or wrote papers on the college's platoon of computers. By 11:00, most students had departed, except Edward and a lonely African student. By midnight, the African departed.

Except on Fridays, Edward studied until 2:00 a.m. Around 12:30 a.m., however, Edward put on his red Tailor College jacket and walked to the 7 Eleven, ten minutes away. He bought a large cup of coffee and a bag of peanuts. He ate the peanuts on the return walk. Fueled by caffeine, Edward continued to study another hour. Then he walked to the parking lot and drove home.

On Saturdays, Edward grocery shopped (frozen pizzas, microwave tacos, bagels, cream cheese, instant coffee), sat alone in the nearly deserted student union, or attended keggers at fraternity houses. But on Saturday nights Edward was home by one, and light from a television flickered through the windows of Edward's apartment.

One Friday afternoon, Alex called up Edward's academic record on the department computer.

> Head, Edward.
> Permanent Address:
> 24 Napoleon, Valparaiso, IN 46383
> Majors: English and European History
> Cumulative GPA: 3.85
> Credits Accumulated: 45
> Advisor: Dr. Lawrence Ray
> College Address
> 112 East Locust

Alex then copied Edward's day schedule: his classes were on Monday, Wednesday, and Friday from 9:00 a.m. to 2:00 p.m.

Alex had all the information he needed. He knew Edward's schedule, his obligations, his habits. As a teen, Alex escaped his shell by pretending to be someone else, and now he imagined himself a Secret Service agent on surveillance. The groundwork was laid, the target's habits were established, the bust was impending.

Tonight, Alex would try a dry run.

By 11:00 p.m., Edward was yawning. The flickering fluorescent lights destroyed his depth of field perception. The literature text, the table upon which it rested, the blue carpet under his feet: all these objects seemed flattened upon a single geometric plane. Edward glanced at his watch every five minutes, and with each glance he groaned to see that only five minutes had elapsed. Rather loudly, one of the fluorescent tubes popped, flared, and blackened. Still, Edward persisted, and after two more groans, he closed his book and pulled on his red Tailor College jacket. Coffee time.

More of the building's lights had failed. The college's maintenance crew was lax, for the lights had started burning out months ago. Now the stairwell was dark, the steps descending into murky black. He remembered that as a child, he directed a flashlight into an abandoned well but would not open his eyes. He feared the beam would reveal a corpse, or a monster. Now, stepping into the crisp late evening air, Edward whistled a rock and roll anthem and hurried to the 7 Eleven.

Behind one of the oaks, Alex smiled as Edward passed. At this point, amidst the oaks, Alex would attack.

Alex would carry the corpse thirty feet to the college's abandoned utility shed. Once inside, Alex would stuff the corpse into a large plastic bag and carry it another forty feet to his car, waiting in the corner of the gym parking lot.

At home, Alex would carry the corpse into the basement, hang it upside down from the ceiling rafters, and sever the carotid artery. The blood would be transferred from buckets to jars. Once in jars, the blood would be kept fresh in the basement freezers; the inevitable stray bits of flesh would make the contents look like pureed tomato. Disposing of the remains would be a snap, and Alex imagined the scene: a cornfield in southern Illinois, the decapitated head, the withered body, a copy of *Helter Skelter*. A death metal CD.

"Howya doin' tonight?" the cashier asked.

"Tired of studying."

Jeff nodded, lit the thirty-first cigarette of his 12:00 to 8:00 a.m. shift.

Edward placed his cup of coffee and bag of peanuts on the counter.

Jeff bared his teeth and wrinkled his nose as he sucked the smoke into his lungs. "You don't know anybody on campus who wants some dope, do you?"

"I'll ask around." Edward wondered why he felt obligated to appease the weed head. He noted Jeff's three-day beard, yellow teeth, glazed eyes. "What're you offering?"

"I got some ditch weed cheap, and some genuine red bud for, uh…" Jeff peeled a drying gob of saliva from his bottom lip. "Damn, I forgot."

"Happens," Edward smiled, gathered his purchases. "Later."

Still hiding behind the tree, Alex mouthed a silent "Until next time," as Edward passed.

"Studyin' late, aren't you?" The maintenance man pushed the door back until the door's hydraulic arm stiffened enough to hold the door in place.

Edward glanced at his watch: 12:15. "You're working late yourself."

"At least I get overtime. You probably noticed that the lights around here ain't for shit." He dragged a stepladder into the classroom. "We got to get everything right for the big occasion."

"What's that?"

The man stepped up the ladder and removed the opaque plastic cover from the light bay. "Somethin' to do with a parent/student week-end. Didn't you come to the college when you was a high school senior to check out the college?" He gingerly removed the dead fluorescent tube.

"No."

"Well, that's what's startin' this Saturday, and we got five days to get this place shiny." He placed a new tube into the bay, replaced the plastic cover. "I been working since eight this morning. And when I get done with that—" He pointed at several fluorescent tubes, upright in a long cardboard box. "—I gotta polish the floor. And startin' tomorrow, I got to paint the hallway." He yawned, almost lost his balance. "But I need that overtime money bad."

The yawn was contagious. Edward looked at his textbook through tired, watering eyes. He still had a chapter to read. "Yeah. I still have work to do myself, but I need some coffee to keep going."

The man put his palms to his temples and groaned.

"What's wrong?"

"Damn headaches." The man stepped carefully off the ladder. "Campus doctor says they're clump headaches, I mean cluster head-aches. They come on faster than hell."

Sympathy and wariness commingled in Edward. He was sorry that the man was in pain, but he did not want to hear about the man's prob-lems. "Do you have aspirin?" he asked. Edward hoped the man would answer "Yes" and leave.

"They don't help much. I'm supposed to take medication but I left it at home." The skin above his right eye reddened, as if smeared with pepper juice. "Advil and aspirin help if I take 'em together, but—" He made a gesture of futility. "I don't have any with me."

"That's too bad," Edward mumbled. He quickly stood up. "Well, time for me to get coffee."

Alex rotated his wrist, trying to read his watch in the rays of a distant vapor lamp. The watch seemed to announce 12:35, but Alex's increasingly poor eyesight made him uncertain. Alex was at least certain that he parked his car in the corner of the gym parking lot at 12:15, put on his latex gloves, and placed the plastic bag in the maintenance shed. He had been waiting at least fifteen minutes. Where the hell was the kid? Dozens of bad scenarios raced through his imagination. Edward Head was sick. He had found a girlfriend. Or a boyfriend. Maybe he had smoked too much grass and was now slumped in a chair, listening to rock CD's. Or he had fallen asleep while studying, nose flattened against the desk. Maybe he had tripped in the darkened stairwell, broken his leg, and was shouting for help.

Alex again tried to read his wristwatch. He was about to take a few steps out of the oaks when he heard steps.

There he was. Hands stuffed deeply into his red Tailor College jacket, head down against the cold. He was in a hurry. He walked more quickly than usual, as if impatient to get his coffee.

Monster and victim nearly brushed shoulders, then the victim was a yard beyond the tree, hands still in his jacket pockets. The monster supposed he was rather humane to let Edward enjoy a last cup of coffee. Soon the victim reappeared on the tracks. In a minute the footsteps were audible.

The red of Edward's varsity jacket passed. The monster took two long steps. His right elbow arced through the air toward the victim's skull. The victim stumbled like a battered prizefighter, and the monster drove his right fist into the victim's kidney. Next he smashed the victim's head with his left fist, hammer style.

The victim fell face forward, his coffee cup skidding across an ice patch.

The utility shed's only window was partially boarded, and the dark was infuriating. Several times, Alex nearly had the body in the bag, but an unruly arm or leg threatened to puncture and tear the plastic. Alex soon lost his patience and stuffed the body into the bag headfirst.

Alex flipped the light switch at the head of the steps, and a bare bulb lighted the narrow stairway. He dragged his prize down the basement steps. The victim's skull bounced on the stairs a couple times.

Alex dragged the bag to the end of the basement, turned on the light switch next to his workbench. The tools were arranged neatly, like silverware on white linen: two hacksaws, three carving knives, ten feet of rope, three buckets, four dozen Ball jars. Alex cut the rope into three sections: one to tie Edward's ankles together, the second to tie his hands behind his back, the third to suspend him from the rafters.

A muffled groan escaped from the bag. Alex ignored it.

He went upstairs to the kitchen, washed the buckets, and dried them carefully. Then he consulted his list: hacksaws, knives, rope, buckets, jars, scissors. Alex had forgotten the scissors! He would use them to cut Edward's hair so the blood could run freely from the carotid artery to the buckets.

Scissors in hand, Alex hurried to the basement, taking three steps at a time.

The bag sat up.

"You're a strong one!" Alex marveled.

Next came the splatter of vomit.

Alex straightened out the bag—it had become wrapped around the neck—and pulled.

"For Christ's sake!" Alex bellowed. He threw the scissors to the floor. "Explain this to me!"

The maintenance man looked up at Alex. His right eye was purple and swollen shut.

"Where the hell is Edward?"

"I'm Marty." He wiped at the blood smeared across his mouth. "I don't know Edward."

"Then what the hell are you doing in his jacket?"

"It belongs to the kid."

"Uh?"

"The bookworm that was studying on the fourth floor."

"That bookworm is Edward Head!"

"I borrowed it to go to the 7 Eleven. He was gonna go for coffee anyway, and I needed some aspirin and Advil for my headache. Marty reached into the jacket pockets, removed two bottles: one bottle contained aspirin, the other contained Advil. "He let me use his jacket because I got some paint on mine at work tonight. I was soaking it in the janitor's closet." He put the bottles back in the pockets, as if he were about to leave.

Rage deformed Alex's narrow face. "Now my plans are all fucked over!" He hurled a hacksaw against a wall, then threw a jar at Marty. The jar cut Marty's scalp and exploded against the wall.

Adrenals pumping, Marty struggled to his feet. Alex was too busy smashing Ball jars to notice. Marty heard two more jars shatter as he was halfway up the stairs. His headache had escalated to surreality: the stairs rippled as if underwater. The pain in his back was enormous: it was too great to be contained in a single human body, and Marty faltered as the pain radiated beyond him to penetrate stairway's walls.

Marty reached the landing. He turned to see Alex marching slowly up the stairs.

"Goddammit! You take one step and I'll drive these —" Alex held up his scissors " —through your eyes."

Stumbling into the kitchen, Marty saw something on the kitchen table. A carving knife. He grabbed it, held it over his head in a threatening pose. Mute with rage, Alex threw down the scissors, crossed the room, and grabbed Marty's shirt.

Marty slashed at Alex's arms with the carving knife.

Alex pushed Marty against the kitchen table, but Marty kept slashing and blood welled through Alex's sleeves.

"Let go of me and I won't kill you!" Marty promised.

Alex let go.

Marty slashed at Alex, missed.

Alex grabbed Marty's head.

Marty heard bones in his neck crack from the sudden jerk, and he saw that he was about to crash against Alex's raised right knee. Blood poured from where his nose had been. I'm surprised my nose doesn't hurt more, Marty thought. My nose, it's, it's—where is it?

No time to think. He collided against the knee again. And again. His blood spattered the knee, his own pants, his work shoes, the floor. I know how to clean, he wanted to tell his assailant, you need to mix ammonia with water to get that out.

The blood on his assailant's pants turned yellow, as if Marty were looking at the negative of a photograph. The once white floor was black, the puddles of blood were dazzling yellow, and the pain became pleasure. Warm waves, like those of a sauna, soothed him.

His headache was gone.

He decided to drop the knife. No need to fight now, everything was fine! But he could not drop the knife: his hand would not obey. With enormous effort, he lifted his head and looked at his disobedient hand.

The knife had impaled his hand: the handle was on top of his hand, and the blade emerged through the palm. Marty tried to shake the knife loose, but a new pain distracted him. The new pain was in his neck and pierced the soothing waves. He tried to ask why the pain had returned, but his question was a gurgle. The new pain faded into a black dot that was surrounded by blacker black.

Out of spite, Alex chewed off half of Marty's neck, pausing only to cough up pieces of gristle. Then he dropped the carcass and went to bed.

The alarm clock sounded at seven thirty, but he was already awake.

His eyes and nose ached as if struck by a ball bat. Burning white spots marred his vision.

Alex walked slowly, but each step aggravated his headache. He dragged Marty's corpse into the basement, then wrapped it in the big plastic bag and pushed it under the workbench. As he walked up the stairs, he saw two small bottles: a bottle of aspirin and a bottle of Advil.

He cursed his bad temper. Tearing Marty's neck open with his teeth, driving the knife through the victim's hand: all of it was stupid and sloppy. He was spinning out of control, and his plans to gain Edward Head's blood were at risk.

Mrs. Mathews clicked her tongue when Alex called in sick. "Goodness. With a headache that bad, you may have to see the doctor. There's an influenza bug going around campus, and..."

Mrs. Mathews set aside her typing to discuss influenza: Alex might be suffering from both bacterial and viral infections; he should eat onions, garlic, and ascorbic acid to build white blood cells. He should check his lymph nodes for swelling. Swollen nodes cause sore throats. Alex should not use an antipyretic unless the fever becomes unbearable.

"Antipyretics are fever reducers," she explained.

"Why not just call them that?" Alex rubbed his eyebrow. It twitched wildly, as if it had grown nostrils and inhaled pepper.

"Antipyretics are the proper name. I was a biology major, you know."

Alex grunted.

"Furthermore—"

"You're right," Alex agreed. "I'm going to the doctor right now." He hung up.

Chapter Eight: Scared of the Dark

Jimmy considered the sacrifice he was making to woo Holly Dish: taking a class he despised. As a rule, Jimmy disliked all his classes, but already he harbored the most sour loathing of Professor Resartus's class. Other students also seemed to despise it, except the English majors: those pretentious grease spots in patched denim and dirty tennis shoes who blathered about metafiction, poststructuralism, metaphor, and metonymy. And Resartus! A half-baked, Alzheimeresque slob who wrote a book that nobody read.

All these woeful crosses to bear, and all for hot Holly Dish. Now, bracing himself to endure Resartus's nonsense, Jimmy waited at the end of the hallway. When Holly breezed by on the way to class, he stealthily fell in behind her. Jimmy guessed that Holly was a virgin ninety-nine times removed, but he did not care. He ached for her sack-smarts, for her thighs clamping his twenty-five inch waist, for her tongue in his nose.

He did not hear her say, "No class." He walked into the empty room.

Holly stood in the doorway. "You're learning to like it here, huh?"

Jimmy tried to snort nonchalantly, but the snort came out as a belch. "See what I think of this class?" he sneered, wiping his mouth with the back of his hand. Jimmy walked past her, hoping she did not see his blush. He was half way down the hallway when he turned around. "Want to grab some java with me at the union?" he asked in his most casual voice.

She was gone.

Jimmy stomped down the stairway and out the building. Cold wind cut through his thin jacket and cotton slacks. The life-affirming joy of a canceled class was gone, so he decided on a solo coffee. The caffeine might restore his spirits.

He forgot about the coffee when he saw Holly talking with Edward Shithead. He tried to reason with himself: she's just after his perfect notes. She doesn't like him. How can anyone like him? Do-it-yourself haircut. Goofy blue sweatshirt and stiff denims a size too large. Eyes that are out of whack. One eye looked higher on the face than the other did, though Jimmy had noted that look on other intellectuals.

As Jimmy reviewed the reasons to hate Edward Know It all, he realized that one of the biggest reasons was gone: that God-awful prissy varsity jacket.

"Nice break from class today, huh?" Jimmy called, approaching Edward and Holly.

Edward looked up, sighed, and moved over to make room for Jimmy.

Jimmy remained standing; he took every opportunity to stand over others.

"Edward was telling me the weirdest thing about his jacket." Holly nodded at Edward to continue his story.

"Yeah, I noticed you weren't wearing that jacket." Jimmy's grin was mocking. "It's a nice jacket."

Edward nodded.

Impatient, Holly offered a summary. "Edward thinks that the guy who stole it was a gambler, and that he got killed or something."

"Well, I don't know if I really believe that," Edward cautioned. "But campus police said it was possible. They'd heard he owed a lot of money."

"Edward was studying late last night, and a maintenance man was replacing all the lights on the fourth floor. He came in to replace the lights in the room Edward was in, and—"

"And he had this bad headache. He said he had a cluster headache."

"Cluster headaches!" Jimmy cackled. "What's that bullshit?"

"I think it was real. A teacher in high school had them. The headaches came in groups. Like two or three, then they'd be gone for a week or two." Edward winced, recalling the teacher's symptoms. "His eye would twitch and his nose and eyes would run."

"So get a Kleenex," Jimmy said.

"Anyway, the maintenance guy was rubbing his head and said he'd left his medicine at home. I was going to get coffee at the 7 Eleven. He said he'd get it for me and pick up some aspirin and Advil at the same time."

"But he had to borrow Edward's jacket," Holly interjected, "because the guy'd spilled paint on his own jacket."

"An hour went by. I went over to the 7 Eleven and asked Jeff if a guy in my jacket had come by."

"Jeff the stoner," Jimmy chuckled.

"And Jeff said that the guy had come in and left a long time ago!" Holly said, excited.

"So today I talked to the campus police," Edward continued. "They said he might be in trouble with some people he owed money to, and he might have just taken off. That didn't make sense to me. They admitted it didn't make sense to them, either."

"Why not?" Jimmy challenged.

"Just leave in the middle of the night, in the middle of his shift? He'd even said he needed money, and that's why he was working a double shift. And what's a Tailor jacket worth? And it's conspicuous to leave with a stolen jacket."

"There must be signs of, a, of a struggle," Holly blurted.

"What?" Edward asked.

"Struggle," Holly repeated. "If the guy got grabbed or jumped or whatever. C'mon let's check it out!"

"Yeah dream on," Jimmy snickered. "What, you think you're a cop and you'll find —"

"Excellent idea!" Edward announced. Holly was right: there might indeed be evidence of a struggle. He and Holly were half way across the room when Jimmy called for them to wait.

Edward, Holly, and Jimmy carefully walked up and down the path that led to the 7 Eleven.

"I don't see any signs of struggle," Jimmy said, trying to sound observant.

"What would they look like?" Holly asked.

Jimmy tried to imagine.

"Probably not much," Edward speculated. "Maybe you'd see a pair of footprints, where they fought. Or maybe some marks in the dirt, if the guy got knocked down."

The three scoured the path, which frequent travel had turned to packed dirt. They could find no such marks. They looked through the tall grass that ran parallel to the tracks, but found nothing.

After an hour, the wind had turned sharper. Holly complained that she was bored and asked to borrow Edward's cell phone. He conceded he did not own one, which made Jimmy snort. When Holly asked for Jimmy's, he conceded he'd left his at the frat house. Increasingly restless, Holly announced her departure. Without Holly's presence, Jimmy lost interest and left too. Edward stayed, looking for anything. He found nothing.

Jimmy cracked open a second after-dinner beer, handed a second to his frat brother Don. Don drank in peace because he had no homework. Jimmy drank in agitation because he had lots of homework. But if he got drunk, he would be incapable of studying, and so he could skip his homework in good conscience.

They passed ninety minutes in gossip: who was sleeping with whom, who was cheating on whom, and who was cheating on his term paper. Don enjoyed Jimmy's serious treatment of gossip. Don even occasionally invented gossip just to savor Jimmy's reaction. Jimmy, the short cynic, considered himself a shrewd operator. He was always looking for the right angle on people and situations.

Who, for example, was the easiest instructor? What girl was break-ing up with what guy? She might be vulnerable, and Jimmy could pro-vide a sympathetic ear, sweet wine, and comforting embrace. Don once lied to Jimmy that Ellen, a tall Italian girl—"Nice black curly hair, and just a faint mustache"—had broken up with her boyfriend back home.

"You know how some of those Roman Catholics are," Don said.

"Of course I do," Jimmy assured, even as he wondered what Don meant.

"This chick was supposed to marry this guy, and she finds him cheating on her. You know," Don improvised, "I think that the guy's name was Jimmy. How about that?"

Jimmy leaned forward in his chair, elbows on his knees. "Where did you hear this?"

"I heard her talking about it between classes with, uh, with…" Don feigned forgetfulness.

"That girl Tracy," Don said. He knew of no Tracy.

"I'm not sure if I know Tracy," Jimmy lied. He also knew of no Tracy. "Whatever. I'll play it cool."

"Yeah, don't let on you know. Let her come out and, you know, con-fide in you."

"I'll play it right."

Jimmy played it wrong. When Ellen did not come to the frat party at nine, as she usually did, Jimmy started drinking heavily. Ellen arrived at eleven, a striking, olive-skinned girl in a red and blue winter coat.

"I'll take your coat," Jimmy offered, but the offer sounded like a drunk's threat.

"I'll keep it." She pushed by and joined a group of friends.

Working his way through the crowd, fending off elbows, biceps, and beer cups, Jimmy approached Ellen.

"Get you a beer?" he demanded.

She frowned at his glazed eyes and unashamed leer. "I've got one." She held up her cup.

"Well so have I!" Jimmy snorted.

"Looks like you've had one too many."

Jimmy noted the foam on her mustache. Her mustache, he thought, is thicker than mine and I've been trying to grow one for six weeks. He wiped at his upper lip, wondering if he too was foamed.

Ellen was self-conscious enough about her mustache. Her free hand darted at her upper lip as if fending off a bee. Now her mustache was two-tone: black on the left half, white on the right.

Revolted, Jimmy turned away then felt beer running down his head and back.

He cursed her. She laughed at him.

"Bearded slut," Jimmy growled at Ellen. He tossed his beer into her face, and foam dripped from her face to her tomato red blouse.

"And you suck on this," demanded someone behind him.

Jimmy turned to see a large fist rocket down at him. He tried to duck, but only fell drunkenly into the punch. Ellen not only was still engaged; her boyfriend Francis had just entered through the back door. Seeing his bride to be, he had waved and navigated through the crowd. As he moved to embrace her, he accidentally spilled his beer on the head of a short person. And even as Francis apologized, the short person threw beer into his fiancé's face.

Don's attention was wandering. He played idly with his empty beer can, staring into space. He was remembering how funny Jimmy looked after Ellen's boyfriend had flattened him: Jimmy on his back, surrounded by feet and legs that must have looked large and long to such a little drunk guy.

Jimmy told Don about the disappearing maintenance man.

"A disappearing maintenance man?" Don asked. He had been only half-listening.

"That's right. Last night. Looks like he got nabbed."

Don was skeptical. He wondered if Jimmy had learned of his deception about Ellen. Was the little creep planning revenge? "Do you think there's anything to it?"

Jimmy cracked his fifth can of beer. "Seems that way. But I guess even a dweeb like Edward Know It All would make up a story just to impress Holly Dish."

Don settled deeper into the battered chair, rested his feet on the fraying ottoman. "Who's she?"

"You know, Holly." Jimmy carved two breasts in the air with his hands.

Don acted nonplused.

"C'mon. Holly. Big jugs."

"Oh yeah. A bit on the thick side, though," he teased.

"That's crap! You'd kill to spool her deep dish tits."

"She's solid, all right," Don admitted. "She belongs on one of those swimsuit magazine covers, with a bikini string up between her cheeks."

"You'd kill to spool her deep dish tits!" Jimmy repeated, vicious.

Booze did not flatter Jimmy; it reminded him he was short, cynical, and manipulative. He responded to these realizations by standing over people (when possible) and becoming more cynical and manipulative. "I'll be spoolin' her and she'll be eating jelly off my –" Jimmy gestured emphatically, and beer spilled over his hand onto the floor. He was shouting directly into Don's face.

Don decided to get Jimmy some fresh air. The little guy was about to blow a gasket. "Let's check out the crime scene."

"Check it out?"

"Before Edward Sherlock Holmes finds something and runs to show Holly Deep Dish."

Alex punched the dashboard several times. It was not enough that he murder the wrong person, drink ill blood, and suffer a crushing headache. No, he had to leave evidence at the murder scene.

After sleeping off his Bushmill's, Alex sat at his kitchen table drinking coffee and chain-smoking Dunhills. Soon he was out of pocket matches. He thought he had picked up a big book last week at the Blue Flamingo; a talkative bartender insisted on giving them to Alex.

A maddening fifteen-minute search recovered several kitchen matches, loose in a kitchen drawer. He lit one by striking the match head against his thumbnail. He noticed some gray fabric under his thumbnail, then saw that the fabric was under all his nails.

Tired of striking matches with his thumbnail, he searched his jacket for matches. Still no matches. But more gray fabric was embedded in the right elbow of the jacket.

Alex then remembered striking Marty with his right elbow, and he remembered how he yanked the wool cap over the victim's face to muffle any shouts. Alex searched the house twice for the wool cap. After a few minutes of futile searching, he decided to search the shed, where he had stuffed Marty into the plastic bag. If the cap had been left behind, Alex reasoned, perhaps so had a book of matches. The odds of being connected to an errant cap or a lousy book of matches were remote in the extreme, but at this point, Alex believed he could not be too careful. The stakes could simply be no higher.

Now, parked in the small faculty lot of the gymnasium, Alex lit a Dunhill, stuck a flashlight in his pocket, and followed the sidewalk around the gym to the abandoned utility shed.

Inside the shed, he searched the cement floor with the flashlight. The flashlight revealed cracks in the cement, oil stains, dirt, a rusty nut and bolt. A fraying broom rested under the window. Alex leaned against the creaking workbench. The beam scanned the floor a second time. Nothing.

Alex next walked slowly around the shed, directing the beam to where wall met ground. The frosted ground glimmered and sparkled under the beam and crackled under each step. No wool cap or matches.

He had circled the shack when the flashlight beam revealed an object: the ski cap. He picked up the cap; the top of it was pinched between the hinged side of the door and the ground. An easy tug freed the cap, and Alex shoved it into his jacket pocket.

Alex guessed that the cap had fallen from Marty's head just as Alex stepped into the shack, and the cap got caught as Alex closed the door. He felt enormous relief. Screw the matches, he reasoned; they were innocuous now that he had the ski cap. And Jesus on his throne, Alex told himself, calm down...you're panicking about every little thing because the stakes are so high...so very high.

The beam of another flashlight stopped him.

Alex hurried behind the shed. Thankfully, the night air was clear, and he could make out two figures among the oaks. One figure searched the ground with a flashlight, the other supervised.

"No, we already looked all over there the whole, all damned afternoon," the supervisor complained.

"What about over there?" The flashlight beam jumped ahead toward the railroad tracks.

"Yeah," the supervisor answered.

"How about over there?" The beam pointed toward the shed.

"Why would you search over there?"

The supervisor sounded irritated. "Mr. Know It All said he always took this path."

"Okay, okay."

"And he didn't stop to enjoy the fine ambiance of an abandoned maintenance shack."

"But he was a maintenance man, so I think we should check it out." Don headed toward the shack. Jimmy stayed behind for a moment, swearing, then caught up.

Alex grinned. Despite his poor memory, he often remembered people whom he disliked, and he instantly recognized the supervisor's voice.

"We're wasting our time!"

"Just shut up for a minute."

Alex waited until the footsteps were close: he heard the crunching of frost under the snoops' steps. The snoops were about to turn the corner. Alex ate the spent cigarette's butt and pulled the cap over his face.

"This is way off the path," Jimmy asserted. "It doesn't make sense that—" Jimmy collided with a thin man in a ski mask. Jimmy yelped like a frightened puppy.

The thin man stood impassively, hands in jacket pockets.

"Watch it, buddy." Jimmy said.

The man nodded an apology and stuck a fresh cigarette into his mouth. "Light?" The request was muffled through the mask's mouth hole, and the eyes narrowed behind the eyeholes. His request was a command.

Don fumbled with the matches he had found on the trail. "Pretty cold for a walk tonight, eh?"

Alex extended a gloved hand. "The matches," he queried in a low Southern accent. "I wonder if I might see them?"

"Sure. I found them just now, on the ground."

Alex accepted the matches, looked at the cover. "The Blue Flamingo," he read tonelessly, though he wanted to laugh. His luck tonight was a blessed marvel.

"It's a bar downtown," Don said. "A dive, really."

Jimmy studied the thin man. Must a have a long nose, Jimmy thought. His nose is stretching that mask like a hard on. "You're welcome. For the matches."

Unfortunately, the ski-masked man had quit talking, and Jimmy did not know how to react to his silence. The silence made the confrontation absurd. If the man carried a pistol, it might fire a colorful flag that proclaimed "Pow!" Or it might fire dumdums.

Jimmy wanted to shout. Or punch. Or faint. He finally stepped back. He tried to study the contours of the man's features behind the ski mask, but the light was poor. "Well, you're sure talkative!" Jimmy blurted.

Alex nodded, and Don told Jimmy that they should get back.

"Why?" Jimmy snapped at Don. "We're not done yet." But Don was already twenty feet away, eager to get home for more beer and his warm room.

Feeling mischievous, Alex stepped forward and drew his gloved hands from his jacket pockets. Then, as Jimmy's eyes bugged, Alex theatrically ran a forefinger across his own throat. Jimmy sprinted across the frozen ground and crunchy, brittle leaves. He imagined that the man chased him in an erratic, demented gate while fanning the air with a knife. His strides felt slow and weak, as if he were running through water. At one point, he stumbled and fell, sliding ten feet on his face.

"You fuck!" he shrieked at Don. "Wait for me!"

Don turned. Muddy snow covered Jimmy's face.

Back in the frat house, Jimmy berated Don for abandoning him with the killer. Don laughed, told Jimmy to stop fantasizing. "That guy's just some townie. Some bum."

"He's said I'm next!" Jimmy insisted.

Don was reduced to helpless laughter, and Jimmy stomped angrily from the room. When Don called for Jimmy to come back, Jimmy threw an empty beer can at him.

Chapter Nine: "I'm the next victim!"

The headaches had first come in waves, but not like waves that lap the shore. The waves were heavy and their impact was painful. Every thirty seconds, it seemed that a refrigerator fell on him.

Now, by Wednesday, the waves had subsided to a dull, seamless ache. His right eye no longer watered, and his forehead was no longer knotted.

Alex muddled through his first three classes, often stopping to gather his thoughts. Walking into Modern British Literature, however, his spirits rose. He looked forward to seeing little Jimmy Stubbs.

But Alex did not call Jimmy a dwarf. Instead, he followed his lecture notes, which his secretary had kindly retyped while Alex was ill, and concluded class with a reminder.

"Our field trip to Chicago begins Thursday afternoon. We leave campus from the library parking lot at 5:00 and arrive at our hotel around..." He consulted his itinerary. "...Yes, around 9:30."

Some of the students looked surprised. Their wrinkled foreheads and slack jaws revealed that they had forgotten about the field trip. Others snickered and smirked with one another. The field trip let them miss Friday classes without penalty.

"Don't forget to bring some heavy clothing. The wind goes right through you on Michigan Avenue. And if the wind is strong and you're along Wacker, you could get blown right into the Chicago River."

Jimmy rolled his eyes. He figured that most of his classmates had not been to Chicago. He, however, had grown up in Worth, a Chicago suburb. I'll show Holly around the city, Jimmy thought. And I'll be her special guide to nightlife.

"Any questions about the trip?" Alex asked, hoping for none.

"What time Friday does the play start?" Edward Head asked.

Would you shut up for once? Alex thought. He resented Edward for botching up the murder, and for the crippling headaches. "I think that information is in the course syllabus," Alex said, though he did not remember.

"No, I think that information isn't there."

Alex's smile was brittle. "Are you sure? Take another look."

"I don't need to." Edward winced; his remark was arrogant. "I mean, I remember. The syllabus said the play is at the Royal George Theater." Edward narrowed his eyes, a study in concentration. "The theater is on Halsted. But the time wasn't stated in the syllabus."

"No further questions then," Alex asserted. "See you Thursday evening in the library parking lot at..." He was irritated that several students were already through the door.

"At 5:00," Edward whispered to himself.

"At 5:00," Jimmy mumbled as he passed Alex.

"5:00," Holly chirped.

Edward saw Holly and Jimmy waiting for him by the stairwell.

"You won't believe what happened last night," Jimmy began. He wanted Holly to marvel at his courage, and he wanted Edward Know It all to see Holly marvel.

They walked to the student union. Jimmy bought coffee for himself, Holly, and Edward, and led them to a table in the back.

"I don't want anyone to hear about this," Jimmy cautioned. Then, voice low, he narrated last night's events. He embellished cleverly. He made hay out of the fact that Don left first, leaving Jimmy alone with the ski masked stranger.

"That jerk took off like a gazelle, and here I am with this maniac. The guy just stands there looking at me, then all of a sudden he comes at me." Jimmy reached across the table, illustrating how "the creep was trying to choke me!"

"He attacked you?" Edward asked.

"Yeah, he choked me." He savored Holly's reaction: her mouth opened slightly, and her eyes bulged. "Fucker had leather gloves on and I tried scratching at his hands but—"

"How long did he choke you?" Edward interrupted.

"Not that long. I had a pencil in my pocket, and I stabbed one of his hands. He let go, and I took off." As Holly gasped, Jimmy shot a quick smirk at Edward.

"But you said he had gloves on," Edward countered.

"So?"

"You're lucky that you managed to drive a pencil through the glove. You said they were leather, right?"

Jimmy ignored him and faced Holly. "I was sprinting. I was about forty yards from Lincolnway, and I'm thinking, 'You got away!' I look behind me and this maniac is right behind me! I'm thinking, 'Christ, I'm next! I'm the next victim!'"

Edward sputtered. "So you know he's the murderer?" He looked to Holly for skepticism, but she was all wide-eyed credulity.

"He said he was!" Jimmy insisted.

"Did he tell you his name too?"

Holly frowned. "Edward, shut up for a moment, will you?"

"No. But he said..." Jimmy paused to enjoy Holly's attention and Edward's frustration. "He said, 'You're next!'"

Chapter Ten: Lights, Camera, but no Action

The students chattered as the bus rumbled north toward Chicago on I 55. A few talked about the play, but most talked about the bars and stores they wanted to see. Students who had been to Chicago assumed the role of guide, including Jimmy Stubbs. But after two hours, the chatter ceased and many students napped.

Alex moved to the back. The last four rows were empty. He eased into the last seat, turned on the overhead exhaust vent, and smoked. After his tenth cigarette, Alex pulled a pint of tequila from his duffel bag. Soon the tequila worked its magic: Alex felt light, free of that damned headache. I'm a simple bastard, he thought. Leave me alone with my cigarettes, drink, and a good play once in a while.

More tequila made him sleepy. His bones felt loose in his skin, like short ribs wrapped loosely in paper. He dozed.

An hour from Chicago, Jimmy ached to boast about his encounter with the ski-masked murderer, but he resisted. He thought that the return trip would be a better time for the story. His classmates would be bored with the long ride and would enjoy the entertainment.

Besides, Edward Know It All was only two rows behind. He would try to steal everyone's attention: I lent the guy my jacket, he would say, and I gave him money to buy coffee for both of us, and I led Jimmy and Holly to the scene of the crime, and fuck man, I'm the hero!

Fortunately, Edward and Holly did not mention the incident, either, so Jimmy looked forward to sharing a thrilling story on the bus ride back.

Alex woke to chatter. The lights of Chicago had excited the students. On the left was Ameritech Field. Directly north, the Sears Tower and Hancock building reached into the foggy night, black monoliths with nearly infinite rows of bright tiny windows.

The bus exited at Lake Shore Drive. The self-appointed travel guides resumed talking. They pointed out the Field Museum of Natural History and the Shed Aquarium. Several students ignored the buildings and marveled at the hundreds of yachts, sleeping in the harbor along Lake Shore.

"There's Soldiers Field, where the Chicago Bears play," a Tailor College football player said.

"It's Soldier Field," Jimmy corrected.

"That's what I said."

"There's no 'S'. It's 'Soldier', not 'Soldiers.'"

"Remind me to apologize to you."

The bus made its way to Michigan Avenue and eased to a stop in front of the Palmer House Hilton. The bus's overhead lights came on, and Alex pushed his empty bottle into his duffel bag. "Exit in an orderly fashion. One at a time, boys and girls. Do not trample one another, do not talk loudly, and do not enjoy yourselves during one moment of this trip." His voice was high and nasal, an expert imitation of a fretting grade school principal. The students laughed and joked, appreciating their professor's good humor.

Inside the enormous plush lobby, the students stood in a group as Alex distributed the students' room keys. Jimmy stood next to Carl Locke. Jimmy and Carl were assigned to share a room. Jimmy was pleased because Carl was only six inches taller than he was, and Carl had never been in Chicago.

"This isn't a bad hotel, but there are a lot fancier ones," Jimmy informed Carl.

"Looks pretty good to me," he grinned. He nodded toward a loud posse of pretty young women.

"It's okay," Jimmy grunted.

Carl noted the numerous vermilion couches, which seemed longer than his car. Floor lamps with ornate stems threw overlapping spheres of warm light across the width and length of the lobby's floor. Circular end tables accompanied overstuffed high back chairs. Businessmen sat drinking cocktails, trading divorce stories.

Edward got his key and visited the coffee shop. A few men sat alone in booths, reviewing sales figures and double-checking ledgers. Edward had a cup of decaf and a salad, then went to his room. He was relieved that his assigned roommate had broken a leg and had to remain at Tailor.

Edward pulled his camcorder from his suitcase. He planned to film a documentary of his class' field trip. He had written a letter to the Field Museum and the Museum of Art, requesting permission to film on their premises. The Art Museum refused permission, and it even threatened to have Edward arrested if he tried to sneak in "any kind, manner, or form of filming device, moving or still camera." But the Field Museum granted permission. The assistant curator requested only that a museum employee accompany Edward.

Once back at Tailor, Edward planned to follow up on his filming by recording an accompanying narrative. The narrative would unify the scenes and serve as clever commentary. Edward hoped to sell the film to the college as an introduction for any class that visited Chicago. Ultimately, he hoped the film would help him get into film school.

"Why not start now?" Edward asked the camcorder. He attached the camcorder to its tripod and pressed the AutoFilm button.

"We're here in Chicago, and we, we..."

Edward got up to make sure the door was locked.

"I am in Chicago as a stranger, having been here only three times. The first time, as an infant with my mother and father. We visited a brother of my mom's. Uncle Slim. The second time, as a thirteen year old with my mother. We visited Uncle Slim again. The third time, as a sixteen year old. My mother and I attended Uncle Slim's funeral."

Edward winced. "Cut." His introduction sounded pretentious, so he tried to be casual.

"My name's Edward. Cut. Damn it."

He cleared his throat. "My name is Ed, and this film will introduce Chicago to you. You'll see some of the city's obvious attractions, and some of its not so obvious attractions."

He realized he was picking his nose. He decided to continue because he could edit later.

"This will be a record of the particular students on the trip. They'll offer you some comments and some insights into the city and its culture."

He turned off the machine, rewound the cassette, and reviewed the intro through the viewfinder.

Edward the viewer cringed at Edward the narrator.

The narrator's nose was oily and, in conspiracy with the dresser lamp, cast a shadow that reached his right ear. The harsh light and shadow made his chin look like an ass. A blushing pimple demanded privacy. The narrator's nostrils flared, as if he had to sneeze.

A flicker, then blackness. Now the narrator reappeared, sitting further away. The nostrils kept flaring. And yes, here it came, the index finger violating a nostril.

Edward erased the introduction. In the bathroom, he examined his chin in the mirror. The pimple was smaller than the camera made it look, but it still had to go. He squeezed. Holding a paper tissue to his purged pimple, Edward knew he could not narrate his documentary. He would have to find someone else.

Edward dropped the tissue and wondered why he had not thought of it earlier. "Holly," he said in a stage whisper, "you look very good on camera. Yes, I really think so. Okay, now just talk naturally into the camera. Try not to look like you're reciting my script."

According to the itinerary, the class was to meet in the coffee shop at 9:30 a.m. By 9:45, all the students had arrived, and they waited for their professor. Jimmy drank coffee with his back to his classmates. He had been up since 5:00 and had already taken a walk up Michigan Avenue to the Chicago River. Last night, he had slept poorly. He was not used to having a stranger in the room with him, and Carl had snored all night. Jimmy lay in bed, staring at the darkness and getting angry. Twice he got out of bed and poked Carl. Carl apologized, fell asleep, and resumed snoring.

Infuriated, Jimmy clamped his hand over Carl's nose.

"What in the hell...!" Carl suffered a coughing jag. "Get me some water!"

"I will if you stop snoring."

"Fuck off, midget." Carl stumbled to the bathroom, stubbing his toe on the way, and drank two glasses of water.

"What the hell's wrong with you, midget?" Carl stood over Jimmy, waving the drinking glass like a club.

Jimmy got back into bed, pulled the covers up to his chin. "Relax. You won't snore any more because I scared you."

Carl cursed again, got into bed, and slept without snoring for a few minutes. Jimmy dressed and left the room.

Now Jimmy looked at his watch: 9:45, and no sign of Resartus. Maybe the guy is sick, Jimmy thought, and will call off the scheduled events. Then Jimmy could concentrate on charming Holly Dish before the return trip. Jimmy hoped that his superior Chicago savvy would put him in charge. Rush Street was not the place to go, he would announce with amusement. Only conventioneers and suburban divorcees went there. River North, once a run down shambles, was now an upscale neighborhood of bars and restaurants. It was, Jimmy thought, the place to be. Or, maybe they'd get up to Wicker Park, another refurbished and suddenly hip neighborhood. Jimmy would promise Holly the real Chicago. Once he gained her confidence, he reasoned, his charm would do the rest.

Jimmy's schemes evaporated when he saw Resartus enter the coffee shop. Jimmy sighed and joined the group.

Carl was waiting for him. "I want to let you know I won't be bothering you any more. I'm bunking with a couple of guys down the hall."

"Your snores will still wake me up."

Alex reviewed the day's schedule: two hours at the Field Museum, lunch break, then two hours at the Museum of Art. At 4:30, the students were on their own until Saturday afternoon, when the class would attend the matinee performance of *St. Joan*.

Throughout the day, Jimmy tried to insinuate himself with Holly. Several attempts at conversation died in the Field Museum. Holly was especially annoyed when Jimmy attempted to speak with her as she gazed at the museum's gem collection.

He should have known better. Her eyes were large and motionless, her lips slightly parted, as she studied a diamond from Ghana. The diamond, flattered by the room's precise lighting, sparkled inside the display case. He tried to look impressed by squinting and pursing his lips.

She did not note his appreciation.

"It's...Yeah...!" He stared at the diamond. Why do women love diamonds so much? he wondered.

Holly nodded, a line of irritation drawn onto her forehead.

"And it's pretty."

"Yes."

Jimmy wanted to add, "You're just as pretty." But just the thought of it made him feel ridiculous. "Pretty," he repeated, tongue darting at the corner of his mouth.

Edward Know It All appeared on the other side of Holly. He whispered something, she nodded, and Edward retreated to the rear of the room.

"You're blocking the view," she whispered.

"Uh?"

"Jimmy, move. Edward has to get a clear shot."

He turned. Edward stood against a wall. He frowned, then pointed his camcorder at Holly.

"You can't bring a camera in here," Jimmy complained to nobody in particular. Then he saw an old white haired man. The old man smiled, pointing with his thumb to the employee badge on his lapel. He mouthed, "It's O.K." at Jimmy.

Jimmy retreated and watched Edward attach the camera to a tripod. A moment later, Holly turned and smiled at the camera. Edward pushed a button on the camera, and the lens closed on Holly. The heft of Holly's bust nicely filled her blue shirtdress, and Edward resisted the urge to make the portrait salacious.

Edward stopped filming and talked to Holly. He controlled her as a star director controls an eager actress. She was attentive and even smiled. The smile suggested understanding, perhaps a shared secret. Others kept a polite distance. Edward's camera gave him authority. He stood straight and gestured confidently.

For a moment, Jimmy admired Edward's savvy. Every girl, Jimmy mused, wants a camera's admiration. But he forced aside the admiration so he could hate Edward. The hate arced past its target, and for a couple minutes he hated Holly too.

Steven D. Vivian

"I think the filming went real well," Edward said. "You seemed confident but not arrogant, like some narrators are."

"That's cool."

Edward and Holly were resting on a bench in the museum lobby. Holly removed her black Nikes and lifted her left foot onto her right knee. She rubbed, and Edward imagined her rubbing his feet.

"I have to edit some things, maybe even do some narration when we get back to campus." Edward adapted a breezy posture, leaning casually on one elbow as Holly kept rubbing her feet. "The narration will take a while, so we can do it right at my place."

"Where do we film next?"

"Probably film along State Street."

"No more filming today?"

Edward could not interpret Holly's tone. Was she relieved or disappointed?

"We can't film inside the art museum, but maybe we…"

Holly pulled on her shoes and stood.

"Where are…I mean, what do you want to do next?" His directorial power was collapsing.

"I'm meeting Kelly and some other girls for lunch." Holly waved to an approaching group of friends. "I think I'm blowing off the art museum." She left with her friends. They argued about where to eat as they passed through the door.

Edward hoped Holly would wave at him. She did not.

More classmates approached the lobby. Edward could not be seen without his starlet. He hurried to the men's room and hid in a stall for twenty minutes, repeatedly extending and collapsing his tripod.

Thank chain-smoking Christ, Alex thought. It was finally 4:30.

His feet and shins ached, and he had wanted a cigarette all day. He had paid reasonable attention at the Field Museum. But the art museum was a muddle of paintings, white walls, and high ceilings. A Dali here, a Turner there, some Monet to end the day. Now, as fatigue settled on him, Alex could not remember the paintings' composition or texture. They congealed into a scalding red that gave him a headache.

Alex rubbed his temples, offered a weary smile as the students gathered in the lobby. He looked forward to tonight's kill. He had only the roughest plan, but he did not care. With luck, the blood would share the virtue of a good wine: soothing, complex, inspiring.

52

Chapter Eleven: Alter Egos

Though Alex was a careless academic, he was a careful monster. He always used a checklist: gloves, knives, rope. Sometimes he scribbled ideas for red herrings, pieces of "evidence" that a killer might leave behind: a packet of cocaine (typically only baking soda, which suggested a drug deal gone sour); a page ripped from the Satanist Bible; a heavy metal CD; Zodiac paperbacks; paperbacks about true-life murders; matchbooks from out of town hotels; clipped newspaper stories of unsolved murders; travel brochures for the Caribbean; maps with circled towns; scribbled phone numbers of overseas hotels.

Alex enjoyed the red herrings, but he knew that the motive of his acts ruined even preliminary investigation. Police ask, "Who wanted this person dead, and why?" Alex was usually not connected to the victim, and the purpose of Alex's kills was never grasped. Edward Head would be an unusual case because the monster knew the victim. But Alex did not worry. His plan would be up to the challenge.

For tonight's kill, Alex chose another fun trick: a disguise. Alex had survived childhood with his disguises. When his schizophrenic episodes reached their peak, he hated to come out of his closet, much less to face parents or friends. Sometimes he feared that strangers with cameras or knives lurked outside his door, so he came out of his room in a disguise. A pirate with hat, peg leg and sword. A baseball player. Frankenstein's monster. He once went a month dressed as Nero, a sheet wrapped around his waist as he scraped away at a toy fiddle.

Tonight, he used a full-length black rug from a "Hair Replacement" company and wiry fake black mustache. With his frumpy gray sports jacket, he fancied himself a struggling car salesman on the town.

"My name is John Lowe," he said to his reflection. "Come see me if you're ever looking for a Chevy." He put on tinted glasses and double-checked the jacket's inner pockets for rubber gloves.

Alex told the cabby to stop at Grand and Ontario. He planned to take a relaxing walk and enter any bar that looked promising. The unseasonably warm temperature, a humid 60 degrees, encouraged strollers. Couples walked hand in hand. Outside a bar, a woman in a dropwaist dress and boater held open the door for her drunken friend. The man was wiping at his leather pants and bitching about the rude bartender who would serve him no more alcohol.

After walking east on Grand, Alex found a jazz bar. The music was good. A piano/bass/drums trio improvised on "Nardis." Alex cased the room. Subdued swag lamps. A long polished bar. Tables along the right wall and in the back. Glossies of visiting acts upon the walls.

Alex took a table against the right wall. He sipped gin and tonics.

He waited.

In his room, Edward reviewed the day's taping. Holly was especially attractive on the mammoth steps of the Field Museum. From a distance, beside one of the fluted columns, she was just one many visitors. But the filming began, and her arm rose in a winning gesture that encompassed the sheer scale of the museum's steps and entrance.

The next shot was the lobby. Holly filled the viewfinder from the waist up. "Welcome to the Field Museum, named after one of Chicago's most prominent families," Holly said pleasantly. "The museum is world-famous. It captures the world's history from prehistoric times to the present."

Edward was impressed. Holly needed little dialogue coaching. He simply wrote out her introductions, she went through them two or three times, and she was ready. The camera was her friend. Never a false start, never a pause, never a fumble. Inside the museum, she introduced the stuffed lions and beavers, eagles and bears. Then Taoist holy texts. Then a recreation of an ancient African village with huts and children.

His favorite shot was filmed in the gem room. Holly stood before the impossibly well polished display case, reverently describing a diamond discovered in Nigeria by a Peace Corps volunteer. "The Nigerian Triumph, as it's called, features over two hundred individual cuts and an unequaled brilliance. Note how the spectrum radiates from the stone's center when…"

Holly ended her discussion, and the camera pulled away. In the distance, a short person stuck out his tongue.

"You jackass!" Edward exclaimed.

Jimmy Stubbs was sticking out his tongue and mouthing words that Edward could not decipher. Don't get so mad, he told himself. Just cut him from the tape. But Edward despised the thought of Jimmy in the same room with Holly and him. The sneering creep violated the intimacy of director and actress.

Edward grabbed the phone, called the operator. "Holly Dish," he said before he could lose his nerve. She would be happy that the taping had gone well. Maybe she would like to see it right now, with some beer or wine.

Ten rings. Fifteen. Twenty.

"No one answers, sir. May I leave a message?"

"No thanks," Edward sighed.

"How do you know that was for you?" asked Kate. She was annoyed at Holly, but silently admitted that nobody would be calling for her.

"It's Edward," Holly answered from the bathroom. She brushed her hair violently. "I'm late already and I don't have time to talk to him. I'll see him tomorrow anyway."

She regarded her image in the mirror. Any mirror triggered the response, just as a physician's rubber mallet triggers a knee's response. Your thighs, she accused, are about to bloom again. You had potato chips two nights in a row, and then that pizza last week. And today at lunch, fried fish! Holly tried to examine her image objectively. Her tummy did not bulge, and her hips were firm. Her thighs looked a shade heavy.

Those thighs are more than a shade heavy, Holly the Trainer told Holly the Hippo. Those thighs held extra poundage. For a girl only five feet five inches, two pounds on each thigh are too much. On Monday, you will get back to two miles on the track every night, and you will have only protein drinks for lunch. And forget about French fries for the next two months. Butter is bad too. You're appearing in a film, and the camera puts twenty pounds on some people, especially women!

Holly the Trainer continued the harangue for twenty minutes. And Holly the Hippo did not retreat. She stood in front of the mirror and took the criticism without self-pity. Self-pity usually led to a French fry binge and five pounds.

Holly Dish had created her alter ego out of necessity. From the age of twelve to fifteen, Holly was overweight. At age 14, when girlfriends were busy with makeup, jewelry, clothes, and boys, Holly was busy with food. A typical lunch was two Big Macs, large fries, and strawberry shake. Or a large pizza and quart of Coke.

At age 15, when girlfriends were dating and immersed in puberty's soap opera, Holly was hiding in her bedroom. She weighed 170 pounds and was humiliated. She once broke down into sobs and tears when the news carried a brief story about the beautiful and semi-literate actress Watusi Brite. She was six months pregnant but, as the correspondent noted, "as lovely and shapely as ever."

The crisis came when the kids on Holly's school bus signed a petition. The petition demanded that Holly save the school football team by replacing the entire defensive line. At the bottom of the petition was a line drawing of Holly, French fries sticking out of her mouth, sitting on top of all the players of a rival team. She held the football in front of her mouth, as if she were about to eat it. The rivals were covered with bandages, bruises, and plaster casts. Stars and bubbles orbited their heads.

And Holly's character was naked.

The kids on the bus were laughing, and Holly had sensed they were laughing at her. As she got on the bus, someone yelled, "Save our football team!" The petition, folded into a paper airplane, fell to her feet. Holly's little sister Geri was laughing and ran past Holly, even though Holly yelled for her to wait. Geri, who weighed exactly half what Holly weighed, was soon out of sight.

Holly cried when she saw that even Geri signed the petition.

One week after the petition incident, Holly joined a health club. She felt obscene in her gym shorts and tee shirt. You're a hippo, Holly told herself, a hippo in a girl's clothing. Eventually, Holly became friendly with one of the trainers whose name, ironically, was Holly. Holly the Trainer had once been overweight herself, and she confided that she too had been the butt of jokes.

At the first sign of Holly the Hippo's tears, Holly the Trainer showed no sympathy.

"You're in the wrong class if you want people to feel sorry for you!" The trainer had just led the class though a half hour of jumping jacks, pushups, and stretches. "Anytime you feel sorry for yourself, stand naked in front of the mirror for one minute. Then tell yourself that you're worth more than French fries or cookies or ice cream or whatever. Tell yourself that you're worth about twenty sit-ups!"

"I can't do five sit-ups!"

"Not yet. But in two months, you'll be doing fifty."

When Holly Dish turned 18, she weighed 120 pounds. Three years of diet and exercise had transformed her. She could do one hundred sit-ups and one hundred pushups. She ran three miles daily. The boys liked her and the girls respected her. Her regime naturally rendered her athletic: she could have modeled for those swimwear magazines such as *Sunned American Buns*. When she went running in her tee and slims, she gave boys a hormone high.

Holly went away to college, and she retained her two personalities, the Trainer and the Hippo, as motivation. She also took the petition, which she had kept taped to her dresser mirror for three years. Once at college, Holly realized she could reinvent herself. She was not fat Holly. She was Holly Dish, a campus spool drool.

Holly soon decided that the best part of college was the social life. She liked talking with people, and people liked talking with her. She discovered a gift of gab, and her advisor recommended public relations.

"Why public relations?"

"You're good around people, and your best grades are in speech. Frankly, your grades aren't so hot otherwise." He paused, reconsidered his words. "And you're an attractive and vibrant young woman. You have confidence, and confidence is what pub. rel. is all about."

"I was thinking of publishing."

"You've taken only a freshman English course, and you got a C minus. That won't do at all."

"I don't want to write." Holly was by now an expert actress, adept at manipulation. She offered her sheepish grin. "I was thinking of being an agent, of representing authors in their deals and stuff."

"I see."

"I know my grades need to be better, but I do want to get into publishing because I want to live in New York."

"Why New York?"

"It's supposed to be..." Holly cocked her head. "Cosmopolitan. Glamorous."

"Why not?" Her advisor shrugged. "Perhaps publishing will be your niche. You'll have to take more English courses. Both literature and writing."

Holly nodded firmly. "I'm prepared for that."

The bartender refilled Sandy's glass. Sandy put the glass to her mouth, savoring the barley and malt, and finished half the beer in two gulps. With another two gulps, the glass was empty.

The customers applauded as the jazz trio finished "Star Eyes". She giggled into her empty glass, imagining that the applause was for her. Sandy imagined the bartender addressing the crowd: A round of applause and a round of drinks for the lady. She's put down four straight beers and is not yet weaving in her seat.

Sandy put down her glass, waited for another refill. She searched through her purse for a smoke. No luck. She tapped the shoulder of the man sitting to her left.

"I'm sorry to bother you, but could I steal a cigarette from you?" Sandy hoped "sorry" and "steal" did not come out as "shorry" and "shteal."

The man kept her back to Sandy. "I don't smoke."

"Oh." Sandy looked over the man's shoulder. The man's companion raised her plucked brows at Sandy. The brows were as sharp as a saber.

Sandy turned to her right. "Say, could I borrow a..." The stool was empty. The man sitting next to her had smoked those stinking Kools, she remembered. But she was now agreeable to any cigarette.

Alex had been sitting by the wall, not ten feet behind Sandy. He had watched for a half hour. She was apparently alone, which surprised him. Though the light made it difficult to be sure, she seemed attractive. Her orange hair and red dress were catchy. When she failed to bum a cigarette from anyone, he took the chance.

"Here," Alex offered. "Have one of mine."

"Thank you."

"You need another beer too. Bartender?" He gestured for two more drinks.

"No thanks," Sandy said. "I can buy my own."

"I'm sure you can. But it's my pleasure." His smile seemed genuine. Many smiles, Sandy thought, were disguised smirks. "If you like, you can buy my drink. If not, that's fine too.

Sandy did not know if she liked the man, but at least he did not seem to be a creep. These days, that was a terrific start. He was dressed sanely: no idiotic gold chains or piercings, and his smile widened into an easy grin.

"My name is John Lowe," the man said. "Come see me if you're ever looking for a Chevy."

"Really? I do need a new car." It was true. Her car had 138,000 miles. "Can you get me a good deal, Mr..." She had forgotten his name.

"John Lowe."

"Sorry. Sandy Chandler."

"It's all right. I forget people's names all the time." He laughed. "I forget all kinds of things all the time." His second laugh was a snort.

Sandy laughed too. She laughed freely at his candid snort, and at her own drunkenness. The room had been tipping left since her third beer.

The bartender delivered Sandy's beer and John's gin & tonic. He waited to see who would pay for the drinks.

"She's paying for the drinks," Alex said.

Sandy laughed again. The laughs were coming so easily. She waved a ten at the bartender.

Alex lightly pushed Sandy's hand away. "Just kidding." He paid the bartender and sat on the stool. "The trio's back," Alex noted. "Let's see if we can name the tune."

"All these jazz tunes sound alike to me."

"You've just got to concentrate." He laughed inwardly. He was alert, witty, focused. He felt wonderful when he had a victim. The anticipation was energizing. His headache had melted like ice cubes in warm water.

The trio kicked into a double time cover of "It's Easy to Remember." He told Sandy the name of the tune, then noted the composers, Rogers and Hart.

"They're famous, aren't they?"

"You'd probably recognize a lot of their tunes." He rocked his head back and forth. "You know, 'Isn't It Romantic?', 'Spring Is Here', stuff like that."

"Geez I don't think so." She found herself leaning toward the man, rolling her shoulders to the music. Her spilling orange curls had loosened and now reached the middle of her back. She realized she was flirting and chuckled. The man understood her chuckle and smiled.

"It's a nice night, isn't it?" Sandy asked.

The thought of Sandy's blood thrilled him. "Very much so."

Alex hummed along with "Blue In Green", the trio's last tune. When the trio left the bandstand, Sandy asked that he walk her to her car. "You can tell me how much I can get on a trade-in," she joked.

They walked toward the parking lot. Alex wanted to remain a gentleman for the moment, so he kept a polite distance. Sandy wanted to close the distance, so she began to walk suggestively. She imagined that her walk was alluring. She offered her new friend a cheesy smile, held it, then raised her eyebrows playfully, then smiled again. I know I'm acting silly, she wanted her eyebrows to say, but I'm loaded and I think I like you.

Sandy wanted Alex to smile at her drunken riot of facial tics. So he smiled.

Once inside the car, she rolled down the window. "Give me your phone number, I'll call you next weekend."

"Give me yours first."

She did. He invented a number with the same prefix.

"What a coincidence. Do you live around here?"

He nodded. "What's your street?"

"Broadway, almost on the corner of California."

"I live just a couple blocks away." He stepped away from the car. "I'll call you soon, okay?"

"You bet."

Alex opened his mouth as if to speak.

Sandy leaned half way out the window. "Did you say something?" she teased.

"Not yet." He looked to his left, to his right. Nobody within thirty yards. "I'm sorry if this is a bit odd, but..."

"I hope really fucking odd." Several more winks and nods to show her good humor.

"Could you give me a lift? I took a taxi down here, you see, and since we live close..."

Chapter Twelve: "You'll wake the neighbors."

Alex sat on a fake leather couch in Sandy's living room. Sandy had stepped into the bathroom ten minutes ago, and he wondered if she had passed out. Her speech was slurred as she wobbled to her apartment building. The lobby elevator was not working, so they took the stairs to her fifth floor apartment. She had fallen twice, but she just laughed. "I'm smashed and it's harder to be hurt when you're, when you're, when you get hammered."

Her apartment was pleasant, and Alex was comfortable. Stucco walls; a miniature forest of houseplants on the floor and on the living room window sill. Light gray carpet, art deco prints, and a gleaming kitchenette to the side of the living room. At the end of the hallway, two bedrooms and a bathroom.

He waited calmly, his senses enlivened with anticipation. He heard her singing "Speak Low". Soon she was walking down the hallway in a bathrobe.

"You're very beautiful," he whispered. "And healthy looking."

She smiled. No facial tics this time, only half closed eyes and candid smile.

He took her in his arms and heard her blood rushing through her. It was especially turbulent in her neck and chest.

"You like this?" She ground her breasts against his chest.

"Very much." He wondered if he should excuse himself to go to the bathroom; he wanted to put on his rubber gloves.

Now she rubbed her tummy against him in a circular fashion. With each completed circle, she pressed her breasts against him and squeezed his buttocks. He smiled, followed her cue. They moved to the middle of the living room.

Her perspiration and rising pulse excited him. He imagined her ca- rotid artery ejaculating into his mouth. He had managed to slip on one glove by thrusting his hips as a distraction.

"Off with that." She began unbuttoning his shirt.

After she unbuttoned the shirt, he shrugged it off and let it fall to the floor. With a big grin, he slipped on the second glove.

She stepped back, eyes widening.

"Don't worry about the gloves," Alex smiled. "You'll like the feel of them."

"Don't be an idiot," she whispered. She backed into the kitchenette, arms folded across her breasts.

He followed.

"Frank, Jesus Christ, Frank."

Alex turned.

A tall swarthy man stared at Alex.

"You asshole, Frank, you asshole. I changed the locks. I'll have you arrested for breaking and entering."

"The goddamned door was not locked. I walk in, and what do I see? I see you naked and crawlin' all over this creep." Frank pointed at Alex, and hate hardened his black eyes. He removed his trench coat, revealing thick hairy arms and a big chest straining against a tee shirt.

"I should kill you both," Frank declared. Sandy blinked through tears.

"No need for hostilities, Frank." Alex tried to sound frightened. "Please. Why don't we sit down and discuss this quietly? There's always a way to settle differences without resorting to hostilities."

Frank removed his cap, tossed it over his shoulder. The gesture was theatrical, and Alex wondered if Frank rehearsed it before a mirror.

"He's right, Frank. Let's talk."

"We'll talk after I pound his goddamned face!" Frank roared, face tense and teeth bared. He evidently mimicked the macho confrontational style common in television police melodramas.

"Please. Civility is most precious at the very moment it's being threatened," Alex suggested.

"Shut up!"

"Suck me off."

"Christ shut up, he'll kill us," Sandy pleaded.

"No really. Suck me off, Frank, and then I'll fuck her."

"Now you shut up!" Frank demanded. "You're a freak."

"And a mass murderer." Alex gripped his own neck and stuck out his tongue, pretending to choke himself.

Sandy starting crying, and Alex, still pretending to choke himself, told Sandy to calm herself and sit. She sat.

"Goddammit, I'm the bastard that gives orders in my apartment," Frank roared. "You don't have nothin' to say in here!"

"You'll wake the neighbors," Sandy warned.

"I don't give a hard shit about the neighbors. They can kiss my— Hey, let go of me!"

Alex had grabbed Frank's neck.

"I'm warning you, let go!" Frank managed to punch Alex.

"Rude host," Alex half-whispered. He stomped Frank's foot.

"Stop it," Sandy pleaded. She tried to pull Alex off her husband.

"Shut up, both of you," Alex ordered. He gripped Frank's neck, squeezed, and smashed his face against Sandy's. A sharp report echoed through the apartment. The sound was exciting, like a baseball player hitting a home run, so Alex crashed their faces together again.

Frank dropped to his knees. A purple bulb disfigured his forehead. Alex removed his knife from his jacket pocket. He was about to cut Frank's throat, but on a whim, he jabbed the knife into Frank's eye. The eye leaked like a runny poached egg. To silence Frank, Alex stuffed Frank's cap into his mouth.

Sandy crawled crookedly from the kitchenette to the living room. Alex watched, fascinated by her halting, awkward motions; she crawled like a partially squashed insect. Finally, she made it to the end table, where the phone was.

Alex took a running start and kicked Sandy's head. Her head struck the end table, and one of the table's legs spun across the room like a cheerleader's errant baton. A bloody clump of flesh and hair stuck to a corner of the table. Alex removed the flesh and ate it.

Alex cut Sandy's throat and sucked. The blood was thick, pungent. Its bouquet filled his senses until the air smelled of warm blood.

After Alex finished, he wiped his mouth and chest with Sandy's bath towel, and dressed. Then he stood over Frank, who breathed noisily through his bloody nostrils.

"You were right," Alex whispered. "You should've killed us both."

Frank tried to grab Alex's ankle, and Alex stomped Frank's head until it split.

Six blocks from Sandy's apartment, Alex hailed a taxi.

The cabby pointed at a police car speeding north. "That's the third one. Busy night."

"Never a dull moment for the cops."

"I got a police scanner in the car here." He pointed to a small box with a row of tiny flashing red lights. "There's different stuff every night. That squad car, it's going up to Broadway."

"What's the trouble?"

"From what I can tell, a domestic dispute. Some guy beating up his wife."

"Or visa versa."

They laughed.

Chapter Thirteen: Tales Out of School

Edward had slept poorly and was glad to see daybreak. He sat on the edge of his bed, rubbing his eyes and yawning. All night he had fretted over his plans to seduce Holly Dish. He had revised and reevaluated his plans, but he was losing hope.

His first plan had been to slyly ingratiate himself with her, to win her confidence, and to sleep with her: as simple as putting on a shoe, lacing it, and tying. But she was not attracted to him. At least not yet.

He stood in front of the dresser mirror. The refection winced. His hair was oily and matted; his skin was pasty, its only color the green circles under his eyes and the red splotches of three pimples on his chin and cheeks; his trunk was pear shaped, with a sunken chest and the start of a spare tire. Edward frowned. He was only twenty-one. How had he gotten so out of shape?

He got on the floor and did ten trembling push-ups, then had to rest his burning arms.

His fatigue increased his frustration. What can I do? he wondered. I've tried courtesy, flattery and humor. I've gotten nowhere. What does it take to get her in bed? The old reliables? Lies, booze, and drugs?

In the coffee shop, Edward played it cool. Holly sat with two other women. When he walked by their booth, he ignored Holly. Holly ignored him.

Alex drank coffee and chatted with a few students, but Edward did not join the discussion. He simply ordered coffee and sulked. When he saw Jimmy Stubbs, Edward pretended to study his fingernails.

"All right, ladies and gentleman," Alex announced. "We have a few hours until the matinee at the Blackstone. You're free to do what you wish until then. We will meet in the lobby at one thirty. The performance starts at two o'clock. Please be on time."

Alex paused, sipped some coffee. Sandy had been healthy, indeed: Alex felt rested, focused, and brisk. He even remembered what this afternoon's play was about. Enjoying his role of learned scholar, Alex summarized *St. Joan*. "Mr. Shaw's play is famous for many reasons. In my opinion, its best quality is the humor. On the one hand, it's the story of a woman who martyrs herself for the French Revolution. On the other hand, it's filled with gallows humor and features an unusually full portrait of Joan. She is not a two dimensional, politically correct plaster saint."

Alex clasped his hands, as he imagined a learned scholar would.

"Rather, she is full blooded and fully human, with all the failings of human beings. Human beings," Alex announced, "are so funny in their failings." Alex smiled at the cliché: if he could bring off that stale observation with verve, he must be fully professorial after all.

The play was over, and Jimmy figured it had been good. He was not sure because he hated plays. But the audience had laughed at several scenes. Edward Know It All had laughed more than anybody. Twice, Jimmy had heard Edward's smart ass snicker when no one else was laughing.

The students boarded the bus. Most were tired, and several complained about classes on Monday. Jimmy did not mind going back. The trip had gone badly. He was still fuming because Edward Know It All was filming Holly. Edward had spent an hour filming Holly in the theater lobby, and he even threw a directorial temper tantrum when an elderly woman walked in front of the camera.

And now Edward was yapping about the play with a couple other fungo heads. Resartus was laughing and talking with them. Jimmy had never seen Resartus so animated. He guessed Resartus had spooled a tart during their field trip.

"Last year," Resartus said, "we didn't make it to Chicago. Some administrator decided the trip was too costly, and the funding was cut."

"That's preposterous," Edward said.

"Farcical," Resartus agreed.

"Really sucks," Holly added.

"But I raised some hell and got the funding back," Resartus continued. "Students always gain so much from the trip, so the money is well spent. And what does the administration need with that money? I don't think one of them would appreciate the play, much less understand it." He laughed. On cue, several other students laughed.

Holly had not understood the play either, but she smiled knowingly. "Culture isn't for everyone." She waited for the group to laugh. No one did. "At least, not for administrators."

She got a tepid chuckle or two and decided to get serious. "Professor Resartus, what plays did the previous class see?"

"The last play we saw was *Oedipus Rex*."

Holly nodded, pretending to know the play.

Edward jumped in. "The Ancient Greeks wrote some good comedies. They were called satyr plays, and they were performed after the tragedies. You know, to lighten the audience's mood." Edward started to give a history of satyr plays, but caught himself.

The group changed topics a few times: they talked about Chicago, about school, about their plans for graduation. Eventually they became quiet, and a few students moved to the back to doze. Holly wanted to

keep talking. She wanted to impress Resartus with her knowledge because she needed his letter of recommendation. But she did not know
what to say, so the conversation died.

She did not, however, move from her seat. She decided to feign
sleep. Sleeping with men gave her power over them, perhaps even if the
sleep was just a nap on a bus.

A half-hour from campus, Jimmy took charge. Holly had woken, and
Edward was talking again. Jimmy moved to the seat behind Alex and
Holly and loudly cleared his throat.

"Holly, "Jimmy asked, "have you got any more theories about the
campus murder?"

"Theories?"

"Yes, theories." Jimmy leaned forward until his face almost touched
the back of Holly's seat. "I think the murderer had to be somebody who's
connected to the campus. Maybe even a student."

"Maybe," Holly allowed. "But that'd be risky. The guy might be
identified."

Alex smiled. "What's this about a murder?"

Holly was surprised. "You haven't heard about it?"

"Well, I knew about the female student that was murdered a while
back, but..."

"Lori was, like, she really got messed up," someone lamented.

"No," Holly said. "This is another murder."

"Where did they find the body?" Alex asked.

"There isn't one," Holly said.

"But there is a body," Jimmy asserted. "I know there is."

Edward, unwilling to let Jimmy enjoy everyone's attention, re-
counted the story of lending his jacket to the maintenance man who
never returned. Jimmy motioned for Edward to hurry, but Edward instead speculated about the murderer and the motive.

"For a while, I thought somebody might be after me," Edward
grinned. "But I doubt anybody wants me dead."

"Well, the guy wants me dead," Jimmy asserted. Several students
scrutinized him. He paused, savoring the attention. Jane Johnston asked
if Jimmy had any enemies.

"Not until I confronted the murderer."

Jane let out a little squeal. "What happened?"

Jimmy explained how he looked for clues to the maintenance man's
disappearance. He could not resist a few embellishments: the murderer
took a swing at him, Jimmy claimed, but Jimmy punched back. The

murderer raised his fist to punch again, but Jimmy challenged him "to take your best shot and hope it lands." The man took a few steps backward, Jimmy explained, then ran off.

"That's amazing!" Jane said. "Where did the guy run to?"

"What do you mean?"

"I mean, where did you chase him to?"

Jimmy smiled, leaned back in his seat. He needed a few seconds to construct an answer.

"I started to, but I fell on the ice. When I got up, my ankle was killing me. I had a hard time walking, much less running." He examined the faces of his audience, trying to gauge their credulity.

"There wasn't any ice there," Edward said.

"Right!" Jimmy snorted. "I guess I slipped on a banana peel."

"Let's not get bogged down in details," Alex said. "This is an amazing story. Anyway, you slipped. When you got up, the guy was gone?" He nodded at Jimmy to continue.

"Yeah, but by then I'd cooled off a bit, you know, and I thought, 'Christ, what are you doing? The guy could have a gun!'"

Jane shook her head, confused. "You said the man wants you dead."

"That's what he told me."

"But he only took a swing at you."

"Yes."

"He was so big that if he hit you, he would have killed you?"

"Oh yeah!" Jimmy's excitement soared, and he struggled to remain calm and credible. "Before he swung at me, he said, 'You're next, pal. I swear to God, you're next.'"

Edward wanted to jump into the conversation, but he could not contradict Jimmy without seeming petulant.

Edward tried to sound reasonable. "Do you think that the murderer thinks there's some connection between you and the maintenance man?"

Jimmy shrugged.

"Maybe the guy has a list of people he wants to kill!" Jane blurted. "There's got to be some connection between you and the maintenance man. And Lori too!"

"If we knew the guy's background, maybe we could find a link," Edward suggested.

"The poor guy," Holly sighed. "He goes out for a walk and gets killed."

"And it could have been you!" Jane pointed at Edward. Edward waved his hand to dismiss the notion.

"No, really. Maybe someone wants you dead," Jane insisted.

Billy Thomas had been listening carefully, and he offered his own theory: "It could have been a case of mistaken identity. Maybe the guy thought the maintenance dude was, you know, was you."

"I doubt it," Edward said.

"But the dude was wearing, he was wearing your coat. How tall was he?"

"I don't know. About average."

"About your height, right?"

"A little taller, I think."

"But in the dark, with your jacket on, the murderer might think it was you. You said that you walked to 7-Eleven every night, and the guy, he was walking there at the same time you did."

"And in your jacket," Jane added.

"The theory is plausible," Alex said cheerfully. He was amused that the students had figured out the cause of the maintenance man's murder, but he was not worried. Murders demanded motives, and his motive was too absurd to be considered.

"I still don't think so," Edward insisted. He was pleased to be the center of attention. He glanced at Jimmy, who fumed. "Nobody wants me dead. I don't owe anyone money, I haven't stolen anything, I'm not worth a lot of money, and I never carry anything valuable."

"No kidding," Jimmy said.

"Second, the maintenance guy really did owe people money. He told me that he needed overtime to pay off some debts. I think that whoever he owed money to got impatient."

"I heard that the guy's wife divorced him because he gambled," Holly said.

"I heard the same thing," Billy said. "But I also heard that he was spooling a married babe in town, a bona fide party ass." He snapped his fingers. "Maybe that Lori was spooling the maintenance guy. The wife found out and she, she…" He ran his index finger across his throat.

"That could be," Holly agreed.

"Or maybe he just took off with the babe," Billy added.

"That could be," Jane said. "There's no proof of a murder, is there? There's no body, no blood, no nothing."

"I think the guy made it look like he got killed or kidnapped," Edward said, "and he just decided to get lost. The cops said the same thing. One of them even said that they'd had trouble with the guy. He got drunk in town once in a while, and he'd have to call his wife to come get him. Maybe if he owed all kinds of money, the best thing for him would be to disappear."

The group nodded in agreement. Billy yawned and said he hoped the trip home would not take much longer. Alex said they were getting close.

Jimmy had been listening, angry that his time in the spotlight was so brief. Now Holly and Jane chattered about their Business Administration exam; Edward and Billy talked about why Billy's Camaro was running badly; Alex monitored the discussions and pretended to sleep.

Jimmy took a deep breath to gather his nerve. "So when this guy comes after me, I'll just tell him, 'This is all a mistake, pal. I can't be your next victim because there was no first victim. That guy just ran away from home.'"

The group looked at Jimmy. His face was flush, and his eyes were hard with anger.

"I hope you're right about the guy not getting killed," Jimmy said. Actually, he did not care what had happened to the guy. "But there's one little problem. Some guy with a ski mask stood in front of me and said he was going to kill me." He tried not to stumble into melodrama, but he could not resist. "I'm going to keep searching for clues," he declared, "and I'm going to keep looking for the killer. There is absolutely a killer. Guys in ski masks don't hang around campus in the middle of the night, right after a maintenance man disappears, and after a student gets murdered. I want to believe he's not after me, but I can't afford to."

Jane and Holly stared with sympathy at Jimmy, and Billy nodded solemnly. Edward frowned.

The silence was awkward. "I'll help you look again," Holly finally said.

Jimmy snorted.

"Really," Holly assured. She felt sorry for Jimmy; he was small and powerless. She joined him in his seat. "We'll go out tomorrow and look for some clues."

He tried to appear grateful by offering a lopsided grin.

"If there are any clues," Holly assured, "we'll find them. We'll keep looking, won't we Edward?"

Her question was a command, but Edward did not mind. He was encouraged that Holly was bossing him around. Perhaps her command was a way of disguising her affection for him.

Jane and Billy volunteered to help too. Edward headed them off by lying: "I'll call you after we get organized."

"What about you, Professor?" Holly asked. "Want to join our detective agency?"

"Why, yes. Certainly." Alex rubbed his eyes, pretending to be barely awake. "I'm happy to offer my own ideas, but as for getting physically involved..." He loudly yawned. "You can't get in the way of the police. If you're not careful, you can destroy evidence."

Edward and Jimmy were arguing about the best way to conduct their investigation. Occasionally one of them asked Holly what she thought. "I don't know," was her answer. She finally got up and moved to the back of the bus to gather her suitcase. Edward and Jimmy kept arguing as she walked past, but their eyes followed her.

So did Alex's.

Jimmy imagined ordering Holly to remove her clothes. She did, and Jimmy forced her to her hands and knees. "I always spool tarts doggy style the first time," he explained. "Now bark."

Edward imagined being ravished in the middle of the night by nude Holly. She asked him to point his camcorder at the bed and remove his pajamas. Later, he hung the camera from his erect penis. She gave him a hosedown, and he in turn gave her a facial. They watched the playback between spools.

Alex imagined sitting in an easy chair, with Holly sitting on his lap. She held an icepick. Together, they counted aloud: "One, two, three." On three, Holly thrust the icepick into her neck, spraying Alex's shirt and chest with her blood.

Holly imagined nothing. She was busy planning.

Edward turned on his television and put on a new DVD. The movie was titled *Love of the Imortals*: the second "m" was absent. The title and credits were in florid red gothic script, and the first scene was a dungeon. A blonde maiden, her white nightgown ripped, was chained to the damp stone floor. She struggled to escape her bondage.

The dungeon door opened, and a rectangle of light fell across the maiden. Her eyes widened and she gasped. Now a shadow fell across the woman.

"I have arrived to help you," a voice announced. "You must put aside your fears."

"But you are my captor," the maiden cried. "You dragged me from my warm bed and took me here by horse and carriage in the middle of the rainy night."

"So I did."

The camera panned across the dungeon to the man. He wore black pants, white shirt, and black vest. His black velvet cape dragged across the floor.

"I shall free you from this dungeon. In fact, I shall free you from mortality."

"You shall?"

The man knelt beside the woman. He grasped her chains and twisted them. The chains, which in a moment of bad editing were revealed to be

plastic, broke into several small pieces. The dubbed sound of a beer can being popped open represented the popping of the chains.

"You are now mine forever," the man declared. He picked up the woman and carried her as a groom carries his bride across the threshold. He lay her on a straw mattress and paused to watch her bosom heave. Then, as she gazed transfixed at him, he removed his clothes.

Edward was pleased. The maiden's tits were deep dish all the way, and they bounced heartily as the man spooled her.

The woman screamed her porno scream: a dub, it seemed, from a game show. But now the man surprised Edward. Rather than bite the maiden's throat, he bit his own wrist and shoved it against the woman's mouth.

"You are immortal, my love! Immortal!"

The woman howled. She already had canine teeth.

Edward swore and stopped the tape. The vampire angle distracted him. He wanted to see a woman with deep-dish tits and high saddle get spooled without the outdated gothic rubbish: the stilted dialogue, the dungeon and candelabra, the brooding vampire as deadly seducer. Edward wanted direct, uncomplicated spooling.

He again imagined himself in bed with Holly. The camcorder was pointed at them, and Edward directed his starlet.

"Your left side is your best," Edward reminded

"Okay," Holly nodded. "I'm ready."

"Action!"

Chapter Fourteen: Smokes

On a Sunday afternoon, Jimmy sat in his room drinking a beer by his open window. A few leaves were sprouting on oaks. Across the street at another frat house, students tossed a Frisbee. Others sat on the porch drinking beer, gossiping, and enjoying the rising temperature.

The semester was moving quickly. Already it was late March, and midterm exams started tomorrow. Jimmy was unprepared. He had spent much of his time scheming of ways to spool Holly Dish. The cause seemed hopeless for a while. She had spent one afternoon with him looking for clues to the campus murder, but she was bored. They tramped back and forth through snow, cursing the brief cold snap.

Besides, Edward Know It All was there too, and he insisted that "the murder victim" was only a runaway husband. Edward then took a half-hour to explain his theory in withering detail. Jimmy admitted that Edward's theory made sense. It seemed ridiculous that a murderer, if there was one, would confront Jimmy and David. The guy was probably a bored townie, wandering around campus to kill time.

Jimmy opened a second beer, moved to the card table in the middle of his room, and forced himself to study for his Ancient History exam. The history exam would be bad enough, Jimmy knew, and the Calculus exam would be awful, too.

And Resartus's exam...Christ. For a few days after the Chicago trip, Resartus was coherent. Now he was back to his old ways: disorganized, obscure, and eccentric. He spewed nonsense such as "dichotomy of head and body," "rhetoric of interpretation," "Yeats's' Spiritus Mundi," "Joyce's multi-level puns," "Semiotics," "Heidegerian phenomenology," etc. Resartus once stopped in mid sentence and stared at the far wall, then burst into laughter.

Jimmy had studied for two hours and was bored, so he was happy to hear the sudden blare of rock music in the living room. He slammed shut his book, grabbed another beer, and hurried down the stairs.

Several students sat drinking beer and smoking sod.

"Party time, little dude," said Robert Beck. "Have an hors d'oeuvre." He gave Jimmy a joint.

Jimmy took a long drag then went into the kitchen. Bill and Stan stood at the keg, serving guests cups of beer. They made sure the women were served first. A student named Carrie smote Stan, and he handed her the cup of beer with excessive courtesy, pinkie finger extended. When she accepted the cup, he bowed. She smiled and bowed back. Stan left Bob at the keg and escorted Carrie into the living room.

Jimmy was next in line for a beer, but a woman cut ahead of him.

"Nice manners," he sneered.

She ignored him.

"We need a better quality of guests," Jimmy complained to Bill.

Bill laughed. "What's bad about her? Did you see her tee tops?"

"No." Jimmy glanced into the living room, but he could not see the woman. The room already teemed with students.

"I know. You've got eyes only for one special woman." Bill winked, as if promising discretion.

Jimmy grabbed his beer and waded past the people in the living room. Crowded rooms were dangerous for Jimmy because he often collided with elbows, cups, and cigarettes. He still had a scar on his scalp where someone had turned around and accidentally burned him with a cigarette.

Kris Hesse, Holly's roommate, was in a corner. She waved him over.

"I'm surprised to see you here," Kris shouted over the din.

"I live here."

She belched and hiccupped at the same time and nearly lost her balance. She leaned on Jimmy's head to stay upright, as a drunk leans on the bar.

"Stupid! I know you live here. But you've got that killer exam coming up in English." She fished a cigarette from her shirt pocket. Jimmy watched closely, which was easy. Kris was tall, and Jimmy's eye level matched Kris's bust level. "Holly's back in the dorm studying her whole wheat buns off for that exam. Says she's got to get an A."

"Too bad for her."

Kris grabbed his face and squeezed as if she were squeezing an infant's.

Suddenly, Jimmy was gregarious. He stood grinning, spittle and whiskey dripping from his chin, and he marveled at the students. They were packed in the living room and kitchen, with barely room to turn around. They talked and drank, laughed and smoked, joked with one another and rubbed against one another. Jimmy wanted to join in the fun. His steps were unsteady and his foot struck a table leg; a bottle of vodka fell to the floor. Jimmy did not notice. He was too busy with his two drinks.

Elbows, backs, chests and breasts were often in Jimmy's face, but he did not mind. He even laughed about it. "Where are the short people around here?" he screamed. Several people laughed, and Jimmy laughed with them.

He tripped, and someone's back stopped him from falling.

"'Scuse me," he said to the back. He tried to gain his balance without spilling his drinks. He felt as if he was leaning face first against a wall with ice underfoot and his hands tied, and he could not stop the slow, face-scraping descent.

The back turned and hands held Jimmy up. He was again face to bust with Kris Hesse.

"I got you a drink but you were gone," he yelled.

Kris could barely hear him and bellowed through cupped hands. "Have you got any cigarettes?"

"Upstairs!" He grabbed her hand and pulled her through the crowd.

She stumbled behind him, laughing.

Jimmy pretended that the door was locked. "I'll have to kick it in!" Two kicks did nothing but hurt his foot, but he did not care.

Jimmy's cheer was contagious, and Kris took her turn. The door remained shut. They kicked the door in unison, and it finally gave way. They searched the room but found no cigarettes. "Dammit Jimmy, I'm dyin' for a smoke," Kris complained.

Jimmy found a peeling cigar in the bottom of a drawer. Kris made a face.

"I'm out of smokes," Jimmy apologized. He pronounced "smokes" as "shmokes." "Somebody downstairs must have some."

"No, everybody's maxed out."

Jimmy opened his refrigerator and removed two beers. He tossed one to Kris. "Let's chug these on the way to your dorm."

"What?"

"You've got some smokes in your room, right?"

She nodded.

"Then let's get 'em!"

He pulled her down the stairs and out the door. Jimmy insisted on holding Kris's hand as they stumbled across campus. He did so in a joking manner, escorting her like a Boy Scout, then jumping up and down like a chimp. But the chimp was drunk. He fell in a mud puddle and rose laughing.

Jimmy congratulated himself on his quick thinking. He planned on walking into Kris's room with her hand in his. He imagined Holly looking up from her textbooks and turning red with envy. He even imagined the two women would get into a cat fight over Jimmy: slapping and clawing and tearing off one another's clothes while Jimmy, nude except for a cigarette, cheered them on. "Don't worry," he would say, "the loser can sleep with me tomorrow night."

They burst into the room.

Holly sat at her desk.

Edward Head sat beside her.

"What happened to you?" Holly asked Jimmy. She pointed at his muddy pants.

"We're here for my cigarettes," Kris announced. She rifled through several desk drawers until she found a pack. She opened it, handed a cigarette to Jimmy.

Jimmy was shocked to see Edward. Distracted, he lit the filter end of the cigarette, then cursed and flung the cigarette across the room into a wastepaper basket.

"You dumb ass!" Kris yelled at Jimmy. She retrieved the cigarette and ground it out in an ashtray.

"Sorry," Jimmy mumbled.

"Don't start a fire!" Kris ordered. She gave Jimmy another cigarette.

Edward stepped forward. "Allow me. We wouldn't want you to hurt yourself."

Jimmy stood seething as Edward produced a lighter. The cigarette was bent and would not draw correctly. Jimmy sucked hard, but the lit end fell to the floor and burned the rug.

Edward laughed. Jimmy stared down at the burn hole, then up at Edward. Now Holly and Kris laughed too. The laughter was self-perpetuating. Soon Holly was laughing so hard that tears rolled down her cheeks, and Edward was doubled over.

Jimmy's red face rendered his blonde mustache white.

Kris pointed at Jimmy. "Look! The little monkey's about to cry!"

Jimmy took another cigarette from the pack and lit it. He took two deep drags to assure it remained lit. When Edward straightened to catch his breath, Jimmy grabbed his right hand.

"Have a cigarette." Jimmy ground out the cigarette in Edward's palm.

Edward yelled and yanked his hand away. Jimmy punched Edward's nose and kicked his shin. Edward fell against the wall and Jimmy kept attacking.

Shouts filled the room. When Jimmy turned around to tell the women to shut up, Kris struck his face with a beer bottle.

Chapter Fifteen: Buddy System

Alex hurried into the classroom, a stack of midterm exams in his arms. At their desks, the students were hunched over their notes, trying to memorize last bits of information. Anxiety lined their faces.

"You can take an extra ten minutes on the test," Alex said soothingly. The test was a dilly; he knew that some students could not pass with an extra ten hours.

He handed a stack of tests to the first person in each row. When he came to Jimmy's row, he noted Jimmy's black eye. When he came to Edward's row, he noted Edward's bandaged hand and bruised forehead. When he came to Holly's row, he noted her suddenly lowered head.

Alex told the students to pace themselves carefully, and to not labor over any section longer than twenty minutes. He wished them good luck then sat at his desk to mull over his outline for a new novel. Alex had started the outline after returning from Chicago. Sandy's blood had revitalized Alex as rain revitalizes the desert. Ideas had bloomed quickly, taking on lively narrative shapes and intense emotional colors; for a few hours, the ideas had sprouted at an exhilarating, even dizzying, pace. The abundance was galvanizing, and he worked quickly. In two days, he had finished half an outline.

But on the third day, Alex's energy flagged and he struggled to finish even a paragraph.

Now Alex stared at the outline, wondering how to proceed. His protagonist was a psychiatrist. The psychiatrist's husband, an inept hospital administer, is having an affair with a young nursing intern. The psychiatrist, possessed of nearly inhuman calculation, decides to murder him and make the death look like suicide. Six months before taking any action, the woman "confides" to a friend that her husband is acting strangely. He has even threatened to hit her. Meanwhile, the nursing intern tells the man that she is pregnant with his child. She threatens to expose their affair if he does not pay for an abortion and give her $100,000 within ninety days.

The psychiatrist begins slipping anti-psychotic drugs into the husband's drinks. His behavior changes as she expected: violent mood swings, bellowing delusions of grandeur, memory loss, paranoia. One evening the wife comes home late from work. She finds blood spattered across the kitchen, and the blood leads to the bedroom. On the dresser, she finds a note torn into small pieces. She assembles the note as best she can and makes out the words "scheme" and "revenge." The note is composed in block printing, so she cannot be sure who wrote it. Worse, she finds a bloody boot print that is larger than her husband's.

At this point, Alex's outline stopped.

Alex had tried to push the story forward for three weeks, but it would not budge. Now Alex sat at his desk, reading the outline, occasionally glancing up at his students, and cussing under his breath. After thirty minutes, the tests began trickling in. The first few were half-finished. The students tossed the tests on Alex's desk and hurried out of the classroom. More tests followed, some unfinished, and others crammed with minute handwriting. The students looked exhausted. One joked that she would be too tired to attend class for a week.

Jimmy Stubbs submitted his test and stomped out. Alex glanced at the test: the first half, composed of multiple choice and short answer, was partially complete. The second half, an essay discussing the link between William Butler Yeats's poetry and his beliefs regarding Irish nationalism, was a mess. The answer started out with bare coherence, then disintegrated into uninformed rambling. The handwriting grew sloppy and the tone desperate. At the bottom Jimmy scrawled, "I give up. Why don't you pull the trigger now and put me out of my misery?"

Alex looked at his watch and announced that two minutes remained. Two students were still writing: Edward and Holly. Edward was calm. With a small smile, he slowly reviewed his answers, pencil poised in his bandaged hand. Holly, however, was frantic. Halfway through the test, she began nervously running her left hand through her hair as she wrote, and now her hair pointed haphazardly in all directions, as if she'd written her test in a malfunctioning wind tunnel.

"Time's up," Alex announced.

Edward gave Alex his test then stood by the doorway, waiting for Holly.

Holly put down her pen, folded her arms across her chest, and remained in her chair. She looked as immovable as an anchor.

Edward asked Holly if she wanted to get some coffee.

She stared straight ahead.

Edward left.

Finally Holly stood up. Her lips trembled, her chin wrinkled, and she cried.

In his office, Alex spent ten minutes calming Holly to the point that she could speak without weeping.

"I really want to apologize, Professor Resartus." She spoke softly, without theatrics. "I made a butt of myself, and I am sorry to bother you like this."

"It's all right."

"I didn't do too well on the test. I do not want any special favor, but..." She shrugged. "Maybe I do. I guess I just want to explain."

Holly said that she had studied hard for the test, but something happened last night that upset her. The trouble started when her roommate and Jimmy Stubbs, both drunk, burst into her room. Soon a fight broke out between Jimmy and Edward. Kris ended the fight by striking Jimmy with a bottle. Holly threw everyone out of the room, but on the way out Edward had mistakenly grabbed several pages of notes.

Holly was telling the truth—except about Edward taking her notes. Her notes were where she had left them, on her desk.

"By then," Holly exclaimed, "I was too angry to phone Edward for the notes and who knows, maybe it wouldn't have helped anyway. I was too bagged to study more."

Alex leaned back in his chair, took out a Dunhill. "I'm sorry about this whole mess, but what do you propose to do about it?"

Holly had hoped that Alex would not count the test, but she could see that she was wrong. He just sat there, smoking and stone-faced.

"If I do better on my other tests maybe it, maybe this one wouldn't count quite as much."

"Did you pass this test?"

"I doubt it."

"I have an idea. I will grade your test with all the others. But I will discount it a bit if you do well on the upcoming term paper and on the final exam. If you do well on the remaining work, that will suggest that you could perhaps have done better on the midterm."

Holly nodded bravely. Already she was making plans for Edward to ghostwrite her term paper.

"I'll do my best." Holly rose from her chair, then asked, "Did you hear about the double murder in Chicago this weekend?"

"No."

"My mother told me about it when I called her the other day. She was shook up." Holly laughed. "She didn't want me to go on the field trip in the first place. Said Chicago was too dangerous. And then two murders. Can you imagine?"

"Your poor mother," Alex smiled.

"The police think it was a love triangle. Somebody murdered a woman and her husband in their apartment. They were separated, and the police think it's the woman's boyfriend."

"Sounds like a melodrama."

"Or a soap opera."

Edward was washing the dishes when he heard a knock on his door. He paused, listened again. Friends of the women upstairs sometimes mistakenly knocked on Edward's door. But the knocking persisted.

"Who is it?"

"Holly Dish."

Edward gulped. It was unthinkable. After last night, he feared that she would never speak to him.

"Just a moment." He ran his hands through his greasy hair, popped a mint into his mouth, then opened the door.

Holly stood in the doorway. She wore sweatpants, sweatshirt, and a generous smile. A six-pack of beer dangled from one hand. "It's about time for a break from the books, don't you think?"

Shrugging happily, Edward led her to the living room. His bowels rumbled with anxiety. Holly Dish in his apartment...with beer!

"What a, a, it's a surprise to see you." His voice seemed an octave higher than normal.

If Holly noticed his high pitch, she did not show it. She handed Edward a beer and took one for herself.

Edward motioned for Holly to sit on the couch; he took the folding chair beside the couch. They talked about the exam. Edward was modest. He had done well, he knew, but suspected that Holly had been nuked.

"I got at least a 'B' on the test," Holly said casually.

"That's terrific!"

"Who knows? Maybe I'll even luck out and get an 'A'."

He thought she was lying, but he was happy to agree with her.

"I want to thank you for helping me study for the test. You really helped me out."

"You're welcome." Edward looked squarely at Holly for a moment, and she did not look away. "And I'm sorry about the stupid fight."

"Maybe you can help me with the final, too?"

"Sure!"

After thanking Edward again, Holly drained her beer in three gulps and began talking about her plans to get into publishing. Then she asked Edward about his plans after graduation.

Edward disliked talking about himself, but the combination of Holly and his second beer excited him. "I want to make movies, so I'll try to get into a film school in California. Maybe UCLA."

"What makes it so good?" She feigned interest with great skill, eyes bright and smile lively.

Edward took the bait and talked ten minutes, pausing only to open his third beer. Holly nodded and smiled at the perfect moments, playing Edward as a virtuoso plays the piano. Soon Edward was talking about his plans to form his own movie company.

"I like your ambition."

Edward's grin made his big ears stand away from his head.

She slowly tucked her legs underneath her bottom. "Do you have any wine, Ed?"

"I—yes, I think I do." He jumped from his chair, sprinted to the kitchen, and rifled through the refrigerator. When he did not see any wine, he panicked. But then he saw the wine lying behind a loaf of bread.

"Hope you don't mind regular drinking glasses," he called.

"Not at all."

Edward carried the bottle and glasses into the living room. Holly was lying on the couch.

With unsteady hands, Edward filled Holly's glass, then his.

"Here's to your movie career," Holly smiled.

"And to your publishing career."

They clicked glasses. Holly downed her drink quickly and looked at Edward. She nodded at him, indicating that he too should chug the wine.

He did. The room was suddenly warm. He giggled.

"I'll pour us another," Holly said. When Edward gave her his glass, she grasped his hand and pulled him on top of her.

"Jesus Christ," Edward managed.

Holly encircled Edward with her arms and pushed her groin against his.

Sweat gathered upon his forehead. He pecked Holly's cheek, as if she were his grandmother.

"Let's spool, Ed."

Edward's eyes bugged.

"But I don't want to marry you. Roll on a shower cap."

"Roll a what?"

"A life jacket, a rubber, a condom, a prophylactic. Whatever you want to call it. Just roll it on."

Edward disentangled himself from her and ran into his bedroom. He peeled off his clothes, did battle with the uncooperative condom, then looked at himself in the mirror, red-faced. He groaned at his reflection: a pasty, bowlegged pear with an erection.

He took a deep breath and turned around. He nearly collided with Holly.

"That looks very nice, Edward." Holly smiled, looked down at Edward's erection. She was fully clothed, and Edward felt ridiculous. He covered his erection with his hands.

"Don't you want to spool?" Holly asked.

"Obviously."

"Good. If I let you spool me, will you do me a favor?"

"What's the favor?" Edward stared at her gym shoes.

"Write a term paper for me."

"A term paper?"

"It's the buddy system," Holly soothed. "You do something for me, I do something for you."

She pulled Edward's hands from his penis. It was sagging. "You're getting a flat." She massaged his penis, and it was erect in three seconds.

"What's so wrong with helping each other out?"

"Nothing at all…if I spool you once a week."

"For an 'A' paper?"

"Of course. I don't write McPapers."

"Okay. But the paper comes before you do."

Edward again covered his erection.

"I need to have the paper in hand. An 'A' paper. Then we spool."

"Then we spool," Edward nodded.

"Got any pop? Maybe a Coke?"

"I don't think so." Edward awkwardly stepped backward, wondering what to do with himself.

"That's OK. I've got to get back anyway."

"Already?" He draped his jacket over his lap, loincloth fashion.

"Hope to see that paper soon, Edward."

"You will, Holly, and then we…"

She was already gone.

Chapter Sixteen: Dream Anatomy, Dream Physiology

Edward and Holly sat in the student union. For different reasons, both pondered their performance on Alex's midterm. Edward had earned an "A". Alex had even scrawled, "Well done. Your answers are well-detailed and direct" on the test. Though Edward was used to "A"'s, he was euphoric. The praise from a Once Respected Author was exciting.

Holly had crumpled her test into a ball and tossed it in a wastepaper basket. She had expected to do poorly, but Christ! Failing the test unnerved her. Walking to the union, she remarked casually that she had done "OK." She hinted that the test maintained her "B" average. In fact, she now had a "D" average. Getting a letter of recommendation would be impossible without an "A" on both the term paper and on the final exam.

Edward did not want to gloat, so he asked about Holly's spring break plans.

"I don't have the money to go to Florida this year," Holly said, "so I'll just stay home and look for some new athletic shoes. Probably a pair of Lambruscos."

Edward wondered why Holly needed new shoes. Her current pair was impressive enough. They looked less like shoes than sports cars: cherry red, with neon blue trim along the uppers' dynamic lines.

"Do those shoes come with a tachometer and four on the floor?"

Holly rolled her eyes: Edward was such a loser. "Anyway. What exciting things are you doing during break?"

"I'm staying here." He leaned forward and spoke with a lowered voice. "I'll work on the term paper."

"What will it be about?"

"What would you like it to be about?"

Holly dismissed the suggestion with a wave of her hand. "Just make it good, and make it look like I wrote it."

Edward enjoyed the irony of her demand. "Your paper will be about...oh..." His fingers drummed the tabletop. "How about Dylan Thomas?"

"Who's she?"

"No, it's a he. He's a poet. We'll read him after spring break." Edward allowed himself a boast. "I've worked ahead of schedule, so I have some ideas. Besides, he's so obscure that you can say just about anything."

Holly nodded, briskly gathered her books. "Well then. See you after break." Then she whispered: "I'll need all of that term paper done when I get back."

Edward blinked.

"All or nothing," she said as she turned away.

Edward bought another coffee and meandered into the deserted TV room. He stretched out on a couch and watched the news. Despite the coffee, he soon nodded off, the TV's light flickering on his face. He woke at seven thirty and trudged across campus toward the parking lot.

At the corner of the Academic Center, Edward ran into something.

Edward found himself on the ground, watching red and blue bubbles orbit his head. He wondered how he had managed to run into the wall. Then he saw Alex Resartus standing over him.

"Sorry, old sport," Alex apologized. He pulled Edward to his feet.

The collision had sprung Alex's briefcase, and Edward winced at the moat of papers that encircled him. Then Edward noticed that Alex was wearing sunglasses in the waning moments of twilight.

They stood looking at one another for an awkward five seconds: Edward staring at the sunglasses, and Alex smiling with the sprung briefcase hanging from his hand. Bothered by Alex's silence and curious smiling, Edward squatted to gather the papers. Alex simply stood there, allowing Edward to do the work. Edward arranged them into a crude pile and handed them to Alex. Alex balanced his open briefcase on one palm and shoved the pile inside; the briefcase bulged and barely locked.

"Thank you," Alex said with incongruous cheer. "Great to see you. And have a good break." Alex nodded and continued on his way. His gait was tentative, as if he walked on ice.

Edward watched Alex until he disappeared from view, then headed to his car. He pondered the odd behavior of writers. Edward guessed that many writers cultivated their eccentricity, as a rocker or a rapper cultivates arrogance or as a salesman cultivates aggression. Alex's oddity, however, seemed genuine.

These musings were interrupted when he kicked something and heard a soft *ping*. An amber prescription bottle rolled off the sidewalk and onto the grass. Edward took it inside the Academic Center to examine it.

The bottle contained a half dozen gelatin capsules filled with something rusty brown. The bottom of the bottle was dusted with the same brownish substance. Edward broke open a capsule and shook out the contents. At first, Edward guessed it was paint. He smeared the stuff across his finger, and it became a shade redder.

Blood.

Must be part of a fraternity hazing ritual, Edward thought. He had heard many stories about frat hazing: pledges keeping a pickle in their anus for a day, pledges gluing beer mugs to their foreheads, pledges wearing giant diapers over their normal clothing. And now capsules of blood. It got weirder each year. Edward tossed the bottle into a wastepaper basket.

Alex studied his face in the mirror. The reflection was unflattering. The cluster headaches were returning, and so were the red patches. The right eye twitched and watered as if an invisible pin were jabbing it. Adding to the eye's odd appearance was a bloom of long eyelashes: Sandy's eyelashes.

Alex needed blood immediately. He rummaged through his briefcase, cursing. That little shit Edward Know It All, Alex thought, running right into me, scattering papers all over the place, me standing there like an idiot with sunglasses to hide a mutating face.

And now the precious bottle was gone. Alex threw the briefcase across the room. It chipped the wall and papers scattered across a dusty pile of books. The missing bottle contained Alex's final supply of blood.

The blood dated back to last year when he had come across a man changing a flat tire. It was three thirty in the morning, a misty moon on highway 7, eight miles from Pokena. Alex had pulled off the road behind a jacked up pick up.

"Bad night for a flat," Alex remarked. He ambled up to the truck, gloved hands in pocket.

"Damn right it is." The man, a stout six-foot and a half, wiped sweat from his forehead.

"Thought you might need some help."

Alex's cold grin alarmed the man. He picked up the tire iron and twirled it like a baton. "Not really."

"Let me help," Alex insisted.

They stood looking at one another for a long moment, then Alex lunged. The man took a step back and struck Alex's shoulder with the tire iron. Alex slipped and took another blow on top of his head; the iron rang like a giant tuning fork.

The steel-tipped toe of the man's boot arced toward Alex. The kick cut his lower lip, and the man cocked his leg for a second kick. Alex grabbed the leg and pulled. The man waved his arms like an unsteady tightrope walker, but Alex's second pull brought the man down.

"I don't have no goddamned money!"

Alex smashed the man's head against the road, and the impact produced a dull thwop, like a hollowed pumpkin dropped on asphalt. Blood erupted from the head's every opening, and Alex lapped the face clean.

The blood was rich and slightly sweet.

The body was worth bleeding.

Alex put the corpse in his trunk. When he got home, he hung the body in the attic and slit the throat. The blood dripped into a bucket. Alex spent a week putting the blood in gelatin capsules. Though not as good as fresh, the blood was Alex's pick-me-up. He used the capsules as others use coffee.

Now, as his headache worsened, Alex resorted to the crude pain-killer of whiskey and sleeping pills. But his sleep was marred by odd dreams. In one dream, he tracked a victim for hours. When he finally cut open the victim's stomach, empty gelatin capsules tumbled out.

In another dream, his lungs were housed in his forehead, his ribs under his cheekbones, and his anus under his chin. The face throbbed with the erratic pulsing rhythm of stop action photography. His dead brother David, rotted flesh dangling from his radius and ulna, gave him a jar filled with lithium.

"How did you recognize me?" Alex managed to ask. His mouth was in his right armpit.

"Medicine time again," David said. "You're getting worse. Crying because your pop lost its fizz is one thing, buddy. This disguise stuff, though, it's too much. You've lost your center."

"I don't like—"

"Stop whining."

"But I don't like—"Alex wept at the futility of explanation. "I can't be around you people, any of you people! Leave me alone, the medicine reminds me that there are people!"

"C'mon, buddy. You can't live in your closet another week."

Alex raised his arm and pushed in the lithium. The shifting of bones and muscle in his face slowed. When David nodded approval, Alex ripped the last of the flesh from David's arm.

Alex woke. He had been sleeping with his head raised six inches above the pillow. He had often slept like that as a teenager, so the pillow's singing would not wake him.

He examined his face with both hands. Now the eyelashes of both eyes had grown. He trudged to the bathroom mirror and laughed.

The eyelashes were half an inch long. His Roman nose was tipped several degrees to the left, as if made of modeling clay. One eye was blue, the other brown. His right earlobe was larger than the left; it was pierced to accept an earring.

"Losing your center?" Alex asked his reflection.

"Very quickly," the reflection agreed.

His condition was declining rapidly, and he wondered if he would grow breasts in another week. He needed a victim in the next day or two. The victim must, Alex thought, be male. He must be about six-foot tall, have dark brown or black hair, and he must be healthy.

Alex stuffed a suitcase with clothes, knives, rope, and rubber gloves. He decided to drive north until he hit Michigan. He had not been in Michigan for several years. Maybe, he thought, my luck will be better there.

Chapter Seventeen: The Name Suits Her

Claire Sweet was often told that her name matched her personality. She was good company. She was industrious and smart, tall and pretty. Her words were kind, and she put the needs of others before her own. So she did not complain when her seven-year marriage ended. First, Claire figured that most people were busy with their own problems. Second, they would not understand how Claire Sweet could become entangled in such a debacle. They would not understand at all.

Claire locked the door to her apartment and hurried down the stairs to the driveway. Mrs. Tandy, the landlord, happened to be looking out the front window.

Mrs. Tandy rapped on the window and waved. "Off to the library?" she called loudly enough to be heard through the window.

Claire nodded.

"Have a nice time."

Claire nodded.

Mrs. Tandy could not have been more pleased with her tenant. Claire worked hard and was dedicated to learning. And she was never a minute late with the rent.

Driving to the library, Claire tried to concentrate on today's task. She still had a lot of research to do. Dr. Smith, her history professor, had assigned the class a twenty page research paper requiring at least thirty sources. Claire liked her topic — the economic aftermath of the Athenian-Spartan War — but she was also intimidated by it. The topic was complex and demanded thorough research.

Despite the task's appeal and enormity, Claire was distracted. She was wondering, as she usually did in her minutes of spare time, if she would ever really graduate. Her immediate answer was always, "Yes." But then again, she never dreamed that she would be divorced at age twenty-five and be a college freshman at twenty-seven. And now to look back and think that marrying Stephen would have ever worked.

"You were an idiot," Claire accused herself for the thousandth time.

To hasten the divorce, she agreed to half the possessions and half the money brought by the house's sale. The bungalow sold for eighty-eight. By the time legal fees and taxes and moving costs and other debts were subtracted, Claire had almost enough make it through four years of tuition and board. If her grades were good enough, she might earn a scholarship. After one semester, she had a 3.6 GPA: good for a Tailor freshman. But not good enough for the money she needed.

The thought of grades pulled her back to today's task. She trotted up the library steps, determined to find twenty sources by five p.m. The library was deserted, thanks to spring break. A librarian smiled as Claire walked past the check out desk.

Edward looked up at the sound of books crashing to the floor. The room had been silent all morning, save for the buzzing of the fluorescent lights overhead. He saw a tallish woman, long brunette hair tied into a ponytail, disappear behind a row of hooks. Edward guessed the woman was a young faculty member, or perhaps a bookish townie.

He returned to his notes about Dylan Thomas. Edward already had an idea for Holly's paper. The paper would examine Thomas's use of sexual metaphor. As he bragged to Holly, Thomas's poetry was so obscure that the paper could claim nearly anything. The challenge would be to imitate Holly's confused and confusing prose, yet write an "A" paper. He decided to write the paper in his own style, then rewrite it to imitate Holly's style later.

Edward wrote five pages in ninety minutes. He liked the paper so far, and figured he could finish it in a few days. He yawned, stretched, and walked to the water fountain. As he bent over for a drink, he heard several books crash to the floor.

He walked across the room and found the tall woman sitting on the floor, surrounded by books.

Startled, Claire looked up.

"Let me help," Edward offered.

"That's been about par for the course," Claire sighed after the last book was replaced. "I've gotten nowhere today." She stood and swept hair from her forehead.

"Me too. I've spun my wheels." Edward wondered why he was lying, then realized that he did not want to upset the woman. She was pleasant, long and lilting. And her slight Southern drawl was charming. He wanted to listen to her talk more. He followed her back to her desk, which was covered with notes and open books.

"What are you looking up?" He glanced at her notes. They were written in a script as graceful as the author.

"The war between Athens and Sparta."

"That's a good topic. I had a class with Dr. Smith, and that was a pretty good war."

"A good war?"

"Yeah. For one thing, it lasted so long. Twenty six years, right?"

"Twenty seven," Claire corrected softly.

"And when your general dies during the second year of the war!"

"You mean the Athenian general? Pericles?"

Edward snapped his fingers. "That's him." Edward launched into a monologue about Pericles's skill in oratory, and how good the general was at inflating the Athenians with righteous indignation. He was about to discuss Pericles's death, but caught himself.

"I don't know when to shut up," he grinned. "Sorry to keep you from your research."

"Not at all." She looked up, her smile brightening the room. "I'm tryin' to find some notes about Socrates's role in the war. It's very interesting."

Then it dawned on Edward. "You're a student, aren't you?"

"Yes. The world's oldest freshman." She felt uneasy admitting she was a freshman at the age of twenty-seven; her uneasiness made her accent more pronounced. "Maybe when I'm forty, I can start on a Masters."

"I think that's terrific." Edward was intrigued. He wondered if he would have the courage to start college at her age. He extended his hand. "My name's Edward Head."

"Claire Sweet." She shook his hand. "And it's a pleasure to meet you, Edward."

Claire's ease disarmed Edward, and he indulged in self-mockery. "Sometimes people call me Edward Know It All because I've such a big mouth, as you already know."

The next day, Edward and Claire shared a desk. They worked efficiently, and got a lot done. At four thirty, Edward closed his books.

"You're a fast worker," Claire remarked.

"And a thirsty one. Let's go get a pop. The library's about to close."

"I could go for a burger too," Claire said, "but I've got to get back. I want to rest a while before I go to work. But I'll see you tomorrow."

Edward savored Claire's walk down the stairs. She was simultaneously casual and elegant in her old shirt and faded jeans. He told himself he was a spaz for being interested in a woman six years older. The thought of even holding her hand made him feel foolish. And the thought of sleeping with Claire...he shook his head. His inexperience embarrassed him, and he feared that, despite Claire's disposition, it would amuse her.

But his banana, he promised himself, was about to be peeled. As soon as he finished the Dylan Thomas paper, he would be in Holly's bucket seat. By the time he got home, he was figuring ways to hide his mini-cam in his bedroom.

The third day of spring break was rainy and dark. Sullen clouds crowded out the sun and dumped an inch of rain. The few students who stayed on campus during break holed themselves up in their rooms, watching soap operas, listening to CD's, or Web surfing.

But the weather did not bother Edward. He dressed quickly, brushed his teeth and gargled thoroughly. Then he drove to the library. The old wiper blades could not remove the rain quickly enough. The humidity did not help either; Edward continually wiped the glass to keep a portion of the windshield clear. Despite the difficulties, Edward whistled and hummed. He was happy.

The librarian's eyes widened, surprised to see him chipper on a rainy morning. Edward shook the water off like an eager puppy and left a water trail up the stairs to the table. His books and papers were on the table, where he had left them yesterday. Claire was not there yet, so he had a chance to comb his hair. He settled down to work and occasionally glanced at the clock.

Ninety minutes passed, and Edward's glances grew frequent. She should be here by now, he thought. By noon, Edward wanted to call Claire and almost looked up her number in the student directory. But he decided that she probably had a cold, or perhaps she had to work.

Or perhaps she was leery.

Yesterday, he had brushed her hand. Despite the innocence of the touch, Edward's hormones sang and soared. He'd even excused himself and walked to the water cooler, waiting for the flush to fade from his face.

His normal pasty color returned, but he remained charged. He fidgeted and grinned like an idiot. At one point, he giggled for no other reason than the joy of sitting across from this lovely woman.

"Punchy?" Claire had asked.

"Are you offering a punch?"

Then he did it. He patted her hand.

The pat was quick and light, but Edward agonized over it all evening. He kept seeing Claire's long bare arm. Now he feared that she had thought about the pat all night too, and she did not like it.

Here you sit, he mocked himself, writing a paper for a fuck. Edward the Know It All knows nothing. A twenty-one year old virgin: something of a curiosity in the new millennium, certainly. Claire isn't interested in you! You have no looks, no wit, no presence! What are you going to do? Write a paper for her too?

He slammed shut the books and hurried to his car. He drove recklessly and even ran a stop sign. He barreled into his driveway, nearly striking the garage door. He sat in the car and wondered why he had come home. The apartment was empty, and he had no guests to invite and no one to talk with on the phone.

Finally, anxiety escalating, he drove to a grocery store and bought two one-quart bottles of beer. He drank in the parking lot. The beer dulled his anxiety, and he began giving names to the grocery shoppers. He wondered what the Forty Year Old Housewife bought for tonight's dinner...pot roast and potatoes? And what about the Elderly Couple? The Old Man was happy to get out of the house, but the Old Woman was pissed because she could not get out of the house without him. And the Scolding Mom? Her Five Year Old threw a tantrum in the store because he could not have a second candy bar.

Edward was on his second bottle of beer when a woman walked out of the store. She pushed a cart full of groceries and nearly bumped into another cart. Edward named her the Worried Wife. He imagined she was fretting about her husband's late nights at the office. His late nights were actually spent with a blonde-from-a-bottle. His cheating enraged her, but she was even more frightened by the future. Her husband's salary was not large; she estimated that he could afford no more than $300 a month of child support. How could she survive on a lousy $300, even if she returned to the Wal-Mart?

The Worried Wife loaded the groceries into her rusted car.

Edward sat up. The Worried Wife was Claire Sweet. Claire got into the car. It coughed oily blue smoke and struggled onto Main Street. Edward waited until Claire was nearly out of view, then started his car. He followed her, careful to remain twenty yards behind.

She turned left onto Pine and followed it to Byron. At the end of Byron was a two-flat. The flat's white paint was peeling, and the old pink paint underneath stood out like scars. With a sack of groceries in each arm, Claire hurried up the steps to her apartment.

Edward had parked twenty yards back. As he trotted down the sidewalk, he saw Claire enter her apartment. The lights went on, and Claire's silhouette appeared behind the white curtains. He wanted to sprint up the stairs and surprise her with a bouquet of roses and a six pack of Coke: "My favorite drink in the world," as she had remarked yesterday.

"You funny Know It All, bringing me Coke and flowers," she would say. They would sit and laugh. He would again pat her hand. And he would entertain the improbable notion that love was more exciting than sex.

He did not run up the stairs with Coke and flowers, or even with his last quart of beer. He did not have the nerve to let love make him act so recklessly.

Still, Edward wanted to do something. He tore a sheet of paper from a notebook and wrote, "Hello. Hope you're well", then left the note on the car's threadbare front seat.

Chapter Eighteen: They Care More at Apex

Alex had driven 75 miles an hour all the way to Benton Harbor. When the sun came up, backlighting the trees atop the vast stretches of Lake Michigan's dunes along 1-94, he checked into a roadside motel. He slept until dusk, then dyed his hair jet black. He put on mirror shades and got into his car.

On the way to a supermarket, he mused that his disguises might soon be pointless. If he did not find good blood soon, his appearance could change wildly. His voice was different—it was higher and raspier, as if his vocal chords had been sanded. His left earlobe had grown a hole too, and the hazel eye was turning black.

At the supermarket he bought five of the bloodiest steaks he could find. Back in his motel room, he took each steak and, gripping both ends, wrung it out like a wet bath towel. He drained the blood into drinking glasses. The steaks filled two glasses, and he drank the blood while watching a re-run of *Clone City*, an old show about embittered human clones and their second class societal status.

The steak blood would hold him for only a day or so. He felt like a starving man who had only houseplants to eat. Worse, his changing physical appearance was a sign of deepening; his irrationality would become an invincible enemy.

He had again dreamed about his deceased brother David. In the dream, David made him swallow haloperidol, a powerful anti-psychotic drug. The haloperidol pulled Alex out of his catatonic state, but the process was painful—Alex felt ripped from a womb into the appalling world of his family's worry-lined faces, their hushed despair, their glaring lamps and loud TV's.

"You're better now," David said. "Let's go outside for a walk."

Frightened, Alex gripped David's head and twisted it clockwise several times. When he could twist no further, he let go. The head spun counterclockwise as if spring-loaded, throwing off a spiral of blood.

The idea of stealing a supply of haloperidol hit him a mile out of Kalamazoo. He saw a billboard for Apex, a chain of pharmacies. "WE CARE MORE AT APEX!" the billboard declared. Beneath the declaration was a photograph of an elderly couple smiling at an Apex pharmacist. The pharmacist's broad smile was as white as his jacket.

Alex might not have had the idea if he had not feared what his appearance would be in thirty or forty years. He might not have the wrinkled skin and narrow sunken mouth of the elderly man on the Apex billboard. But he would look different: he imagined himself with an Asian eye, a Nordic profile, the smirking mouth of teenage boy, and the chronic cough of a drunk with TB.

The pharmacy on the corner of Grant and Wilson was old fashioned. Chocolates and a stack of newspapers were displayed in the front window. A modest rack of liquor ran along the rear wall. The teen cashier had left five minutes earlier. The pharmacist, jacket across his arm, was halfway out the door.

"I need a prescription," Alex said with a broad Southern accent. Alex's grungy fake beard and plaid hunting cap had rendered him a bit whimsical.

"Sorry sir, we're closed." The pharmacist, a hefty man in his early thirties, extended an arm toward the sidewalk. "Please come back tomorrow."

"But I need —"

"There's an Apex Drugs on the north side. They're open 24 hours."

Alex drove a shoulder into the pharmacist's chest. The pharmacist fell, and Alex shut the door.

"I need haloperidol." Alex grabbed the man's neck and yanked him to his feet.

"There's a law that, that —" The pharmacist was frightened by the ease with which the nut lifted him. "I'll need a physician's prescription."

"Shut up."

"Federal law requires a —"

"Just shut up and get it." Alex slapped the pharmacist.

Face tingling, the pharmacist walked gingerly to the back room. Alex followed. Pharmaceuticals filled two dozen gray metal shelves. Hands unsteady, the pharmacist reached for the top of the third shelf. He removed two white boxes. Each box held four two-hundred count plastic bottles of haloperidol. "Anything else?"

"Just one thing. A personal question."

"Personal?"

"Two questions, really. First, what's your name? Second, do you have any health problems?"

"No."

"Your name is 'no'?"

"Bruno."

"Goodness," Alex smiled. "What a charming Old World name." Alex put an arm around Bruno's shoulders, as if consoling a distraught friend. "Okay Bruno. Do you have bad headaches? Ulcers? Maybe respiration problems? What about cancer?"

Bruno tried to step away, but Alex tightened his grasp. "Any serious health problems in your family? What about extreme blood pressure?

What about, oh — what about gout? Diabetes?"

Bruno feared that Alex was joking, perhaps leading up to a psycho punch line that ended with a knife. As Alex continued asking, Bruno realized Alex was serious. The realization frightened him further.

"You seem to be really healthy," Alex said brightly. He hugged the pharmacist.

Bruno stood stiffly as Alex's bear hug briefly tightened, then sighed in relief when Alex stepped back. He closed his eyes and took several deep breaths, fighting to stay calm. He did not want to startle the nut, who was happily shaking bottles of haloperidol like castanets. The crazy bastard's going to leave, Bruno thought. I'll call the cops a minute after he's gone and he'll wish...

The pain started at Bruno's neck and tore throughout his head.

Bruno tried to loosen Alex's mouth from his neck, but the struggle only deepened the pain. Still, he managed to get one foot against the wall. He set himself and pushed. Alex stumbled back two steps before regaining his balance.

Bruno stared at Alex, straining to grasp what he saw.

Alex sucked in a stringy piece of skin just as a clowning child sucks in a length of spaghetti. He chewed slowly, in an exaggerated manner, and noisily swallowed. Bruno probed the wound in his neck with a shaking pinkie.

"You just standing there with a hole in your neck!" Alex teased.

Bruno felt divided into two parts: one was trapped inside his body and shook from the wound's pain. The other stood outside his body, motionless and numb.

Bruno bolted only when he saw his blood on the floor. Alex attacked and forced a hand inside the wound. His fingers pushed past the slippery torn skin and found the carotid artery. He pulled.

As Bruno lie twitching, Alex squatted and clenched his fists. The blood turbo-charged him. He was higher by the nanosecond and felt like a kid on the world's biggest, most brightly-lit Ferris wheel.

The Ferris wheel spun faster. Wind burned Alex's face and G-forces juggled his stomach. The wheel's lights blurred into a spinning red circle composed of thin, multiple queues. As the speed increased, the circle's arc grew bigger and brighter. Alex could see nothing but the circle; everything else faded into a black background.

Alex squeezed his head and rocked back and forth: the Ferris wheel had raced beyond the point of mere fun, and he was suddenly anxious. The circle's lines grew erratic and elliptical, and tiny white spots, like stars on the night sky, marred the black background. Alex wished it would stop — the ellipses were throwing off sparks.

Alex found himself whispering, "Stop...stop...stop."

Finally the spinning stopped. Wiping his mouth, struggling for breath, he looked at Bruno and recalled his latest dream about David.

Alex reached down and gripped Bruno's head. He twisted: once, twice, three times. After the initial protest of noisy cervicals, the head turned freely.

Ron Daley was halfway home when he remembered. He trotted back toward the pharmacy, hoping Mr. Anderson was still there. Ron had gotten paid today. Yet when Mr. Anderson told him he could quit early tonight, Ron had yelled thanks and was through the door without his check.

The front door was locked. He was about to try the side door when he saw movement in the back. "Mr. Anderson I forgot my check!"

Mr. Anderson had a nosebleed. Then he saw that Mr. Anderson's entire face was bloody. Then he saw that the bloody face did not belong to Mr. Anderson.

Ron sprinted across the street toward the corner pay phone to call the police. He was searching his pockets frantically for change when he heard shattering glass. The pharmacy's front window was gone, save for a few jagged pieces that glimmered in the streetlights like knives. A passing car swerved to avoid the body that was suddenly in the street. Ron covered his ears as a pick up rear-ended the car. Quiet Grant Street was suddenly riotous with shouts, broken glass, and blood. A woman stood before the headless body and screamed. A pot-bellied man gripped her shoulders and tried to calm her, but she kept screaming.

Ron heard a hollow thunk behind him.

Mr. Anderson's head engaged Ron in a stare-down. Ron's limbs went prickly and he could not avert his eyes from Mr. Anderson's stare. He was still staring when the police car arrived two minutes later.

Alex was hiding under somebody's mini-van. The damned kid, running across the street to the pay phone! Alex had to distract the kid, if only for a few seconds. The headless body had crashed through the front window with spectacular noise. Then the fender-bender, the screaming woman. It was perfect. On a whim, Alex had picked up the head and heaved it through the window. It bounced a couple times and landed a yard from the kid's feet. Alex cackled at the bloody slapstick, even as a tiny inner voice demanded discipline.

Running out of the pharmacy, Alex had dropped a bottle of haloperidol. He was about to grab it when he saw a cop car barreling down the street. Alex cut across several lawns and into an alley. He kept running until he saw the mini-van.

Now, as he fished through his shirt pocket for a cigarette, he heard the clicking of boots on cement. Someone in cowboy boots approached. The boots paused by the driver's side, and Alex heard the jangle of a key ring. My goddamned luck, he thought, is finally getting better. The driver's door swung open and the driver got in. As the driver pulled on the door, Alex extended his arm. The door slammed against his palm then bounced back.

"You fuckin' kids! Get out from under the van," Carl demanded. Last night, kids had egged his house. He had a mind to boot their asses across the street. The kids never tired of hassling him. Carl got out of the van, lowered himself to his hands and knees.

Carl was struck in the face. "I'll kill you little shits!" He was struck again and fell back onto his haunches.

As he struggled to clear his head, Alex rolled out from under the van and, gripping Carl by his jacket, walked him to the driver's side of the vehicle. Carl struggled to resist, but his head was ringing and he found himself shoved across the driver's seat and into the passenger seat. Alex followed him in and occupied the driver's seat.

"Where's the pharmacy, that one on the corner?" Alex demanded. His beard was caked with dried blood. So was his shirt.

Carl cursed his luck — the nut had been hiding right under his van.

Carl tried not to choke. The sergeant had told him the killer was probably a psycho.

"Which one?"

"The one that's two or three blocks from here. The little brick one, on the corner."

"That's Bruno Anderson's pharmacy. He's my pharmacist."

"Why don't you direct me toward it?"

"Just take this street three blocks down, then turn left."

Alex was halfway to the pharmacy when he saw the billy club. It was halfway under the passenger seat. He sighed and pulled over.

"We're not there yet," Carl said. He inched his hands toward the .38 on his right hip.

Alex noted Carl's blue windbreaker: the words "County Sheriff's Police" were emblazoned in yellow script above the jacket's pocket.

"One goddamned nightmare after another!" Alex complained. "You wouldn't believe my fucking luck tonight. First the kid, then I drop one of the bottles." He faced the cop, eyes bugging. "To top it off, I choose to hide under your van. Why the hell don't you have a police decal on the damned thing? What, are you ashamed of your profession?"

"What?"

"Well are you? Ashamed?" A laugh frolicked its way past Alex's rage.

"I can help you, buddy. Just be calm."

"I don't think you really want to help me." He glanced at the police scanner/phone, then saw a sheet of paper taped to the door of the glove box. Various police codes were printed on the paper.

"I do want to help you." Carl quickly raised his pistol to Alex's head. "Just stay calm."

Alex tore the police scanner/phone handset out of its receiver, then tossed it over his shoulder into the back seat. The cop's hand was unsteady, and the barrel trembled six inches from Alex's face.

"Go ahead and shoot," Alex dared.

"Get out of the van, buddy."

Alex opened the door, slowly stepped out.

Carl sprang out of the passenger side and pointed the pistol at Alex's head. He would make Alex lie on his stomach. Then he would cuff Alex's wrists and ankles, use his cell phone, and wait for assistance.

"On the ground, buddy, and put your hands on the back of your head." Alex obeyed, then asked the cop what street he was lying on. The cop laughed. "Brown."

"It's a nice neighborhood," Alex remarked to the asphalt. The cop cuffed him. "Don't go away, buddy," Carl mocked. He was elated — already, he saw the headlines and the stories about how Carl Martinez, a rookie Sheriff's cop, collared a genuine psycho killer. His wife Sherry would be so proud. She'd screw him morning, noon, and night for a month. Then he cursed: his cell phone had lost its charge. He'd have to use a neighbor's phone.

A middle-aged man, coffee mug in hand, answered Carl's knock. Carl showed the man his badge.

"What's wrong, officer?"

"I've apprehended a suspected murderer," Carl stated in his best Joe Friday tone. "Call the sheriff, I'll be right outside." Carl held up a reassuring hand when the man gasped.

"Everything's under control, sir. Just call the sheriff and give them your address. They'll be here immediately."

Mouth agape, the man ran to his phone.

Carl approached his car. He heard something metallic, and the hair on his neck raised.

Alex whipped the handcuffs across Carl's face. Carl dropped to one knee, and Alex kicked him. Alex noted the house's address, then ran into the house, dragging Carl by the jacket with him. Just inside the front door, Alex saw the middle-aged man with the phone. He had just pushed the "9" button on his phone to dial 911. When he heard someone approach behind him, he paused and turned with a relieved smile. "Here, I'll let you call in and —"

When he saw a thin bearded man with a bloody face, he dropped the phone.

Alex put the phone back in its cradle.

The man dropped to his hands and knees to beg for mercy.

"Shut up and give me your car keys."

The man pulled them from his pants pocket. "It's a brand new BMW! A beauty. Take it!"

Alex punched him.

White smoke with red streaks painted the black sky. The sirens, flashing lights, and crackling radios soon lured the neighborhood residents onto the street. Two more squad cars squealed to a stop in front of the house.

"This is a son of a bitch," a fireman yelled to his partner. He wiped soot from his forehead and wondered how the fire started.

It had started ten minutes earlier. Alex found a can of gas in the garage. He poured a trail of gas through the living room to the kitchen and den, then up the stairs to the bedrooms. He backed the BMW out of the garage and, with the car idling in the driveway, tossed a lit kitchen match down the stairs. To keep everyone occupied, Alex turned on the gas range before driving away.

Alex admired the car. It was midnight blue and had leather upholstery, CD player, and moon roof. He fleetingly thought of stealing it, but knew he could not. He spotted his own car and kept driving, just to be safe. In a few minutes, the entire town's police and fire force would be fully occupied, struggling to contain the unforgiving fire and to control neighborhood panic. He would park the BMW, walk freely to his own car, and be on the highway in fifteen minutes.

Chapter Nineteen: A prestige project

The east horizon was turning pink. Sullen auto factories churned white smoke. Alex exited at Flint and checked into a Cut Rate Inn. He pulled the blinds, turned on all the lights, and examined himself in the mirror.

The pharmacist's blood had helped. Alex's nose was regaining its original shape. The eyelashes were still long, but the holes in his earlobes had filled in. His irises resembled an artist's messy palette, with several colors mixed into seaweed green. Alex took four haloperidols and hoped his vision improved.

His dream was wonderful.

Alex sat on a leather couch. The room was filled with men in tuxedos and women in sleek dresses. Someone produced a bottle of champagne. The cork bounced off the ceiling, and everyone applauded.

"To our most prized author!" the executive vice president of Conglomerate Publishing declared. He sounded a dramatic chord on the grand piano, and the guests chuckled. "*My Life as a Dead Man* will be on the *New York Times* best seller list this week."

Alex nodded modestly.

"More than that," the veep continued. "I'm terribly pleased to tell you that *My Life as a Dead Man* will enter the best seller list at…" He shook his head, as if disbelieving his own words, "…at number one!"

Applause and cheers. A woman in a crushed black velvet puff dress sat beside Alex. She rested her hand on his thigh. "May I be the first to congratulate you for such a feat?" She had a French accent, which Alex found exotic and exciting. She kissed Alex's cheek.

"You're the literary story of the year," a bald man exclaimed. He removed his wire-rimmed glasses and shook them to punctuate his words. "To return after years of anonymity! It's sensational! You might be the next Pynchon."

"What about movie rights?" the French woman asked. She re-filled Alex's champagne glass.

"Authors are often seduced by the film industry, and I'll admit that I'm attracted to it," Alex confessed. "She's a beautiful seductress." The din of conversation stopped as Alex expounded.

"But beautiful seductresses can make great demands. And they can distract us from doing the work that brought us success. You know, one of my favorite authors is Nathanael West. Bless him, he got me through a few tough times as a teenager. His *Day of the Locust* is a really marvelous evocation of lost Hollywood. What's interesting about Hollywood is that she's beautiful and odious at the same time." A camera's flash blinded Alex for a moment, then he continued. "In *Locust*, people come to Hollywood to find their dreams. The people have no genuine purpose, no genuine spirit, and so they hope to find it in Hollywood. Of course, Hollywood's spirit is artificial. If Hollywood is a church, it is the church you find on movie lots: two-dimensional. The front looks like a church, but behind it you find only two-by-fours, nails, carpenters and key grips."

A young man with a platinum coiffure sighed. "You're right, Alexander. But *My Life as a Dead Man* could be a huge hit."

"Financial and artistic success are both desirable," Alex conceded. "But they're often mutually exclusive." He accepted a slice of bread lightly covered in caviar. "Of course, there are exceptions."

The veep agreed. "Our company is well connected in Hollywood. We think *My Life as a Dead Man* could be a prestige project. Several studios are interested."

Several hours later, the party ended. The French woman, Simone, clasped Alex's arm and guided him to the elevator. The elevator whisked them skyward, and they entered an apartment with a sunken living room and loft bedrooms. Hand in hand, they walked to the window, which reached from floor to ceiling.

"New York is so lovely from forty floors up," the woman remarked. "Lovely." "You must feel wonderful tonight, very high. Forty floors for you, it is nothing. Tell me, how did you come to write such a book?"

"It took a long time." Alex narrowed his eyes. "My career was dead. I had to start over.

"Rebuild?"

"Re-invent myself. I studied people, examined them, saw what their best qualities were. I'm self-made. I decided what qualities I needed to write again, and I pursued them until I had them."

Simone stroked Alex's hair. "You are fascinating."

"How candid of you."

He took her in his arms. She leaned back, neck exposed, in romantic surrender. Alex carried her up the stairs to a bed.

"Oh, but you're a clever fellow," she sighed. Her thighs squeezed Alex's roving hand.

He undressed her slowly, pausing to unhook her black lace brassiere with his teeth. Simone took a knife from the dresser and cut a line across her chest, from nipple to nipple.

Alex woke at 4:30. The dream had been so pleasant, and like a child he wished that the dream would come true. He wondered who Simone might be. He recalled no French women. And he had never been in a

Manhattan high-rise with black suits, black dresses, and black grand pianos. And had never seen, nor thought of, the title My Life as a Dead Man. But he liked the ring of it.

He rose and washed his face. His lips were sore, and he remembered having cracked lips as a teenager. The dry mouth and lips, side effects of the anti-psychotics, had been a bad sign. Alex had learned that if his mouth was dry, the drugs would soon drag him up the tunnel toward glaring light and clamorous voices. And so he had to face his family, endure their dinner table talk, suffer their repulsive emotions.

But now, years later, the dry lips were a good sign: the haloperidol was working.

Alex realized that he felt better this afternoon than he had felt in months. The pharmacist's good blood and good medicine were a tonic. He was frisky and wanted some fun: Bruno must have been, in his natural life, a high-spirited fellow.

Alex drove north on 10 for three hours. Each hour, he swallowed a haloperidol and sipped bottled water. The rhythm of tires along road pleased him and added to his good mood. He turned on the radio and hummed along with country tunes.

At nine o'clock, the news reported a tragedy:

"Police are investigating a murder and fire in Portage, Michigan just west of Kalamazoo. According to police, the owner of an Apex pharmacy was murdered shortly after closing. One hour later in Portage, a house fire claimed the life of Sherman Park and a sheriff's policeman. The police believe the robbery and fire are connected.

Alex congratulated himself for thinking of leaving a few pills in the cop's van. He was setting the table perfectly.

The blue neon sign—"Cal Clyde's Elks Lounge and NiteSpot"—flickered erratically, as if drunk. The NiteSpot was a cinder block dump with fake log cabin trim, torn awnings, and a gravel parking lot. Alex pulled a greasy denim jacket from the trunk and put it on. He also put on a floppy cowboy hat and filmy reading glasses.

Alex ambled in, cigarette dangling. The bar was on the right, and half the stools were claimed. The customers drank, belched, smoked, and swore. The bartender was thin and wore a white blouse and blue jeans; her dyed black hair was decorated with a red ribbon. Eight scarred wooden booths leaned against the left wall, where the occupants necked or bellyached.

Alex took the stool at the end of the bar. In the back, a country and western band acknowledged tepid applause before launching into "How Much I Lied". The singer forgot the lyrics whenever he tried to strum his six string.

"What's yer pleasure tuhnot?" the bartender asked.

"Laht beer and uh glayas," Alex replied through his nose. He drank and smoked silently, casing the joint. The cash register was ancient: no electronic keypad or digital display. After a couple beers, Alex walked to the back of the bar, pretending to use the washroom. The washrooms faced one another in a short hallway, and the emergency exit was at the hallway's end.

"How's about another beer?" Alex asked the bartender. She had been busy with a drunken customer whom she refused to serve further.

The woman pushed a gray strand of her black hair from her forehead. "Sorry. That jerk there's had too much too drink."

"Well, as long as he pays for it," Alex remarked.

"But he can get killed if he goes out drivin' after drinkin' like he has."

"And then he'd sue ya," Alex added sympathetically.

"If a dead man could, he would." The bartender snorted. Her dentures slipped, and her smile was all gums.

The man beside Alex said, "That drunk's a prick."

"A prick?"

"A prick." The customer stroked his ragged black beard. "Last year, he smashed up a new Ford Ranger on county road 8, up by Petoskey. Ran over three mailboxes and landed upside down in a ditch."

"Lucky to be alive," Alex suggested.

"Agreed. But he managed to scramble outta that truck and run away before the sheriff came. Even left his wife in the truck to fend for herself.

"And so she divorced him and got child support. The kid was left behind in the truck too, did I tell you? But half the time now he don't pay his child support. And of course, he's got another brand new Ford Ranger. It's jet black and has a CB, I mean a CD player."

Alex leaned forward and looked lengthwise down the bar to get a better look. The fellow was skinny, with a bobbing Adam's apple and arms thin as pipe cleaners. He was resting his forehead atop an empty beer glass.

"I think he sells dope since he lost his job. I see he's got some cow with him tonight," the bartender said. She wrinkled her nose and tended to her other customers.

Alex looked at the prick's companion. She outweighed him by fifty pounds. Her hair was dyed the color of straw, and her face was burnt red from a sunlamp. She let him lap at her beer as a dog laps at water.

"What's that prick's name?" Alex asked the man beside him.

"Lee Howell. You know him?"

"I thought maybe I did." Alex squinted, feigning concentration. "But

I don't." Alex shrugged. "Anyway."

The man stopped stroking his beard and extended his hand. "My name's Marty Hesse. Yours?"

"William Yeats." Alex shook his new friend's hand; it was as thick as Alex's foot.

Marty nodded and kept talking about the Soo Locks. His talking was structured by geography, moving south from Sault St. Marie to Mt. Pleasant to Alma. Alex pretended to listen, mumbling "Yes" or "Uh huh" or "No kidding." He kept his eye on Lee Howell.

The band had been on break for a half hour. The members were dragging themselves back to the bandstand, which was plywood supported by milk crates. They played "Sweet Dreams", and a few couples slow-danced. One man vomited on his girlfriend's shoulder. She slapped him and used his blue windbreaker to wipe off the vomit. When she returned to the dance floor, Lee Howell was with her. They leaned against the Wurlitzer to lick each other's tongues.

Alex excused himself and approached Lee Howell's straw-haired companion. "How 'bout a dance, ma'am?"

Val sat coolly at the bar, as if she were a beauty used to rejecting dances, and looked Alex up and down. "I've got a few minutes."

Alex took the lead and nudged Val across the dance floor. They were next to Lee and his freshly-wiped dance partner. Lee did not notice his company at first. Lee was sucking his partner's neck; she embraced him and tipped her head back in drunken rapture.

When Val saw her man Lee with another woman, she gripped Alex's waist and thrust her hips.

Alex twirled Val around. In doing so, he elbowed Lee. Lee removed his mouth from his partner—he was now working on her cheek and eye—and looked at Alex. Lee's eyes were glassy from booze, and his mouth was slack. A string of saliva, tinted peach with his partner's makeup, swung from his chin.

Alex held Lee's gaze for a moment, then stuck his tongue into Val's mouth. She squeezed his ass in return. Alex extracted his tongue from Val's cigarette-flavored mouth and pushed his tongue up her cigarette-flavored nostril. She snorted and wiped at her nose, but she was grinning. Alex smiled back and stuck a hand between Val's thighs.

Lee pushed his partner away and stepped forward. He stared at Alex, but Alex kept thrusting his hand between Val's thighs. She began unbuttoning Alex's shirt.

"You bitch," Lee muttered.

"You dancin' with a blow-job vendor like Amy Johnson!" Val nodded at Amy, who offered a drunken smile in return. "And you call me the bitch in the bar?"

"Touché!" Alex laughed.

"Quit rubbin' her box," Lee ordered.

Alex shook his head. "She likes it."

"Stop it, you whore." Lee kicked Val in the ass. She whirled and swung at Lee. Lee backhanded her and Val fell over a chair. Lee spit in Alex's face and yelled, "You hit my woman!"

The band stopped its interpretation of "Faster Horses". The patrons turned to the confrontation. A retiree at the pool table asked if anyone wanted to make wagers on the fistfight.

"Wait until I tell your daughter what Daddy's doing on weekends. Gettin' drunk and slappin' women." Alex wiped the spit from his face, then gripped the lapels of Lee's shirt. He pulled sharply, as if opening curtains, and the buttons popped off.

Lee quickly yanked his shirttail back over the pistol he'd stuck in his pants, but Alex saw the handle between Lee's bony hip and jeans.

"You're chickenshit, carrying a gun," Alex whispered. Nobody else saw the gun. The customers, along with the band's three musicians, formed a circle around Alex and Lee. The bartender enjoyed the excitement. She lit a cigarette, poured herself a whiskey, and put her feet up.

Alex heard the retiree taking bets. "I'm not much of a fighter, but I'd still bet on me to whip this cornholer." He pulled his cowboy hat down until it shaded his forehead and eyes. The betting increased, and in one minute the retiree had seventy eight dollars crumpled in his fist. "Winner of the fight gets free drinks and ten bucks."

"Twenty bucks," Lee yelled.

Val had risen and pulled twenty dollars out of her purse. "I bet on the cowboy."

"You gonna stand there faggot, or you gonna fight?" Lee stuck his thumbs into his pocket and sneered.

"I'm gonna stick my fist up your ass, queer." Alex parodied Lee's pose, fists on hips and lips pursed.

The customers laughed. Lee began to laugh along with them, but he suddenly threw a haymaker. The punch missed. Alex swung back, but Lee ducked and landed a one-two. Alex pawed at his bleeding nose.

Another one-two struck Alex's mouth. Alex's counterpunch was feeble, as if thrown by an arthritic. Lee wind-milled several shots to Alex's face and stomach. Alex dropped to one knee and Lee kicked his chest. The impact was loud, and the customers roared.

"Kill him, Lee!" someone screamed.

Lee whooped and kicked Alex's head. Alex fell onto his side and shielded his face with his hands. Lee kicked him three more times, exhilarated. "Rip my shirt, ya shit! Faggot!" He lifted a chair over his head. Val screamed at Lee to stop, and the retiree laughed. As Alex rolled onto his stomach, Lee gripped one leg of the chair and swung hard. The chair crashed against Alex's head and broke in half. Only the chair's leg remained in Lee's grip, and he twirled it like a gunfighter twirling his smoking six-shooter.

Three customers pulled Lee away. Marty, who had bet on Alex, hunched over Alex and wondered what to do. Alex was motionless, and Marty poked cautiously at him, as if he were a frog squished on the road.

Lee wiped his mouth with the back of his hand and demanded half the kitty. "Never laid a hand on me," Lee boasted.

"I'll still kick your ass," Alex announced. His claim was muffled because his face was flat against the greasy wood floor. "Up that kitty to two hundred."

"Enough's enough," Marty told the crowd. "I'll buy these two bums a drink. Let's call it a night."

Alex ordered the retiree to take more bets. "Make it double or nothing. Easiest money you'll ever make."

Nobody took the bet. The crowd doubted that Alex could stand, much less fight. But Alex pulled himself up with a table and chair and faced Lee. He raised his fists awkwardly and demanded a second chance.

"Nobody's bettin'. Why should I whip you again?"

"You haven't whipped me once."

Lee gripped Alex's collar with his left hand, drew back his right, and launched his haymaker. The blow landed with a sharp report on Alex's head.

A pained yell excited the crowd. The bartender grimaced, afraid that Lee might kill Alex. She was walking to the pay phone to call the police when she heard Alex laugh.

Lee clutched his broken right hand to his chest.

"Somebody should have bet on me," Alex laughed. Lee swung at Alex with his left fist. Alex lowered his head so the punch struck his forehead. Lee howled. Both hands were broken. He tried to strike Alex with an elbow, chicken-wing style, but Alex slapped him. The slap spun him 360 degrees, like a top.

Lee realized his face was on the floor. He rolled over, peering through his fingers like a child watching a horror movie. But the horror was real. Six arms held twelve chairs over him. The chairs struck him in unison.

With a guffaw, Alex faced the spectators. They stared at him, slack-jawed and unbelieving. The retiree handed Alex the wad of bills. "Best fight I ever saw," he said.

"Thank you." Alex stuffed the money into a pocket and punched the retiree in the face. The retiree imploded into an awkward heap at Alex's feet.

"What the fuck!" Marty yelled. He swung at Alex, missed badly, and ineptly covered his head in self-defense.

"Watch this!" Alex roared to nobody in particular. He kicked Marty's knee, then his shin, and Marty fell on top of the retiree. Marty was still conscious, and Alex stilled him with a kick to the head.

The bartender held the pay phone's handset with a shaking hand. "Put that goddamned phone down!" Alex barked. Frightened, the bartender hesitated. Alex ran across the bar and pulled the handset out of the wall. The bartender swore at him, and Alex hit her over the head with the severed handset. When a man tried to help her, Alex choked him with the phone's armored cord, then locked the front door and pulled the neon light's power cord from the wall.

The three musicians were trying to sneak out the back. "I've got a gun!" Alex yelled. They stopped.

Alex crossed the room and grabbed Lee's pistol. "Turn around, you guitar pickers." The trio obeyed. Alex approached them, pistol pointed.

The bassist panicked and turned to run.

Alex shot him in the back, and the bassist lurched twice before hitting the floor.

"Why didn't you stop him?" Alex yelled at the remaining two.

"You told us to stop!" the drummer answered.

"Shut up!" Alex shot the drummer, then the guitarist.

Val, Amy, and a rosy cheeked young man in mechanic's overalls were the last living customers. The three huddled beside an empty beer keg. "Don't hurt us," the mechanic pleaded. He fumbled with his cell phone, then dropped it.

"Hey, watch this." Theatrically, Alex held the barrel against his outstretched left palm. The trio whimpered in fear, and Alex shushed them. Then he took a deep breath and pulled the trigger. The blood sprayed the trio and the beer keg. Alex suppressed a yell: not a yell of pain, though the pain was enormous, but a yell of elation.

He held his hand in the air. The overhead lights highlighted the hand's bloody hole.

Val and Amy fainted.

"You try it." Alex dangled the gun in front of the mechanic.

"I don't like guns," the mechanic insisted, eyes shut.

Alex fired. The bullet left a hole beside the mechanic's nose; Alex mused that the hole resembled a third nostril. Alex sucked blood from the hole until the mechanic's face was ashen. Then he dragged Lee's corpse next to Val, fit Lee's fingers around his pistol, and pushed the barrel into Lee's mouth.

Alex was in a Battle Creek hotel room when the afternoon TV news carried a story of an "apparent suicide/multiple murder" in northern Gratiot County.

"Gratiot County Sheriff Chief Jonathan Snively announced that Lee Howell of Gratiot County apparently beat and shot several people in Cal Clyde's Elks Lounge and NiteSpot, then turned the gun on himself. Chief Snively-Goodheart speculates, however, that Howell may have shot the others and then tried to burn down the tavern before killing himself. Much of the interior was burned, and investigators are struggling to cope with the extensive fire and smoke damage."

An early morning shot of the Nitespot appeared. Several trucks were parked outside. Smoke escaped from a broken window, blending with the morning fog. A brief shot of the interior showed the blackened chairs, tables, and bar.

"Authorities believe there is a connection between the tragedy at the Elks Lounge and three recent murders in Portage, Michigan. Police found capsules of the drug haloperidol in Howell's Ford Ranger. The drug was stolen from a Portage pharmacy, and the pharmacy owner was murdered. Furthermore, fire consumed the home of another Portage murder victim. Police are investigating the possibility that Howell was involved in the recent Portage murders and fire, either directly or through an acquaintance."

Chapter Twenty: Monkeyshines

Jimmy cursed as he trudged to his first class. He cursed for the same reason an angry infant screams: to vent rage. The curses made no sense, but they felt good, a random string of words and images. Jimmy told himself that goddamned spring break went faster than tits on a dolphin and I hate that fucker Resartus more than a tart hates boils on my, on my ass.

However, Jimmy didn't hate Algebra enough to stay awake. He sat in the back, chin on his hand, and kept his snores to a minimum.

He did hate his history course enough to stay awake. Pompous Dr. Jones. A four hundred pounder whose ten-year-old suits were stained, and whose yellowed shirts strained at each button.

But Resartus was the worst. Jimmy had expended a lot of energy hating Professor Jones's nasal self-importance, and he was tired. He fantasized that Resartus had called in sick.

No such luck. Resartus was already in front of the lectern, shuffling his notes. Jimmy hurried to the last row and wondered what bullshit Resartus would fry up today.

Alex adjusted his sky blue tie before beginning his lecture. He had not worn a tie in several years, and it felt alien. But he liked it. He felt refreshed and wanted to convey his refreshment with the tie, and with the rather sporty tweed jacket.

"I hope your spring break was as good as mine was, ladies and gentleman." A few murmurs, mostly frowns.

"That's wonderful," Alex smiled. "Now. Let me see if I can reduce you to tears of boredom by 2:50." He took a deep breath, like a tenor before his solo, and launched into his lecture. "We are nearing that section of the course where we study black humor and its underlying philosophy. The philosophy of black humor is wonderfully uncomplicated: life is absurd. In other words, it's pointless. If we look for meaning, we don't find it. Nothingness. Religion? Might as well forget it! God? Another childish wish. Love? It's really just the small comfort of someone's company before you or the lover gets sick and dies. Or dumps you. Philosophy? A distraction for shut-ins. Absurdism is in direct opposition to much of our most venerable Western thought. For instance, Plato argued that when we followed reason..."

Students furiously took notes, periodically pausing to shake their cramping hands. Others simply stared at Alex. His energy and organization shocked them.

His voice was effortlessly audible — in fact, it soared. He gestured, he paused dramatically, he even abandoned his notes and offered a mini-lecture on Jean Paul Sartre: "...and many modern authors are inspired by Sartre's novel *Nausea,* in which the protagonist viscerally confronts the pointlessness of his existence. Furthermore, the protagonist finds that..." And out poured a fraction of the countless hours of reading Alex had committed as a teen and young man, locked in a bedroom or exiled in an apartment, address unknown.

Alex picked up steam as the hour unfolded. As class was about to end, Alex stepped forward. "I've enjoyed this lecture tremendously, as I'm sure you have."

The students grinned.

"You're deserving of the great lecture I've given you. Let's continue our quest for knowledge tomorrow. More excellence is in store for you." A pause, a sporty loosening of the tie. "I'll remember you in my next novel." Alex strode from the room, grand as an Oxford don.

Jimmy smiled despite himself. He had almost enjoyed Alex's lecture, and the hour had gone quickly.

He paused on his way out of the classroom, making way for Holly Dish. He had not spoken to her since he had stormed drunkenly into her room. She walked slowly, head down, mumbling.

"Go ahead and ignore me." Jimmy bowed and extended his arm toward the door.

Holly was halfway down the hall when the light bulb appeared and levitated over her head. The bulb was 250 watt, and it warmed Holly's head.

"Hello Jimmy. Haven't talked to you since you got drunk and got punched out."

Jimmy smiled cautiously at Holly's extended hand.

"Let's forget about that night," Holly suggested. "I was in a bad mood and you were smashed."

"Yeah, you sure were a bitch," Jimmy agreed. He gladly took Holly's hand. Her physicality, blooming in the spring, made him itch.

Jimmy and Holly finished their third cup of coffee. The stimulation of the caffeine and their plan reduced them to giggling children. Or rather, Jimmy was reduced to a giggling child. The turn of events thrilled him. Holly Dish was sitting across from him, leaning forward and speaking low. Her large eyes, her round face framed with her new pageboy, her deep-dish tits — what a way to resume the semester.

Holly, a convincing actress, giggled along with Jimmy. She had to be convincing. Edward Shithead was suddenly making demands of Holly, and she did not give in to demands.

She should have sensed trouble immediately. After she returned from spring break Sunday afternoon, Holly called Edward about the Dylan Thomas paper. He said it was done, but he was busy and could not make the transaction. She said she would take the paper tonight and deliver her end another night. Edward refused and told her to call tomorrow.

She suspected that he was not done with the paper and called Monday afternoon.

"I'm here, and so's the paper," Edward remarked.

Holly arrived in fifteen minutes, resplendent in white body shirt and black slims.

"Here's your essay," Edward said. He was nude and held a stapled pile of pages in front of his groin, like a loincloth. "Come get it."

"Is it good?"

"The paper or my sausage?"

"Are you drunk?"

"No. But I've got a bottle of Bleak House chilling in the 'fridge."

"I'd like to see the paper first."

"Trust me — the paper's good. Now step out of those slims."

Holly wondered if Edward had a plan to counteract her plan. But she did not argue. She removed her body shirt, then purposely fumbled with the hooks of her brassiere. Her breasts were brazen, even cocksure, in their D cups, and Edward waited with half-open mouth and popping eyes.

"Time out!" She grabbed the essay and tried to glance at the first page, but Edward mashed her mouth against hers. She dropped the essay; Edward tried to pull down her slims.

"Not here," Holly said. Her protest was garbled because Edward's tongue was tickling her tonsils.

Edward guided her into his bedroom. He had worked her slims halfway down her thighs. But Holly bowed her legs and the slims would descend no further.

"Lie down," Holly ordered.

Edward obeyed.

She lowered herself onto Edward and pushed her breasts against his sunken chest. She suppressed a snicker at Edward's erect nipples.

"It's a very good paper," Edward grunted.

"You don't have on a shower cap," Holly accused.

"I'll be careful," Edward whispered.

"I'm not going to be another knocked-up teenager who drops out of school then whines her whole life that the system kept her down." She snorted in contempt, though Edward was not sure if the contempt was for him or the nation's legion of knocked-up teenagers. "You're putting on a rubber!" she ordered.

He scrambled to his dresser. In his excitement, he ripped a hole in the first condom. He got on the second one and turned to embrace Holly.

She was gone.

Edward looked through the doorway. Holly was hopping on one leg, pulling on her slims. He enjoyed the sight: her bouncing milk-white breasts, the essay hanging from her clenched teeth.

"I wish my camera was filming this," Edward said. He crossed his arms and leaned against the doorjamb.

"I have to go." The essay dropped from her mouth. She retrieved it and hurried toward the door. "I'll be back—I just have to make sure the essay is good."

"You've got the wrong one," Edward shouted.

Holly was already half way to her car. She returned with slow, heavy steps. "Did I hear you correctly?"

"That's the first draft. I have the final draft in my bedroom."

Holly scanned the first few sentences. "Looks okay to me. You're trying to trick me."

"I had to have a backup plan." He shrugged. "I know you think I'm really gross. I knew you'd try to get out of it."

Holly was reading page two. With each sentence, her jaw grew harder. "You grease spot! This looks like it was written by a seventh-grader."

"I agree. I tried to make it dumb." He crossed the room, took the essay from Holly. "Dylan Thomas is really a good poet," Edward recited. "His poems are filled with deep meanings. He's got lots to say. One of them is called 'Alterwise By Ow Light.' It's very deep with lots of meaning. Another good one is 'If I Were Tickled by the Rub of Love.' It's about a metaphor." Edward paused. "And the spelling errors! I even spelled 'Dylan' as 'Dillon' a few times."

"Buttspray!"

"If you want the final version—" Edward nodded toward the bedroom door. "You'll have to spool me ten times."

Holly rolled her eyes.

"Once for each page."

"I'd rather fuck a dyke," Holly declared.

"Once for each page," Edward calmly repeated.

Now, sitting with Jimmy, Holly told her story, though she changed some details. For instance, she told Jimmy that she had merely asked Edward to type and proofread her work, and to insure the citations and bibliography were correct. "It's the same thing as an editor does with a writer's manuscript," she explained. Edward, she said, announced that he needed more money—or a week of Holly-spooling. "Can you believe that jerk's nerve?" Holly complained.

Jimmy admired the jerk's nerve. "Turn him into the witches in the Feminist Studies department. They'll tar and feather him."

"Nah, it's not worth it. I got the draft back. But I need to find a typist fast." Jimmy wondered if he could learn to type in a day or two.

"Can you type?"

"Yes." Jimmy now wondered whom he could pay to type.

Reconsidering, Holly pursed her lips. "Thanks anyway. I can get it done myself." She saw the disappointment darken Jimmy's eyes. Now was the moment. "Did you understand one thing Resartus said today?"

"Sort of. He said that a guy wrote about nausea and that life is mean-ingless. And that's what inspires writers to write."

"My existence will be meaningless if I don't ace his final." Holly slouched in the booth, wearily pushed a lock of hair from her forehead. "If it wasn't cheating, I swear—What am I saying? I must be really des-perate." She finished her cold coffee with a smile.

"What have you got in mind?"

Holly leaned forward, close enough to see Jimmy's nose hairs. "I'd feel a lot better about this class if I knew what was on the final."

"I agree. We've got about six weeks to make a plan."

"I wish I had some ideas."

"I've got some. Let's talk on Wednesday after class."

Jimmy marveled at the difference seven hours can make. At 9:00 a.m., he had suffered through his classes and winced at the thought of another month and a half of classes. Now, at 4:00 p.m., he was euphoric. Tomorrow he would begin Plan A by casing the Academic Center.

But tonight he started plan Plan B: the harassment of Ed Shithead. The gall of that pencilneck, demanding that Holly spool him for typing a paper! Jimmy hated Edward for being gutsy enough to even try it. If Jimmy was going to spool Holly Dish—his belated New Year's resolu-tion—he had to work quickly.

Jimmy got to work on Plan B—which he called Operation Shit-storm—with high enthusiasm. He consulted the phone book and found Edward Head's number and address. Next, he called the phone com-pany.

"This is Tracy. How may I help you?"

"Good morning. My name is James Head, and I need to talk with someone about customer service." Jimmy spoke in a raspy, authoritative voice, aided by a filterless cigarette.

"I can help you, sir."

"My son Edward is a Tailor College student. He's had to leave school early this semester because of illness. Shingles, in fact. I'm calling his utility companies to discontinue services."

"What is his phone number and address?"

Jimmy told her.

"Very good, sir. Service will be terminated at the end of the business day."

"You've been very helpful."

Turning off Edward's phone was so easy that Jimmy cut classes the next day to devise another prank. He walked downtown to the hardware store for supplies. On the way back, he stopped by the post office and asked the clerk for a change-of-address form. The clerk smilingly gave the form to Jimmy; she even noted that he could fill it out later and drop it in any mailbox.

"That's pretty convenient," Jimmy beamed. "But I'll do it right here."

"Whatever you prefer."

"Thank you."

He jotted Edward Head's name and address into the "Old Address" section. In the "New Address" section, he wrote "120 Oak Street." Next he opened the zip code directory and randomly chose a town and zip code: St. John, Indiana. 46373.

"Thanks again," Jimmy told the clerk. He departed whistling.

Chapter Twenty One: "By the rub of love…"

Each morning, Holly Dish stood nude before the mirror. She placed her hands flat against her belly, pushed out her breasts as a GI pushes out the chest, and commenced inspection. On some mornings, her thighs seemed fleshy. On other mornings, the shadow of a spare tire seemed to darken her abdomen.

This morning, Holly the Trainer could find no faults. She was pleased by her abdomen's tightness, by her skin's smoothness. She remembered Edward Head squeezing her hips and stroking her concave belly.

She laughed at her control over him.

But he had laughed at his control over her. He distrusted her enough to write a phony essay. Perhaps he had planned to sleep with her the rest of the semester, demanding sex for each page. Or paragraph. Or word. His yellow fingers on her creamy shoulders, his yeast-coated tongue on her lips…She closed her eyes and shook away the images.

Holly returned to her reflection. Her stomach and thighs had responded well to her spring break regimen. First, a three mile run in the morning. For breakfast, a bowl of Fiber Feast, a cored apple, a cup of strained peaches, and iced tea. For lunch, a patty of tuna on toast, and water. For dinner, either a bowl of boiled pasta (no oil or margarine) and salad, or a skinless baked chicken breast and baked potato (no oil or margarine).

Following dinner, Holly grunted out two-hundred stomach crunches, twenty one-armed pushups (ten an arm), and two-hundred leg raises. The leg raises were performed with twenty pound ankle weights. The pain nearly made her weep. Before bedtime, Holly jogged for a mile. She thought of spring as a runner thinks of a big race. The gun had been fired, and the race was on.

Summer was the finish line, and countless other women were racing toward it. Beyond the finish line was the beach, where the winners of the race — posing in their nearly-nude swim wear — enjoyed the beach studs' attention. Some women had already dropped out of the race. They consoled themselves with chips, dip, pop, and pizzas.

Holly's only class on Tuesdays was astronomy. Astronomy bored her more than most courses. Professor Nova droned about red stars, red dwarfs, the parallax view, and other stupid stuff. She usually skipped on Tuesdays and spent the day lounging. She did a quick fifty pushups every hour or so, watched her soaps *Tyrannies* and *Love and Spite*, and sipped low-cal gin and tonics.

But today Holly had to work.

She had torn off the first page of Edward's Dylan Thomas essay. At least the introduction was good: it stated the theme of sexual metaphors and narrowed the discussion to three poems. She had not read the poems, and she did not want to. But she pushed aside these complaints and opened her copy of *The Collected Poems of Dylan Thomas*.

The first poem mentioned in the introduction was "If I Were Tickled by the Rub of Love". Holly liked the title. It evoked a fantasy of sharing a hot tub with a 1950's era Paul Newman. Unfortunately, the poem was incomprehensible. She sighed and willed herself to read it a second time. Then a third.

Let's try the second poem, she thought. Sounds easier. "Fern Hill".

An hour later, exasperated, she turned to the third poem, "Alterwise By Owl Light".

On the library's third floor, one level above Holly Dish, Edward Head approached Claire Sweet. Edward had not seen her since the day he left the note in her car. He wondered if she were avoiding him.

She saw him and smiled instantly.

He returned the smile and asked if he could sit down.

He could.

"Around here it's, well, the library's been less pleasant lately," Edward said.

"Why's that?"

How many reasons do you want? he thought. Because your hair is long and wavy. Because you're five feet nine and wear blue jeans and cotton blouses. Because you don't wear makeup and your skin is perfect.

Edward shrugged. "You're good company."

"So are you." Claire pushed away her books and gracefully covered her yawn. "But I've been holed up at home with the flu. I'm fine now, though."

He wanted to be as serene and peaceful as she. Christ, even her nostrils were lovely. He was wondering what to say when she offered to buy him a cup of coffee.

On the way to the student union, Claire wondered what to say. She did not want to hurt Edward's feelings. But she could not let him think romance was possible. She promised herself to gently approach the subject after the first cup of coffee.

After the second cup, she lost her nerve. She hated confrontations, even those that were not confrontational. She decided to play it by ear and broach the subject only if necessary.

Edward had relaxed a bit. He was talking about his plans to study film. "I think I can write well enough. At least well enough to write a script. If I can get a 3.75 grade point average this year, I can get in a good film school."

"Have you made any short movies yet?" Claire imagined Edward in a director's chair, surrounded by technicians and equipment. The image fit him.

"I actually started one on a field trip to Chicago, but I don't think it'll work out." He imagined pointing his camcorder at Claire: She sat on a sunny hillside, wearing jeans and a sleeveless cotton blouse. Her knees were drawn to her chest, and a cooling afternoon breeze rippled her hair.

"Wish I had your ambition," Claire said. "I'd have a lot more —"

She paused: in the periphery of her vision, she noticed someone waving, or pointing.

Edward saw it too: Holly Dish stood ten feet away, thrusting her middle finger at him. He rested his forehead in the crook of thumb and forefinger and pretended not to see her.

Holly approached the table, anger rolling off her. "What kind of agreement are you making with her, Edward? Hand jobs for short papers, legs in stirrups for a long paper?"

Edward jumped up. "Thanks for the coffee, Claire!"

"Of course!" Claire blurted.

"I'm sorry," Holly said to Claire. "Excuse me for the —"

"Of course!"

" — the intrusion, but I've got to talk with him."

Holly followed Edward out of the room. She was asking about pen-wah balls and foot-long pearl jams. Fleetingly, Claire wondered what Edward had done to make the woman so mad. She looked like those aerobic women on the cover of women's fitness magazines. And she could probably kick Edward's ass.

Edward refused to talk to Holly, or to even face her. She had planned to tear into him, perhaps shame him enough to write the paper for her without any sex in return. But he hurried away, leaving her seething in the middle of the union courtyard. With Edward gone, Holly found herself thinking of Claire: specifically, she was critiquing Claire's appearance. The critique was not triggered by Claire's possible involvement with Edward. Please, Holly thought, take the grease spot! The critique was simply reflexive, like a drunk downing a free drink. Holly had worked hard for her figure, and she was always aware of other attractive women.

At first, Holly was unsettled. Claire made her feel fifteen pounds heavier. That familiar and loathsome dread of weight grew in Holly, and she had to jog around the campus a few times to calm down.

The jog cleared her head. Now she could critique Claire more objectively. Yes, she was attractive. Nice long legs—but on the bony side—and graceful white arms. Good hair, but kind of messy. The eyes were good: they demanded attention without any makeup. But the bust. Not the best. No banana tits, but they looked small—lucky to be a C cup. And her rear end was probably flat.

But her age was the clincher. She was twenty-five or twenty-six if a day! Must be a loser, still in college at that age. No need to worry. In five or six more years, Holly would be at her peak, and Claire would be finished: she'd be in her thirties.

Edward sat fidgeting in his darkened apartment. Maybe Holly is nuts, he mused. She had stood defiantly, jabbed the air with her middle finger, and did not care who saw her. His face was still sweaty and flush.

Finally Edward turned on the floor lamp. He paced for a few minutes, then scrubbed his face with a new acne soap that smelled like cough syrup and made his face burn. The soap had tiny abrasives that "invigorated old skin" and "made way for vibrant, healthy skin." Edward imagined that his nose's oil-clogged pores were being purged and tightened. He risked a look in the mirror. His skin was certainly clean, but it looked as if he had scrubbed with sandpaper.

Edward fell asleep counting the pimples on his face. Later, he dreamed he sat in the union with Claire Sweet. He was naked. He did not want to stand up because Claire would see his pocked, pimpled buttocks. Holly appeared. She pointed a camcorder at Edward.

"Stand up, tart," Holly ordered Edward. "Make love to the camera."

Edward clumsily shook his ass.

Edward awoke with a start. He cursed himself—his raw skin, his embarrassing virginity, his tedious booksmarts. He realized that his plans for spooling Holly and Claire were moronic. Trying to seduce Holly with a camera...what a loser! And hoping a pat on the hand would lure Claire into the sack.

Pathetic.

Chapter Twenty Two: The Day He was Born Again

Dressed in black jeans and black shirt, Jimmy Stubbs drove around the block several times. The neighborhood was quiet. Cars slumbered in driveways while people slumbered in houses. Jimmy took a final drive around the block, reviewed his plan, then parked thirty yards from Edward's apartment. He walked silently, his supplies in a lunch sack.

Jimmy followed an alley to the rear of Edward's apartment, then crouched beside a tree. A porch light brightened Edward's back door. To the right stood a garage, which would shield Jimmy from the neighbor's view. To the left was a row of shrubs, which offered further protection. The only hazard was the top apartment's kitchen window, just to the right of Edward's entrance. But the window was dark. Jimmy reasoned that if he worked quietly, the top tenants would have no reason to look out the window.

He crouched before the entrance and slowly opened the screened door. It squeaked only once. He positioned himself between the screened door and wood door. Silence was crucial, so attaching the hasp took forty-five minutes. Slow turn by slow turn, his screwdriver drove the screws into the door's old wood, then into the door frame.

He slipped the padlock through the hasp. The padlock yielded a confidence-inspiring click.

The next target, Edward's car, was parked outside the garage. The car was a riskier target because Jimmy would be in the open. Still, working quickly would reduce the risk. He crouched at the rear of the car and pushed several packets of firecrackers deep into the tail pipe until they dropped into the muffler.

"Have a nice day, loser," Jimmy whispered toward Edward's apartment.

Edward woke at 7:30 and took a quick shower. After a candy bar and a Coke, he gathered his books and headed for campus. Or rather, he tried to head for campus. The door would not open. He yanked hard on the doorknob several times and managed only to hurt his hand.

Realizing he would have to bust out, Edward slammed his shoulder against the door. Twice. Thrice. The door stubbornly remained shut. Edward ate a second candy bar in two mouth-stretching bites and tried to reason out the problem. Perhaps one of the women upstairs had gotten drunk and parked the car against the door. He stood on a chair and looked out the basement window that faced the driveway, but the window was dirty and he could see only his car.

Edward cranked open the window that faced the back yard. Although wide open, it was too small for even a child to squeeze through. Edward considered his two options: beat the door down or call...who? The police? The idea of calling the police embarrassed him, so he tried slamming into the door again. Three more futile and painful slams persuaded him to call the police.

He tapped the phone plunger several times — no dial tone. He hung up, picked up the receiver. Still no dial tone. The absurdity of his plight was sinking in. He laughed bitterly before slamming the phone against the wall, wishing he were not one of the last hundred students in America who owned no cell phone.

Dr. John Fear, the English department chair, was used to Alex's odd ailments: sensitivity to sunlight, outbreaks of eczema, changes in hair color, lung-ripping coughs, lurching limps and sideways stumbles. But even John asked if Alex was all right when Alex wore wrap-around black shades to work Tuesday.

"I'm fine," Alex assured. Be casual, he thought. Just another odd symptom. He took two steps back: John had an unnerving habit of standing three inches away and talking directly at one's face. "My eyes are medicated and, I mean, the medication is — "

"Bothering your eyes, yes." John studied his fun-house reflection in the shades.

"I feel good." Speaking was difficult. The haloperidol had dried Alex's mouth. The medication aggravated Alex's light intolerance, too. Even with the shades, Alex squinted at table lamps as if they were klieg lights.

John leaned to the left, then to the right, trying to see Alex's eyes. "Alex, we have to talk. How about my office?"

Alex nodded in agreement and followed.

"I've always liked you Alex," the chairman lied.

John had written three "serious" novels. "My novels," John sometimes sniffed, "are about larger ideas." Publishers returned the manuscripts with form-letter rejections. Only one publisher responded personally to John's third manuscript, *This Sad Evening's Swan Song*. The editor wrote she could not read beyond the first paragraph, which "at least made the manuscript stand out."

Now that Alex had no literary reputation, John was relaxed enough to tolerate Alex. John occasionally watched Alex walk, or limp, or cough down the hallways, or get lost on his way to class. If that's what the literary life is about, John periodically mused, I want no part of it.

"And so you want me to see a doctor," Alex sighed. "You think I'm cracking, don't you?"

"I didn't say that." John poured two cups of coffee. "But your little, uh, performance yesterday didn't go over well with the administration."

"Then it couldn't have been all bad." He waved a hand at John's frown. "Those humorless, good for nothing leaches. Gives them something to gossip about before their lunch break, doesn't it?"

"Still…"

"Okay, you have a point." Actually, Alex was foggy about what he had done. He remembered only tearing up a copy of *The Best Year of His Life* in front of his freshman composition class. One alarmed student ran out of the classroom.

"I just took too much medication."

"There've been rumors of a — well, of your condition. Just rumors." John spoke gently, as if comforting a sick friend.

"I do have bad headaches," Alex confided. "Sometimes they cross my eyes. Maybe my medication discourages the, well, discourages my inhibitions."

" — Headaches?" John marveled that a headache would drive a man to tear off his own shirt. Not to mention tear up his own novel.

Alex struggled to remember what he had done. "Tell me what the rumors are, and I'll tell you what really happened. After I get a laugh from the exaggeration."

John related what he had heard: Alex had stopped in the middle of an English 101 lecture, complained of the heat, and removed his shoes. A few minutes later, he had torn off his shirt. A student giggled nervously, so Alex folded his arms across his chest and announced that he was a world-class author and was therefore a libertine in the social graces.

"Are my sources accurate so far?" John asked.

"A little." He recognized one of haloperidol's notorious side effects: delusions of grandeur. "But anyway. What happened next, according to your sources?"

"After your tore off your shirt, you tore up a copy of your novel. Then you yelled that the shirt and the book were equally useless to you. That they were both just trappings. Or that they both trapped you and had to be destroyed." John scratched his chin. "At this point, I'm sure the rumors make the truth unrecognizable."

"Unrecognizable," Alex agreed.

"And you implored the students to do the same."

"Rip up their shirts?"

"And photos of their parents."

"I think I said photos of their siblings," Alex smiled.

"Whatever."

Alex tried to remember, but his vague and fractured recollections refused to cohere.

"Since the class was reading Thoreau, I suppose you were trying to dramatize the reading," John suggested. "The need for simplicity, the seduction of possessions, and all the usual clichés."

"I've never compared myself to Thoreau."

"Of course not. But really, Alex. You can imagine all the freshman coeds, burning up the phone lines that evening to their mothers and fathers. The Dean has had five phone calls from worried parents already. And one from a major contributor."

"I should have known," Alex sneered. "It's about money."

"Of course it's about money," John snapped. "And spare me the Thoreau nonsense. He isolated himself in the woods. You really don't want to do the same, do you?"

"But it was the medication."

"For a headache. Yes." John stood up, peered out his office window. "How is your more serious condition?" John asked delicately.

"It's no secret I have mild schizophrenia," Alex noted almost cheerfully. "Actually, my case comes closest to what's called 'simple' schizophrenia. You know, the retreat into silence, the inability to participate in life emotionally. The occasional odd response to things." Alex adopted a broad German accent. "But you take zee medication und you vill be fine!"

"You're not having a relapse?"

"No."

John smiled weakly.

Alex solemnly removed his glasses. The pain was extreme: his eyes felt like pincushions, pierced by a thousand pins. "As I said before, I'm fine. If the administration wants to force me to see a doctor, then—"

"No! It's nothing like that." John shrugged. "We're just concerned."

"I appreciate your concern. I guess I got out of hand yesterday. But you know how dull classes can be near the end of the semester," Alex deadpanned.

John nodded.

"It wasn't the medication, I think, as much as the pressures of writing my manuscript."

"You're writing again?" John instantly forgot about Alex's odd behavior. "Is it coming along? Are you happy with it?"

"Sort of," Alex lied. He had not written a word. But the Eccentric Author role mitigated odd behavior.

"What's it called?"

Alex blinked. "*My Life as a Dead Man.*"

"Good title." The old envy bit into John's stomach, like a dormant ulcer come back to life. "What's it about?"

"It's — like I said, I've only written a chapter or so. But so far it's about a guy who's dead but doesn't behave appropriately."

"Does he know he's dead?"

"Yes. But he keeps going to work, takes his kids to the ballpark, kisses his wife — "

"A horror story?" John asked skeptically. He disdained horror fiction.

"Sort of. It's gruesome, sure. But it's also funny." Alex nodded enthusiastically. Excitement lifted his voice and his mood. He rolled his fingers against his thumb, wished he had a pen to record his ideas.

"Funny?"

"Sure. Because he's dead, and everything's got extra humor for the deceased."

John blinked at Alex.

"It's all a metaphor for, uh, for society's deadening effects, how it sanctions proper behavior and punishes nonconformists."

John again hated Alex. "I'm glad we straightened this matter out," he said officiously. "I know the administration will be thrilled to know you're writing again. It's been such a damned long time, hasn't it?" He opened the door and bid Alex good day.

Back at home, Alex dropped a haloperidol into a glass of beer and began writing. The words came slowly. Alex felt like a clogged water faucet that merely drips. But he persisted. When he got stuck, he bit his wrist and tongued the wound. After an hour, he paused for a cigarette and re-read his work:

> Terrence's mother was a martyr. Every day, she reminded her husband and her child that she sacrificed. "I gave up my youth for you two, and my beauty, and my promising singing career." She sighed, ran her wrinkled hands over her leathery face.
>
> Terrence had never heard his mother sing or even hum. When his father was on his deathbed, Terrence asked, "Did Mom ever sing?" Father shook his head. "Was she beautiful?"
>
> Another shake. "I don't even think," father sighed, "she was ever young, either. Or maybe she just went straight from nineteen to fifty."
>
> Terrence was forgiving, however, and he tried to look be-

yond his mother's self-absorption and lies. He imagined that his mother sincerely wanted to contribute, to struggle, to sacrifice. Was it her fault that she possessed no beauty or talent to sacrifice in the first place?

On the day of his high school graduation — mother could not come because she believed she suddenly had a Dowager's hump — Terrence decided to become a martyr for his mother's martyrdom. He would be a doctor.

And he did.

He treated the poor and the demented, the dishonest and the devious.

"I'm not in it for the money," he proudly told his fellow physicians. He loved beating them over the head with his purity, and they hated him.

Even his mother grew weary of his sacrifices. "I've worked my fingers to the bone to put you through medical school. Why can't you show your gratitude by buying me a car, or a new house?"

"I'm not in it for the money."

"Cheapskate!"

Nobody cared when Terrence was run over by an ungrateful patient. Few people attended the funeral. Those who attended struggled to hide their disdain, and they criticized him as soon as he was buried. His mother dabbed tears from her painted, bony cheek and sniffed, "All I did for him, and I'm left with nothing."

Inside his casket, Terrence chuckled at their complaints.

That evening, he clawed his way from the grave. His muscles were stiff, and he had to pull the mortician's stitching and cotton from his mouth. He limbered up with a stroll around the town. Then he went home, got a good night's rest. The house was empty, as his wife and children were staying with relatives across town. He resumed his practice the next morning.

Nurse Kane was speechless when Terrence walked into the clinic, and she never spoke again. But she kept working for Terrence — where else could a mute nurse work?

BUT THAT BASTARD BROTHER OF MINE. When I see him again I'll pull each finger off his hand. I'm the best thing that ever happened to him. He tried to make his reputation off me, trotting me out in front of his moron colleagues to demonstrate my "progress" from schizoid to nearly-functioning citizen. Their white coats, their smug nods, their whispers just out of earshot.

"I know you're talking about ME!" I screamed, and my brother patted me on the shoulder. "Not you. Your condition."

His smug smile.

"Of course, and gentlemen, controlling the schizophrenic's inappropriate emotional responses takes time"

"You let me go back to sleep!" I closed my eyes and covered my ears. I couldn't stop laughing, laughing at them. My bastard brother needed me. I didn't need him. If he died tomorrow, I'd be FREE.

Alex crossed out the final four paragraphs, paused for another cigarette. The paragraphs were another explosion of drug behavior. The medication had done all it could do. Now it was turning on him. It still helped him concentrate, and it slowed the physical changes: no more suddenly red hair, or feminine titter, or smoker's cough, or cluster headaches. But its efficacy would wane, and the side effects would increase: dry mouth and throat, sore eyes, the bursts of grandiosity.

And now, the four paragraphs of ranting.

Haloperidol had stimulated the withdrawn part of Alex's personality, dragging it toward daylight. But the withdrawn part was angry. The withdrawn part was again raging at long-dead David.

After a second beer—no haloperidol chaser—Alex stretched out on the couch and mulled over the writing.

He liked the character Terrence. But why does he have to be a doctor?

A doctor: Terrence the doctor was David, his brother.

Alex laughed like a gleeful child. I couldn't have revenge in life, Alex thought, so I'll have it in a book. That bastard minced my brain with pills. Now I'll mince his life in a book.

Before nodding off, Alex decided to replace the name Terrence with David. The name reverberated in his skull. The name became a mantra, and Alex chanted it in his sleep. Then he dreamed.

But the dream was not fiction.

It was a documentary of the day he was born again:

On the day he was born again, Alex was visiting David before meeting his publisher. David was using the visit to evaluate his brother's condition; if Alex seemed too agitated or withdrawn, David would accompany him to the publisher.

"You seem pretty good," David allowed. "You're taking your prescriptions?"

"Sure," Alex lied. He avoided David's gaze by studying his broccoli. Then David's pager sounded and David rose from the table to call the hospital. Alex was left to play with his food for a few moments. "We gotta hurry!" David called, running past Alex. "Knife wounds, and Vic and Mary are out of town!" David did not want to leave Alex in the house.

Alex's stomach twisted. He hated hospitals. David ignored a red light and cursed a slow moving van. Alex was in the back seat, face between his knees. He kept asking David to inflate the tires. "Maybe they're going flat," Alex pleaded. "We might get in a wreck."

"Relax, Alex. Here." David thrust two tranquilizers into Alex's hand. Alex stared at them. "Damn it. You're meeting your editors in two days. Take them!"

Alex swallowed them and lowered his head. He was ashamed to be seen like this, and he was angry at David for bossing him.

David double-parked outside the emergency entrance, told Alex to follow him, and ran inside. A nurse held up four fingers, indicating that the patient was in room four.

The patient lay on his side. His knees were drawn to his bloody chest, and his hands trembled. Alex peeked over his brother's shoulder at the patient's contorting face. Alex imitated the patient by contorting his own face.

"Settle down, Alex." David put a firm hand on Alex's shoulder and directed him to a corner. Alex cooperated, but he kept imitating the patient.

The nurse studied Alex as he waited in the corner.

"He's fine," David assured. "He's between medications, and he's meeting his publishers on Thursday." He winked. "He's not fond of meeting new people."

"I'd heard he's a writer." The nurse marveled that Alex could scrawl even his initials.

David turned to the patient, who had rolled onto his stomach. "The poor guy needs some street fighting lessons." He peeled the bloody bandage from the man's neck. "Christ." He bent over to better see the two wounds in the neck. They were deep and long; the ripped red flesh on the neck's surface contrasted sharply with the white flesh deeper down.

The patient's breathing became labored. He jerked his head away from David, and the wounds flexed and foamed like the red gills of a dying fish. "Help me get him on his back, Nurse Kane."

David moved to the rear of the cot as Nurse Kane moved to the middle.

She worked her hands and arms underneath the patient's belly, and David reached under the shoulders. David nodded, and they began slowly turning the patient over.

Alex had dropped to the floor and onto his belly. Slowly, he rolled over. When the patient's right arm got caught behind his neck, Alex's arm did the same. The patient wailed. Alex wailed.

The patient twisted free and fell to the floor. Nurse Kane kneeled to help him, but the patient grabbed her head. When Nurse Kane tried to escape, the patient lunged at her and bit off her nose.

David pushed the emergency button then tried to pull the patient off Nurse Kane. He got the patient in a bear hug and struggled to heave him into a corner—the corner where Alex writhed, as if he too were struggling in a bear hug.

"Jesus Christ, Alex! Move! Go for help and—" David choked. The patient had his hand down David's throat.

Alex stopped moving.

The patient jerked his hand from David's mouth; the hand clutched a hunk of wiggly flesh. The patient winced at the flesh, as a child winces at raw fish on his dinner plate. He kept wincing as he ate it.

Alex stared.

Thirty seconds later, a male nurse and two security guards burst in. One guard wretched, the other screamed. The male nurse, more used to blood and guts, slapped the guards and told them to help.

David's body was on top of Nurse Kane's.

The patient and Alex sat in the corner. The patient wore Nurse Kane's blood-spotted cap and sucked loudly at Alex's bloody neck. Alex ignored the patient and juggled Nurse Kane's nose.

One guard pushed the nurse out of the room while the second opened fire on the patient. The patient scrambled to the door. Halfway down the hall he trampled the second guard and the nurse, who were screaming for assistance.

The patient dove through a plate glass window and fell two stories onto a doctor's parked car. He rolled off the car hood and ran ten yards before the afternoon sun drove him to his knees. A rancid, oily smoke rolled off him, then he burst into flame.

Meanwhile, Alex sat in another room, fingering the holes in his neck. The doctors kept asking if he were all right. "I'm fine," Alex repeated.

And he really was fine. He could not remember ever feeling so calm. He sat on a cot, surrounded by doctors and nurses, and he was relaxed. The worried stares, muffled talk, and glaring overhead lights did not bother him. "I feel good, truly good."

Alex was born again, the blood and saliva of the walking dead mixed with his own. The husk of human personality left behind in Alex's skin was perfectly content to be a kind of dead man for whom the world of other people—that loud repellant world of expectations, demands, and disappointments—meant nothing. For most of his natural life, Alex had bitterly wished that he cared nothing for other people, that he could wall himself from their grotesque emotions and maddening motives.

Now the wish was miraculously granted.

After a doctor bandaged Alex's neck wounds, he put a comforting hand on Alex's shoulder. "I'm sorry to tell you that your brother is dead."

Alex nodded solemnly. "I'll just have to make the best of it." He glanced at his watch. "Starting now."

He stood, thanked everyone for their help, and reluctantly accepted a ride to his brother's house. He watched the news: the "brutal multiple murders" at the county hospital were the evening's big news. Officials explained that the murderous drug addict evidently used propellant to immolate himself. The hospital staff tried to forget the incident, and they eventually did.

As years passed, David often tried to recall that baptismal afternoon. Sometimes when he bit a victim's neck, images flashed across his closed eyes: David's bloody unbelieving face, Nurse Kane's severed nose, the demented patient baring bloody teeth. Yet the images remained opaque and fragmented, like an often-spliced movie illuminated by a dim projector.

Now, as Alex woke from the dream, he smiled. The once fragmented images cohered into a thrilling gestalt. Finally, he could recall the second birth that freed him from the curse of his first birth. Fleetingly, Alex realized that people would be appalled by his gratitudes: grateful for his brother's murder, grateful for the bite of the dead. And unspeakably grateful to escape the demands of the living.

Chapter Twenty Three: *Deus Ex Machina* after the late shift

Claire Sweet was anxious. She could not find her notes about two books, *The Greek Idea* and *The Ideals of Greek Culture*. After searching her apartment three times, she searched her car three times. The Chevy was filled with paper cups, fast food napkins, and candy bar wrappers. But no notes. Claire slouched into the driver's seat and battled the urge to cry. A cry would release a lot of tension, but she could not spare the time.

She resigned herself to the fact that the notes were gone. She made up her mind to pull an all-nighter at the library to catch up. As she trudged back into her apartment, the phone rang.

"This is Mr. Nixon. I need to talk to Claire Sweet."

"Speaking—"

"I need you at work tonight, Claire."

"I can't," Claire said weakly.

"I'm sorry. We try to stick to schedules, but I need you here by 5:00."

She hung up the phone. "Goodbye 'A' in History," she muttered. She smoked a stale cigarette and cried.

Mr. Nixon was behind the cash register, ringing up a little boy's 16-ounce Zip Gun slush.

"Glad you're here," Mr. Nixon admitted. His mood was sour because he had been stuck with the busy afternoon shift. School kids streamed in, shouting, pushing, and buying the candy, pop, and chips they could not safely steal.

Claire took over at the register. As Mr. Nixon removed his orange florescent Zip-Quick apron, he studied Claire's rear. Another boy, a bag of Cheezie Corn in his hand, followed Mr. Nixon's gaze to Claire's rear.

She turned. "Yes, Mr. Nixon?"

His toothy grin was vaguely perverse. "Pardon me, but there's a note stuck to your, stuck on your jeans." He retreated to his office in the rear.

Claire reached around and pulled. The note was written on a small square of paper with an adhesive strip. "Hope You're Well," the note declared in neat handwriting: Edward's handwriting. She had been busy that week and had not been to the library. She knew she was avoiding the problem. How, she wondered, do you fend off a boy's crush?

"He's a nice kid," she whispered to herself. "It's a nice note." She tossed the note away, then a revelation struck her: Edward must have her notes! They had shared a messy table at the library, and he must have mistakenly picked up her notebook.

She found his number in the directory and called.

"The number you have called," the recording chirped, "is no longer in service."

Claire decided to visit Edward tonight. Her stomach knotted at the thought, but she told herself to be calm. True, appearing at lovestruck Edward's door past midnight with heavy eyelids might give the wrong impression. I'll just have to explain, she thought, that I really need those notes.

The evening passed slowly. Teenagers did more loitering than buy-ing. The occasional drunk or pothead wandered in for more wine, more cigarettes, or more rolling papers. At midnight, Claire waved wearily as Marsha entered. "Thank God you're here," Claire half-shouted.

"I can tell you're tired, kid." Marsha winked as she ran a comb through her graying hair. "Your drawl is comin' out."

"And I'm gettin' out of here."

"Just give me a sec to hit the restroom, OK?" Marsha disappeared into the rear to sit on the toilet and have a smoke.

A man with unkempt hair and tired, red-rimmed eyes walked slowly down the aisles. He stopped, mumbled, and kept walking. Then he fidgeted before the cooler. Claire fleetingly wondered if he was an in-competent shoplifter. He slowly turned and approached Claire.

"Pardon me." He licked his cracked lips. "Do you have any bottled water?"

"I think you went right by it. Aisle two."

"I also need orange juice."

He looked familiar. She had seen him in the college's Academic Cen-ter. "There's orange juice in aisle three."

She studied him as he gathered the water and juice. It took him a long time. He stared vacantly at the bottled water before taking it. When he found the jug of orange juice, he shook it several times, then studied it. Finally, he nodded and brought the items to the check out.

He pointed at the cigarette rack behind Claire. "I'd also like a pack of Dunhills, please."

After paying, the man immediately opened the cigarette pack, took out a cigarette. "Got a light?"

Claire handed him a book of matches. His hands were dry, too: red and cracked. He blinked through the cigarette smoke, and she recog-nized him. "You teach at the college, don't you?"

"Sorry." He smiled rather sheepishly through his cigarette's smoke. "I don't remember names too well."

"I've not had you for a course. I'm just a freshman myself."

"Ah."

She hurriedly explained: "Took me a little while to get the money together. I've got some scholarship money, but—" She chuckled to hide her discomfort. "It still doesn't pay the bills, so I work here, too."

"Working, saving, keeping up your grades..." The notion fatigued Alex. "You must be in peak fitness, right?"

"Sure," she joked. "It's all the coffee and pop that keeps me going."

"I should try that myself."

"Oh." Claire extended her hand. "My name's Claire. What's yours?"

Alex shook Claire's hand. "Alex Resartus. I'm in the English department."

"You're a writer, aren't you?" She was intrigued by Alex's palpable weirdness. He was like a surrealist painting: the more she looked, the more odd detail she saw. Only one side of his face was shaved, she noted, and his eyes moved independently, like a lizard's.

Alex nodded, gathered his juice and water. "I'm trying to be one. It's not easy."

"I imagine so."

"Nice meeting you."

As Claire drove across town toward Edward's apartment, she imagined the scene that might await her:

Claire: I'm sorry it's so late (Tone apologetic yet businesslike), but I think I left some important notes on the library table and—

Edward: Nice of you to come by. (Grin indicates that he misunderstands visit) Let me get you a drink.

Claire: The notebook would be enough, thanks. (Wonders how she can take the notes and run with a minimum of discourtesy)

Edward: I'm glad you're here because (Takes a deep breath) I need to tell you something. I love—

Claire: —I'm sorry, but there's just no way, Edward—! (Runs out the door without her notes).

She walked to the rear of the apartment and broken glass crunched under her steps. The basement window was shattered. She squatted and peered inside. Darkness. The shattered window seemed too small for a thief to squeeze through, but Claire was still worried. She hurried to the back door.

She knocked, waited a half-minute, then knocked harder.

"Who's there?"

"Claire Sweet. I'm sorry to come here at such at an hour, but—" She heard him tromp toward the door, wheezing. "Christ Edward, are you all right?"

"I'm trapped in here!" His voice cracked, and Claire wondered if he was laughing or crying. "Somebody locked me in."

Claire looked down. A padlock, barely visible in the darkness, rested snugly in a thick hasp.

"I need a locksmith."

"No you don't. All you need is a—well, I need a big screwdriver. Pass it to me through the broken window."

She waited by the broken window, listened to Edward bang around. He cursed loudly when he stubbed his toe against a kitchen chair. His curse was followed by a crash as he dropped his toolbox.

Finally, breathing heavily, he appeared at the window.

"Turn on the lights, why don't you?"

"I don't have any electricity. Fuck. I can't tell you how glad I am you showed up."

"This is weird," she said, as much to herself as to Edward. She took the screwdriver and went to work. The screws were deeply set: it would have taken ten Edwards to force down the door.

Twenty minutes later the last screw came out. Claire slowly opened the door, and Edward stood in front of her. She could see only his outline, but she sensed he was not fully clothed.

"Are you with someone?"

"Only you." His reeked of booze.

"Why don't we sit down for a moment?"

The neighbor's vapor lamp provided the only light. She stepped over several beer bottles. Edward sat on the couch, Claire on a wobbly kitchen chair. Edward talked almost non-stop for twenty minutes, and his monologue was so preposterous that Claire forgot about her notes.

Yesterday morning, Edward explained, he woke to find that he was trapped in his apartment. When he could not force open the door, he finally decided to call the police. "Was I embarrassed calling the cops!" he announced. He tried not to belch, then belched. "I was actually relieved when the phone was dead."

The women upstairs didn't seem to be around, so Edward resigned himself to staying in the apartment for a while. Edward decided to have a beer—"first of a multitude"—and wondered what to do. He stopped wondering after the fifth beer. He turned on his transistor radio, drank a bottle of wine, and enjoyed a respite from the real world. Eventually he fell asleep.

When he woke, the apartment was dark. None of the lights worked and the refrigerator was warm.

"I was a little panicked," Edward confessed, "what with the power still out. So I broke the window and called for help."

"I would have been screamin'."

"I would have, but I was still embarrassed. By the time you showed up though, I was about to fall asleep."

"Who did this to you?"

"An old girlfriend I think," Edward blundered. "We had a fight, nothing more than a spat, really, but you know how women — well some women, especially young ones — they can over-react."

"Not that it matters, Edward, but are you naked?"

"I'm wearing underwear. Black."

"Lacy, I suppose."

"No. Crotchless."

"Why wear any at all then?"

"Because I've got company." He belched again. "Actually, the bedroom door locked behind me, and I can't find that stupid skeleton key that opens it."

The thought of naked Edward trying to break open the bedroom door made Claire wince.

"Want a beer?"

"No thank you."

"Why did you come over?"

"Did you accidentally pick up my notes at the library?"

"No."

"Shit."

"It was no accident."

"Edward?" She tried to sound angry. If he were her type, she would be flattered.

"It was just an excuse to see you, but I got — "

Claire could not help but laugh. "Locked in, yes."

"They're locked in the bedroom. We can try to get in there and — "

"Just bring them to the library tomorrow."

Hidden behind a tree, Jimmy Stubbs watched the tall woman leave. He angrily chewed his lower lip. Christ, Edward Shithead already had a tart over!

Jimmy had arrived a half-hour earlier. He planned to sit against a tree, have a few smokes, and enjoy Edward's imprisonment. Jimmy had hoped to hear Edward yelling for help, or weeping. When Jimmy arrived, he was surprised to see an unfamiliar car in the driveway. He crept closer to Edward's entrance and saw that the door was open. He wondered how Edward had so quickly escaped his lockup.

"I swear to God I'll nail you yet," Jimmy promised. He pretended that the tree was Edward's shin and kicked it.

Chapter Twenty Four: Some Gumption

Final exams were two weeks away, and Holly needed a miracle to earn a "B" in Alex Resartus's class. She was satisfied with her other grades: "C" in algebra, "C" in history, "B" in business administration. But Christ! A "D" in English if she did not earn "A"'s on her final paper and her final exam. Her letter of recommendation was almost out of reach.

The special situation demanded special action: therefore, she was lurking in the Academic Center at 11:00 p.m. with Jimmy Stubbs. Jimmy needed an "A" on the English exam to just pass. His plan was simple: steal a copy of the exam. He had been casing the Academic Center for a week, he boasted, and he believed his plan was foolproof.

Jimmy learned that the janitor began cleaning faculty offices at about 8:00 p.m. The janitor got to the English department—the fourth floor— between 11:05 and 11:15 p.m. The faculty offices were in two suites: one suite on the east side of the building, the other on the west. After mopping the long classroom hallway, the janitor entered the suites, and the double-doors closed and locked behind him. The only trick was to get past the double-doors that separated the suites from the hallway. Fortunately, one door closed slowly. As the janitor walked around the corner, Jimmy could slip past the slowly closing door.

Inside the suites, the janitor had a slick routine. He unlocked each office and mopped the floors. He kept each office door open as he went to the next office. He needed ten minutes to "clean" the eighteen offices. The janitor then locked his sweeper in a closet. On his second trip around the suites, he emptied the wastepaper baskets, sprayed air freshener, and locked each office.

"It's made to order," Jimmy whispered. "I'll come up here each night and slip into Resartus's office. I'll hide under his desk, wait for the janitor to leave the building, and go through Resartus's office." Jimmy excitedly chewed his foreknuckle. "That exam is bound to be in there."

"Fine. But what do you need me up here for?" Holly ventured.

"I really don't," Jimmy allowed. "I just wanted to show you how well planned out this is. You know, so you'd understand."

"—Understand what?"

"Understand the plan."

She slowly nodded.

"Well isn't it?"

"What—?"

"Well planned!"

"Sure."

"Fucking right!" Jimmy asserted. "And Edward Shithead won't be the only one to ace the exam."

A corner of Holly's mouth lifted. "What's that about the last laugher, or is it—" Holly's eyes widened and she pressed a forefinger to her lips. The janitor was wheeling his bucket and mop down the hallway.

Jimmy's pulse quickened at the sight of Holly's erect finger against her mouth. He grabbed the finger and led her into an empty classroom. When he put an arm around Holly's waist, she pushed him away and whispered to quit clowning.

"Bag your whining," he whispered through clenched teeth. "I just wanted to get us out of the way." He looked out the classroom and motioned at Holly to follow. The janitor had just gone through the double-doors. Jimmy and Holly slipped past the slowly closing door, surprised by their own nerve.

When the janitor headed for the west suite, Holly and Jimmy tiptoed away.

They stopped in front of Resartus's open office. Two identical yellowed posters for a Shakespeare festival covered one wall. An overflowing bookcase covered another wall. A pile of paperbacks erupted from one corner, spilling toward the desk.

"Here I go," Jimmy whispered. He felt simultaneously romantic and brave. Perhaps she'd finally grow a crush on him. Such gallantry! he mused. He squeezed Holly's hand, stepped inside the office, and slipped under Alex's desk. He glimpsed Holly's running shoes and ankle socks outside the doorway. Then they were gone.

The janitor would be coming in about three minutes. Two and a half minutes later, Jimmy heard the footsteps. He smiled and told himself he was a fucking genius.

Holly jogged across campus to her dormitory. She was terribly nervous about Jimmy's plan, but it was her last hope for a letter of recommendation. She tried to put the plan's shortcomings out of her mind. But she kept imagining Jimmy being caught under the desk by the janitor, or falling asleep and being caught by Resartus. The little blowhard would bawl out the whole scheme.

Holly was constructing a counter plan—what to do if Jimmy was caught—as she approached her dorm room. An envelope was taped to the door.

Inside the envelope was a typed note:

Dear H:

You probably think it's ridiculous, but I really believe we should be together. I think we can be closer than you thought two people could be. I think I understand you more than you would know.

A friend

That creep Edward, Holly fumed, just won't let up. He's relentless, and he's the reason I'm caught up in this stunt with Jimmy Stubbs.

The janitor had emptied the wastepaper basket, sprayed the air freshener, and slammed the door. Jimmy waited a half-hour to ensure the janitor was out of the building. He waited another half-hour to be doubly sure. Then he crawled out from under the desk, removed the penlight from his shirt pocket, and began searching the office.

Resartus had one metal file cabinet, unlocked and unused. Jimmy next searched the desktop. A computer, two piles of student essays, a memo about next year's committee assignments. A copy of *Animal Farm* and a dictionary were side by side. So the guy reads kiddy books and can't even spell! Jimmy thought scornfully. How did the fraud get a job teaching college?

The desk was unlocked. The first drawer was empty, the second filled with old class handouts. The third was empty too. He sighed, resigned to search the hard drive of Resartus's computer. The computer's desktop was blank; the machine seemed virtually unused. glanced at the raucous bookshelf, but decided not to search it. If Resartus was scattered enough to use his bookcase as a filing cabinet, then Jimmy was out of luck. But Jimmy believed he was very much in luck. He believed that within two weeks, he would find the final exam.

Chapter Twenty Five: "The tradition of black humor."

"You're sure he won't mind?" Claire asked.

"Absolutely impossible." Edward strode briskly toward Professor Alex Resartus's office. "Professors love flattery."

"Maybe you should be a professor."

Edward enjoyed Claire's barbs. Since she had rescued him from his apartment last week, he was oddly liberated. She had seen him at his most ridiculous: trapped, drunk, and wearing only underwear. Now he could not hide behind his Edward Know It All role, and he did not want to.

He knocked on the professor's door.

"Come in."

Alex was scribbling notes about his novel, and the intrusion irritated him. He looked up balefully, expecting to see a screwball student: "I haven't been in class for nine weeks, but I need an 'A.'"

"Oh." Alex put down his pen. "Mr. Head. Edward Head." He smiled. Edward grinned, thinking that the professor enjoyed his company.

In fact, Alex was grinning at the woman standing shyly behind Edward.

Remarkably, Alex remembered her: she was the student who worked at the Zip Quick convenience store. She had said she was in peak fitness.

"I was wondering if you could sign a copy of your novel for a friend of mine," Edward said.

Claire stepped forward, holding a hardcover across her chest.

"I'm surprised," Alex smiled. "Now I've met two people who've read my book."

"To tell the truth," Claire confided, "I've read only the first chapter, but I really truly like it. Edward loaned me his copy and —"

Edward faced Claire. "No. It's yours to keep."

"I ordered a copy online," Claire said.

"Please, I can't take it!" Alex laughed. He raised his hands as if pleading for mercy. "I know my book isn't in every bookstore and in every mall and in every drugstore. But I just happen to have..." He stood up and scanned the top of his bookcase. "Here it is." He handed the book to Claire. "For you."

Claire handled the book as if it were delicate. "Thank you, but I really can't."

"Go on," Alex assured. "I've got a few more copies up there some-where." He sat back down, lit a cigarette. "It's funny. I'd forgotten I had copies in my bookcase, and I was looking for a book—can't remember what it was—and I came across my novel."

"It's even got the dust cover on it," Edward noted, a bit envious.

"Don't remind me," Alex said. "I don't like to see how much I've aged over the years."

Claire had already opened the book to examine the photo of Alex on the inside flap. He looked only slightly younger in the picture, and his hair was longer, and he still looked odd, with eyes that seemed to strain upon a distant object. "You don't look that much older," Claire said.

"You're just being kind."

"I can't believe you forgot where you'd put copies of your own novel," Edward remarked.

"Why not? After you finish writing a book, it doesn't matter to you anymore."

"Not even a little bit?" Claire asked.

"Not even a little bit. Once I was finished with that book, I had no feelings about it. It was like a dead person to me. A corpse." Alex laughed as if he had made a hilarious joke.

Edward and Claire stood awkwardly and watched him laugh. It took him half a minute to calm himself. Claire wondered if Alex were suffer-ing a nervous breakdown.

"Sorry." Alex paused to wipe his running eyes. "I don't know what got into me—" He laughed again. The laugh was percussive, like a gun being fired, and Edward fleetingly had the urge to run away.

"Let me sign that book for you," he said to Claire. He scribbled his name and the date. The date was three days off, but Claire said nothing.

"Now you," Alex said to Edward. As he autographed Edward's copy, he laughed yet again, and his signature was illegible.

"I apologize," he said after catching his breath. "I've been working too hard, I guess."

He wanted to add, And I'm amused that your blood, my fine young man, will help me write again.

"Do you want to be a writer, Edward?" Alex asked.

"I've thought about it." Edward pretended not to see the snot run-ning from Alex's nose.

"I think you will be writer." He returned the autographed book to Edward. "Maybe you'll even carry on in my humble tradition."

"The tradition of black humor, of course." Edward was almost shouting from nervousness: why didn't the professor wipe his nose? Edward turned to Claire, trying to pretend that nothing was wrong. "Black humor came out of the early and mid sixties. Authors like Joseph Heller, Donleavy, Stewart, and of course professor Resartus."

But Claire did not listen. She was studying Alex intently. "You poor man." She was no longer Claire the student; she was Claire the nurse's daughter. "You have been working too hard, and you're on the verge of a collapse."

Edward watched impotently as Claire pulled an unopened bottle of spring water from her book bag. She also produced two sedatives and insisted that Alex take them.

"I don't like to take medication," Alex protested.

"They're just tranquilizers, silly." She smiled. "Now don't turn me in for dispensing medication without a license." She balled up a tissue and discreetly wiped Alex's nose.

Alex swallowed the tiny blue pills. "Thank you," he heard himself saying. "I'm...I'm grateful to you." He had another laughing attack, and Edward and Claire excused themselves.

Edward and Claire sipped coffee in the union.

"That guy's really coming off his rocker," Edward suggested.

"I think he's just over-tired." She felt protective of the professor.

"He's nuts," Edward insisted.

"No...he's a genuine eccentric, and there aren't many of those around. Too many people pretend to be eccentric because their own lives are boring, or empty, or conventional."

"Come off it," Edward snapped. He wanted Claire's attention spent on him, not Resartus.

"Study your peers. They're so damned bored with their lives they wear tee shirts with 'Party' and 'Go Crazy' emblazoned across their chest. They put most of their energy into getting drunk and trying hard not to learn too much at school."

Edward grunted. He owned a tee shirt that proclaimed "Crazy Party Dick", but he was too embarrassed to wear it.

"I'm not romanticizing real insanity, Edward. When you're crazy, it's really not funny. But he's not really crazy—just, you know, a real eccentric. All he needs is a rest."

"Hmm." Edward avoided Claire's gaze. He wanted to lean across the table and whisper, "I'll show you what crazy is," and thrust his tongue in her lovely mouth. Instead, he pretended to review his class notes.

Claire rose, bought a second cup of coffee. She sipped and Edward pretended to study. The silence grew longer, and Edward's petulance grew stronger. Claire wanted to joke Edward out of his mood, but the silence soured her mood, too.

If men can't fuck you, Claire thought, they hate you. And why should I humor him? Nose buried in his notes…the pompous little ass.

"Catch you later," she said.

"Right." He kept his face in his notes for a half-hour, and each minute made him feel stronger.

He had not given in to her overtures for pointless conversation. And she was too old for him anyway!

He stood to get more coffee. Professor Resartus was sitting at the other end of the room, and he waved. Claire, sitting with Alex, did not wave.

The pop bottle shattered against the wall, and so did the coffee mug. But the clock radio was stubborn, and Edward had to stomp on it several times before the casing split. A tangle of wires emerged through a crack, and Edward kicked the radio across the room.

"Bitch!"

He picked up a kitchen chair and struck the wall with it. Fatigue made him quit, but he was still angry, so he slapped his face twice, once with each hand.

"Bitch!" he declared again, but his tone was tainted with regret. "You bitch…" Now only an emotionless utterance. He tried to imagine the bitch's face: the brown eyes and hair, serene face and graceful neck. The image was fuzzy and gave way to another: large blue eyes, round face, page boy.

It was no use. He conceded that neither Claire nor Holly was the bitch. He stood before the bathroom mirror.

"You're the bitch, Edward," his reflection smiled.

"I know."

"Yes—"

"And pull out that unsightly hair."

"Which one?" Edward tilted his head, studied his nostrils.

Edward's reflection continued to berate Edward until the hate was expended. Edward retreated to the couch and wondered what to do next. He guessed that most males would resort to drink, but the thought of even a beer gagged him. He still had a headache from the twenty-four hours he was trapped in his basement, so he stared for hours into blackness.

"And this lecture on Yeats's cosmology brings our course to a virtual end," Alex announced. "We have only two remaining days of class. On Friday, I'll have some review material to help you study for the final, which I'm dutifully revising this week."

Jimmy Stubbs and Holly Dish glanced at one another. Jimmy flashed a smirk; his confidence was brimming. Last night, he had found half of the final exam, hand-written, in Alex's office.

"I'll be happy to answer any questions about the exam on Friday, but the review sheets will probably help the most. Good day."

Holly had been postponing her talk with Alex, and she had to act now. She followed him to his office.

"May I speak with you for a few minutes, Mr. Resartus?"

Alex gestured for Holly to sit down. "What can I do for you, Miss —"

"Dish."

"Yes, Miss Dish." Alex smiled at her outfit: sweatpants, tee shirt, and 36-inch bust. He guessed she was a hit at the frat parties, especially when the jocks played indoor football: she was probably the lucky coed who got to be the ball.

"I'm a senior this year, Professor Resartus, and I'm getting ready to pursue a publishing career."

"It's a good field. Profitable, I imagine."

"My advisor recommended I should ask —" Holly feigned a sneeze. She felt ridiculous: a "D" student asking for a recommendation. " — for a letter of recommendation. You're a writer yourself, an actual author really, and your letter would be a wonderful help."

"I'm always pleased to help out students." He opened his grade book. "You're in my 1:00 class, Miss Dish?"

"2:00." Holly's smile froze on her face. You're doomed, she told herself. She had not figured Alex would look at her grades in front of her — she suddenly felt fifty pounds overweight and naked.

Alex studied the grade book. His eyebrows furrowed, his forehead grew lined. He glanced at Holly, then back at the grade book.

Holly forced herself to remain seated. Humiliation's good for character, she told herself. Humiliation's something you know all about.

"Very interesting."

"I know that I haven't taken the final yet. I do want you to know I'm studying very hard for it. Maybe you'd like to wait —"

Alex waved away her protests. "Your grades are, well, extraordinary."

"I suppose you could say that," Holly said, face in her hands.

"No, that's the word exactly."

Holly wondered if she should leave now, or wait for Alex to kick her out.

"I'll gladly write a letter for you, Miss Dish. You've got nearly a high 'B' average."

Holly winced. The guy was sadistic—couldn't he just say "No letter"? She looked between her fingers. Alex was re-checking the grade book, and his face did not have a trace of sarcasm.

"I guess I, I didn't realize."

Alex smiled and pushed the grade book across the desk.

Holly stared and kept her jaw from hanging open. Beside her name were two 'A's and three 'B's. "I guess, um, that's right. I remember now."

"I'll write the letter in a week or so after the semester ends. Just be sure to remind me," Alex grinned. "My memory isn't reliable."

"Oh I'll remind you for sure!" Holly gushed. "And, and thanks so much!"

"Certainly."

She nearly tripped over the wastepaper basket as she hurried from Alex's office. "Thanks again!" she called over her shoulder.

Alex was surprised. Though he rarely remembered students' grades, he was still pleasantly taken aback by Holly's high average. She usually looked so bored in class.

Holly saw Jimmy waiting at the end of the hallway. His smirk told Holly everything. She ran up to him and squeezed him until he coughed.

"You little weasel," she said lovingly.

Jimmy looked away, blushing. "Ya silly bitch."

"How'd you manage to—"

Jimmy clamped a hand across her mouth. "Let's get a coffee."

Jimmy explained how he transformed Holly from a poor to a fine student. He reveled in Holly's full attention and full affection. He wondered if he could spool her now.

"There's not much to do up there in his office, you know, just waiting for the janitor to leave the building. Anyway, I found his grade book about the second or third night I was in there. I didn't even think of changing the grades until I found a pile of blank grade book pages."

"What a break!"

"So I saw that the student names were printed on the left side of the sheet, along with the social security numbers."

"So you copied his handwriting?"

"No. Every student's name is printed out by a computer onto the class list."

Holly remembered: her name was in caps on the left-hand side, followed by her SS number. Then came the righteous row of glorious grades.

"See, what I did was—" Jimmy leaned forward. "—I copied everyone's name and number down, then I took a few of those blank grade sheets. Last week I found a printer in the lab that printed out just like those grade sheets, so I used a word-processing program and entered each student name and number onto the new sheet."

"Color me impressed!"

He laughed. "It was a breeze. Except when I came to your name, I must have…" He raised his eyebrows. "Put in the wrong grades."

"What about your grades?"

"I didn't want to push my luck. I just changed one grade to a 'C'. Resartus is a senile idiot, but he still might remember how bad my grades suck."

Holly was already daydreaming of a publishing gig in Manhattan: a suite of offices, deep pile blue carpeting and leather furniture, private secretary, and a massive oak desk on which rested a computer, TV-sized plasma monitor, and fax/copier/printer.

"Now all I need is that paper," Holly said. She did not see how she could get it from Edward, but she was not worried. She simply had to get it. So she would.

"Can't you write a paper yourself?"

"Sure, if I want to get a 'D' or a 'C' if I'm lucky."

"I can get it for you."

"I didn't know you and Edward are on speaking terms."

"Doesn't matter."

She was starting to appreciate Jimmy. He had brass, and obstacles did not bother him. She rewarded him with a toothy grin.

"You've done way too much for me," Holly said quietly, "and there's no way I can ever pay you back."

Yes there is, Jimmy thought.

"I'll get the paper back from Edward myself."

"But if you need a little help—" Jimmy nodded meaningfully.

"I wouldn't hesitate to ask."

"This is Holly Dish, and I want to apologize."

"For what?"

"What do you think?"

"There's more than one thing to choose from. By the way, how did you know my phone would be back in service?"

"Try to make just a little sense, and we'll go from there."

Edward's forced laugh sounded like a bark. "You play dumb pretty well, but you can't keep up the act. You're really not dumb."

Do I act dumb? she wondered. "I called to apologize, Edward, and I have. I don't know what you're talking about and I guess I don't care."

"You really don't know?" Edward did not believe her, but he wanted to keep her on the line. "You didn't call the power company? The phone company?"

"God you're weird."

"You didn't lock me in my apartment? Didn't push firecrackers down my car's muffler?"

"Fuck off."

"Thanks for calling. Apology accepted."

"Good." She frowned. She was not any closer to getting the term paper about Dylan Thomas — if it existed.

"Let's forget about the whole thing," Edward suggested.

"Forgotten."

Like a chess player, Edward made his move: "I'm having an end of the semester party. Just to show what a good sport I am, I'm inviting you."

"Maybe I can make it. What day?"

Edward had not decided, but Friday sounded good. "I've got a previous engagement on Friday," Holly lied.

"Did I say Friday? I meant Saturday."

"In that case, I'm free. Who are you inviting?"

"Several people. You'll see."

He had not invited anyone else yet, and she knew it. "Maybe I'll bring a friend."

"Sure. How about your roommate Kris?"

"She's too busy writing essays that were due last month. She'll be locked in the dorm until next Christmas trying to catch up."

Chapter Twenty Seven: Finally, a Thank You

Alex had been anxious about the letter, but he did not expect such a quick reply. His heart rate actually increased—a curious vestige of human behavior—when he examined his mail. The return address almost shouted at him: Herman Adler Literary Agency, 54660 Fifth Avenue, New York, New York. Alex wondered if Herman still ran the agency. Was he even alive? Herman was middle-aged, overweight, and sweaty when Alex first met him. Herman took his high blood pressure medication between cigarettes, and he waved off David's warnings about smoking. Alex liked Herman; anybody who cheerily dismissed David, the smug family star, was likable.

"That guy'll be dead soon," David said spitefully after the meeting. On the flight home, David kept talking about Herman's nicotine-stained fingertips and shortness of breath. "Don't ever smoke, Alex." David gripped Alex's face and twisted it toward him. "I mean it. Smoking will kill you, just like it will kill that fat agent."

Alex grinned at the memory, lit a cigarette, and read the letter.

My dear friend Alex:

How good to hear from you! I could scarcely believe my eyes when I saw the outline from you, but then I remembered: you're a special case. Why should I be surprised? I've occasionally wondered about you and what you were doing. I even planned to call you once, but I had a heart attack that very afternoon—I kid you not! And that afternoon was three years ago! I decided you were bad luck, and that I should wait for you to call me (just kidding. I was ordered to not engage in any business lest I suffer stress, and unfortunately as I've grown older I get so agitated over anything). I've just gotten back in a workaday routine in the last eight or nine months.

I'm intrigued by your proposal, and I enjoyed your sample chapters. Actually, parts are as polished as a final draft. You've still got the knack, my boy, of writing some major league work! Some problems, to be sure (seems the doctor's business would not suffer because of his mishap—as a revived corpse, would not the desperately ill seek him out?) but I don't think they are serious and we can work out the thematic kinks and blind spots, of which there are very few to be sure. Send me the manuscript when it's done. Can you get it done in six months? Good, I thought you could.

I won't kid you. Your career does not exist. You will be, as far as publishers are concerned, almost a new author. But such matters are trivial. I'm so pleased you've fought bravely against schizophrenia. You're something of a miracle, my boy. Some schizophrenics suffer debilitating language deterioration as they get older—but then again, you're not really old yet, are you? And as I asserted earlier, you're a special case certainly.

Cheers,

Herman

Alex carefully folded the letter and placed it in his file cabinet. Now he needed blood for energy, blood for endurance, blood for concentration. Edward Head's blood. After he had the blood in capsules, Alex could fly through the manuscript.

He lit another Dunhill and decided to celebrate Herman's letter by writing a page or two. He looked on his desk in the den, but the manuscript was not there. It was not in the living room or bathroom.

Jimmy held his breath when he heard the rattling of the janitor's keys. What was he doing here now? Jimmy wondered. He should be in the other suite. Jimmy cursed silently and scrambled beneath Alex's desk.

The light came on and footsteps approached the desk.

"I'll be damned," a voice said. "There you are, right where I left you." When he realized the voice was Alex Resartus's, Jimmy clasped his hands, closed his eyes, and silently prayed: Please God, protect me from this jackass. I need to graduate, and I won't graduate if I get caught in this office at 11:30 p.m. Professors aren't that understanding.

Alex frowned at the papers scattered on his desktop. He never left papers scattered on his desk. No matter how many he had, he forced himself to sort them carefully and place them in neat stacks. Without this habit, Alex would never find anything.

"Who the hell do they hire these day!" Alex yelled. He never did like the janitor for this building: pony-tailed little twerp, blue shirt bunched around his waist and pants sliding down his hips. He always left the wastepaper basket by the door, and Alex liked it next to his desk. "Can't do the simplest goddamn things right!" He struck the desktop, and the computer monitor did a little dance.

Alex gathered his manuscript, put the wastepaper basket by his desk, and slammed the door.

Jimmy trembled under the desk for ten minutes before gathering the nerve to move. His neck and back were stiff, and he stood up slowly. He swore when he felt something wet.

He had pissed his pants.

Red-faced and wet-crotched, he cracked open the office window and smoked. After five cigarettes, he was calm enough to think about walking to the frat house. He double-checked for cigarette ashes. When his nerves failed him, he had one more cigarette. The lit end of the cigarette fell to the desk and landed atop a sheet of paper. Jimmy instantly flicked the ash with his middle finger. It rolled, a tiny ember, across the desk and disappeared over the edge.

Keys jangled outside the door.

Jimmy had called Holly Tuesday morning and told her to meet him in the union. He sounded upset and refused to talk over the phone.

He sat in the corner, back to the windows. Shoulders hunched and hair uncombed, he looked hung over. He did not look at her when she sat down.

"Hi."

"You won't believe what happened to me last night."

"Then don't bother telling me."

"I have to." He looked forlornly at his coffee cup.

"Cut the drama." Her heart raced. She wanted to pull Jimmy's hair and slap the pout off his little face.

"I was in the office last night, looking for the test. I heard some keys jangling. You know, like on a key ring. I hid under the desk and who comes in but Resartus. He was looking for something, too."

Holly ordinarily would have enjoyed the image of Jimmy Stubbs trembling under a desk. But not today. She was tense, waiting to hear what she dreaded: *I told him you're in on it!*

"What did he say?"

"To me?"

"No, to the walls, you little piss ant."

"What a partner in crime you've turned out to be." Jimmy looked at

Holly with disdain, paused to light a cigarette. "Well, to the walls he said something like, 'Goddammit, who works around here,' and 'I'll rip off his face,' or 'I'll stuff him into the goddamned wastepaper basket. Maybe he'll put it in the right place.' He hit the desk, too."

"He didn't hit you?" She hoped so.

"No. He didn't see me."

"He didn't see — then what happened?"

"Just what I said." He cackled. "He was looking for something, and I guess he was mangled at the janitor. He seemed really mangled about the wastepaper basket being in the wrong place. You know, just stupid stuff like that."

"I should slap the butt off your face for scaring me like that!"

"And just as I was about to leave, I heard the key ring again, but it was the janitor. He was swearing, too. 'Who does he think he is?' and 'I'll tell him to kiss my ass' and so on. I thought, 'I'm screwed!' but he only straightened Resartus's desk and emptied the wastepaper basket. Resartus must have yelled at him about cleaning better."

Jimmy took a long pull on his cigarette and performed a parlor trick: exhaling the smoke through one nostril then the other.

"That was a nice little adventure, but we still need the test. The final exam is on Thursday. That's the day after tomorrow, in case you've lost your calendar."

Jimmy inserted the cigarette into his left nostril. "I've got the test." The cigarette tip glowed, and smoke streamed from his right nostril.

"Sure. The janitor gave it to you, right?"

"Sort of." Jimmy removed a folded sheet of paper from his shirt pocket. "When the janitor straightened up the desk, he must have re-arranged the papers or something. The funny thing is that I messed up the desk. I'd just started looking through the papers, then decided to look in the wastepaper basket when Resartus came in."

Jimmy removed the cigarette from his left nostril and inserted it into the right. "Anyway, there it was on top of the desk. I helped myself to a blank sheet of paper and wrote out the questions."

"You're a genius."

"Don't I get a thank you?"

Holly's eyes narrowed. "Thank you."

"Now we're in a pact. We have to seal the pact by — "

"Fat chance," Holly blurted.

" — by sharing a cigarette." Jimmy removed the cigarette from his nostril and held it, little finger extended, in front of Holly.

"I will not."

"Then you won't see the test."

Holly wanted to scream. But before she could sicken herself with the thought, she took the cigarette.

She coughed and gagged, but she finished the cigarette.

"Want to study together?" He had been daydreaming about an all-night study session: Holly yawns, stretches, and rests her head on Jimmy's lap. Jimmy gently changes positions and rests his head between her breasts.

"No."

He snorted like a petulant twelve-year-old.

She did not look up from the test, but she pointed at her notebook. "You can copy my notes, though."

"You're a real bitch sometimes."

"Thank you for noticing."

Edward had hoped to find Holly in the union, trying to bum class notes from more serious students. He wanted to follow up on their phone conversation and make sure she was attending his party. He had not expected to see her sitting with Stubby Jimmy.

Then it made sense: Stinking Jim had locked Edward in his apartment; Stinking Jim had turned off his power and re-routed his mail. Edward wanted to punch him. But then again, Jimmy was dealing Holly just as he was dealing Holly. Each used any available advantage. All's fair, etc.

What the hell? he thought. Why not invite him to the party and turn the tables on him?

Coffee cup in hand, Edward strode to the table.

Holly saw him approaching. She quickly folded the test and slipped it into a textbook.

Jimmy groaned as Edward pulled up a chair.

"It's you," Jimmy remarked.

"Indeed." Edward glanced at the notes. "Buckling down for Resartus's test?"

"No," Jimmy said. "This stuff is just so interesting that we study it for fun."

"A scholar!"

"Enough, you guys." Holly tried to sound irritated. She enjoyed the sniping: Edward and Jimmy were like two inept roosters strutting to impress the hen.

"I suppose you're ready for the test," Jimmy said to Edward.

"Pretty much."

He winked at Holly. "Quick, Jimmy. What author made stream of consciousness a credible technique?"

To hide his ignorance, Jimmy played dumb. "What's the name of that river, I mean stream?"

"Out of time!" Edward imitated the electronic buzzer on a game show and turned to Holly. "The answer?"

"Stop," Holly whined. "I'm not ready for this."

"Give us the answer," Jimmy ordered.

"I'll tell you Saturday night."

"Saturday?"

"I'm having a party Saturday night, and you're invited."

Holly raised her eyebrows.

"The exam's on Thursday," Jimmy sneered. "Saturday's a little late for the answer."

"If I tell you, will you come to my party? Holly's coming, aren't you?"

Jimmy glared at Holly. "You are?"

"Sure. It's fun to kick back and enjoy a few brews. Besides, the last big frat parties are Friday night."

Edward ignored the barb. "Bring a friend along. I'm supplying the liquor."

Jimmy accepted the invitation. "Now tell me who the author is." When Holly snickered at his bad manners, Jimmy did his best to smile without sarcasm.

"Thanks for the invite. I'll even bring a bottle. Now please tell me."

"Christopher Marlowe."

"You're a sport, Ed Head," Jimmy smiled.

Edward nodded and left the table. He had to invite two more guests.

Chapter Twenty Eight: Joyride

Alex was laboring over a chapter of *My Life as a Dead Man* when the phone rang. He glanced at his watch: quarter to eleven. Who would call at this hour?

"Professor Resartus?" The voice was hard with anxiety.

"I think so."

The laughter was forced, but Alex recognized the voice: the voice of his Savior.

"This is Edward Head. I'm in your 2:00 modern literature course."

"I agree. Do you need an extension on the final paper?"

"No, nothing like that. I'm calling to invite you to a party. A little gathering to celebrate the end of the school year."

"That's very thoughtful." Alex rarely received such invitations, which suited him. But his instincts told him to accept. Fate was dealing Alex a full house. He only had to play his hand shrewdly. "When do these festivities begin?"

"Saturday at eight thirty sharp more or less. Nothing elaborate. Just a few people." Edward could not truthfully call his guests "friends." Perhaps after the party.

"Good. I prefer small groups."

"Then you'll come?"

"I'd be honored."

"Great. I'll give you directions after the final exam."

"On Wednesday."

"On Thursday," Edward gently corrected.

"Of course. I guess I've been working too hard."

"Yes, professor." Edward remembered Alex's minor breakdown in front of Claire and him. "I look forward to seeing you Saturday."

"And I you."

Alex thought longingly of Edward Head's blood. He needed a plan, and he needed it now. His months of scheming were coming to a head. After an hour of pacing and planning, he was tired. He needed inspiration.

He went for a drive.

By 12:45 a.m., Alex had found a target. A new Holiday Inn had been built across town, off 1-55, and the cocktail lounge was already popular. Alex parked at the farthest end of the lot, hidden from view by two dumpsters.

A red pick-up looked interesting, but the door was locked. Alex did not want to risk forcing the car open because it was too close to the entrance. He scanned the other cars.

A new Camaro caught his eye. Alex approached casually. A lovely break, he thought: the driver's side door was open.

He crept into the back and got as comfortable as he could, hunched over behind the front seat. He waited. With nothing else to do, he resumed thinking of ways to murder Edward Head.

An hour later, the driver's door swung open and the driver hesitated — Alex wondered if the driver had somehow seen him. Then Alex heard the scratchings of a stubborn match. A man eased into the car, cigarette in mouth.

The man started, then turned and stared.

Alex smiled dumbly, as if only half-aware that he was caught.

"You made a big mistake." He reached over and pulled up the car thief by the hair. "My name's Wayne," the man announced. "I'm takin' you to the police station. But first I'm gonna pound the shit out of you." The man's breath was aflame with gin.

Wayne's right hand nearly encircled Alex's neck.

"Christ, you're strong!" Alex remarked. Wayne's forearm was thick as a thigh.

"State lifting champ, 2001. I coach at Illinois State part-time." With a grunt, he pulled Alex halfway over the seat.

Alex was amused. Wayne's strength gave him a hint of what his own victims must feel.

"I've never lifted weights," Alex admitted.

"I believe it, you skinny shit. I don't think you could pop a grape." Wayne pulled Alex further. Alex's face was soon on the floor, and his trunk and legs were draped awkwardly across the passenger seat.

"Do you have a gun or knife?" Wayne demanded.

"No, but you can frisk me."

"Are you a faggot?" Wayne roared.

"Afraid to frisk me?"

Wayne started the car and raced the engine dramatically. Over the roaring of the engine, he yelled at Alex. "I'm not gonna take you to the police, you pussy. I'm gonna take you for a rougher ride." He raced out of the parking lot and onto the highway.

Alex pulled himself upright. He settled into the passenger seat and put a cigarette in his mouth. "Got a light?"

"Shut up!"

Wayne slapped Alex, but Alex only smiled, then casually depressed the car's cigarette lighter. He drummed his fingers on the dashboard until the lighter popped back, then lit the cigarette and stared at Wayne.

"What the hell are you looking at?"

"You."

Wayne drove alertly, with his left hand on the wheel and his right hand gripping Alex's collar.

Three miles later, Wayne exited. He turned right and followed a pothole filled dirt road, then suddenly turned left onto a goat path. He drove for a mile and a half down a long-abandoned utility service road. Several times, Wayne gripped Alex's collar harder; he was certain that Alex would panic and attack, or try to flee.

Wayne eased to a stop beside a scum-covered pond. On the pond's weed-covered shore were several rusted "Polluted—No Swimming" signs.

"Get out of the car, faggot."

"What's with all this 'faggot' stuff?"

Wayne pointed at the pond. The moon's reflection had all the greasy colors of an oil slick. "Back in high school, the faggots used to come out here and blow each other. One time a bunch of us on the football team came out here. We made the faggots get on their hands and knees, then we beat 'em like drums." He smiled at the memory. "Ever since then, I don't think anybody's used this pond for anything but dumping."

Alex yawned.

"Two of those faggots tried to get away. They came runnin' up the hill—" Wayne nodded toward a grade thick with weeds—"and got into the car. I about shit. But we lucked out because their car wouldn't start!"

Alex smiled through the smoke of another cigarette. "I can tell that night was the highlight of your high school career. Life has just never measured up since that night, has it?"

"Faggot car thieves shouldn't talk so much. What were you gonna do, drive my car down to Key West and live on the beach with your boy-friends all summer?" Wayne slapped Alex hard, and his hand tingled with satisfaction.

"Ouch," Alex offered.

Offended by Alex's nonchalance, Wayne raised his fist. But before he could launch the blow, Alex slapped him. A sharp schopp! filled the car. Wayne grunted with surprise. The slap hurt.

Wayne swung as hard as he could. Alex did not try to move. The blow landed.

Nothing happened.

Wayne stared. Alex returned the stare, eyes glassy with the excitement of the impending kill.

"Ever been fisted?" Alex whispered.

Wayne tried to open the car door, but Alex slapped him again.

Wayne raised his hands, but he could not block the blows that tore through his inexplicably feeble guard. Wayne could not find his voice to even yell or plead. Or maybe he was screaming and could not hear over the slaps and the pain. He heard only the deafening blows—the sound penetrated his skull, which suddenly felt paper-thin.

He managed to open the door, falling out of the car onto the weeds and dirt. He lie on his back, staring at the stars. The stars were bright, a thousand suns.

Alex gripped Wayne's skull and twisted.

The thousand suns were gone. Wayne's face was mashed into the dirt and weeds. The sensations bewildered him: lying on his back, his face on the ground, he felt his spine twisting and splintering. He tried to move but could move only his toes.

Alex spoke to the back of Wayne's head. "Before I kill you, I want to thank you. You've really helped me with something. Damn it, are you listening?"

Wayne tried to nod.

"When you told me about the car that wouldn't start, you really gave me an idea."

Wayne tried to snort the dirt from his nostrils but found he had no air in his lungs.

Alex parked Wayne's car on the far side of Holiday Inn lot, far from other cars and out of view of the lobby entrance. He strode to his car, whistling "On Blueberry Hill". A couple staggered out of the lounge. They did not look up as Alex got into his car and drove away.

The night air was exhilarating, sweet with spring's bloom. Alex honked at a young couple walking hand in hand down the sidewalk. They waved back. Sometimes, Alex thought, the world and its inhabitants are interesting, even enjoyable. He took advantage of the stoplight to grin at himself in the rear view mirror. His reflection grinned back and ran its tongue across its bloody front teeth.

Chapter Twenty Nine: In Your Pink Sissy Pants

Edward rose from his book-littered kitchen table and dialed again. He had been trying every half-hour, but the line was always busy.

And it was busy again.

Who could she be talking to? he wondered. Probably nobody. She was probably busy with books and notes. Between working and studying, Claire had little time for small talk. Especially with me, Edward thought. But Edward did not taunt himself. He had made a pact with himself: no more taunts, no more self-torture. After four years of textbooks, coffee, porno DVD's and hand jobs, Edward was ready to grip flesh other than his own: he had made a promise to himself, and it was time to act, not whine.

He pushed his literature notes away for a moment and, in a mood of pleasant indulgence, tried to rank Claire and Holly. Who was best? He would take whoever was willing, but what if his plans went beyond his most glorious hormonal dreams? What if he had to choose between them?

Edward dialed Claire's number again. His heart raced when he heard a ring instead of a busy tone, but nobody answered.

"Please. I've got to study." Holly extended her middle finger at the phone.

"So do I!" Jimmy exclaimed. "Listen, I got a copy of the test for us, right?"

Holly re-thrust the middle finger.

"Right?"

"Don't go pooh-pooh in your pink sissy pants."

"The least you can do is take twenty minutes and give me some information from your notes."

"I did! You've called six times in the last three hours."

"Some gratitude."

"Do you know where my middle finger is?"

"In your nose?"

"Fine, fine. What do you need to know?"

For the seventh time, Jimmy asked questions. And for the seventh time, Holly's answers made little sense. They made little sense because Jimmy understood neither the professor's questions or Holly's notes, and Holly understood neither the professor's questions or her notes. She read her notes almost randomly, hoping to stumble into understanding.

"You don't know much more of this crap than me!"

"I would if you'd leave me alone to study!"

"Call him!"

"No."

"You've got to, or we'll both fail!"

"No."

"Did you know I've got the original grade sheet? The one with your name followed by a bunch of failing grades?" Jimmy smiled at her silence. He felt powerful, as he did when he stepped on insects. She hung up, but he did not get angry. He knew she would call him.

"Hi Edward. It's Holly."

"Uh huh."

"Sorry to bother you, but—"

"Not at all."

" —I'm just a little stuck on a couple things from Resartus's class."

"What's the question?" he asked professorially.

"Uh, there's something in my notes," she fumbled, looking at the test. "I mean something I remember Resartus talking about, and it's about the connection between, of the connection of World War I and the pessimism of modern literature."

"Oh sure." Edward's answer took fifteen minutes, and Holly scribbled quickly, occasionally muttering an intelligent "Uh huh." She did not dare pause to shake out her writer's cramp.

"That's really a help, Edward," she enthused as Edward concluded his answer.

"Anytime."

He waited for the next question.

"Well, there's just one other thing I'm confused about." Her question took five minutes, and it made no sense.

"Are you asking about Irish nationalism in British literature?"

She looked at the test question: "Discuss the significance of Irish nationalism in British literature."

"Yeah I guess."

His answer took twenty minutes, and she scribbled each word. Edward knew she was scribbling, so he kindly slowed down near the end of his answer.

Chapter Thirty: Final Rehearsals

The students were tense. Those who had often skipped class knew they were doomed, and they stared into space with the stoicism of a criminal awaiting sentencing. Three members of the baseball team sat in a corner, skimming notes they had bought from a member of the swim team. The swimmer had dropped the class five weeks ago, so the notes were incomplete, but the ball players could not tell.

Holly and Jimmy glanced at one another and nodded. At 7:00 a.m., Jimmy had pounded on Holly's door. Holly answered in a sweat-soaked tee shirt and shorts; she had been doing pushups with the notes between her hands. Jimmy demanded they write the answers before taking the test.

Holly hesitated, and Jimmy smacked his forehead with an open palm. "What's the worry? We have the test, and we've gone over the questions enough to make me puke. Let's get the answers done now."

To cool off, Holly grasped the bottom of her tee shirt and shook it back and forth. Jimmy glanced at her belly: flat, flush, shiny.

"Just take off your clothes and do your jumping jacks, why don't you." Her display of flesh irritated Jimmy. Bitches that tease, he believed, should at least give a finger fuck.

She glanced at her desk clock. "I guess we've got time. How do you want to divide up the work?"

"Huh?"

"Do you want to take every other question, or do you want the first half, or what?"

"You just don't know how to take advantage of this. We'll both do all the questions. We've got time. Then we'll compare the answers, blend the information together, and have even better answers."

"So we'll have identical answers. How will we explain that?"

Jimmy had not considered that.

"Let's just both write our own answers. At least we can help each other out."

They finished at 1:45, fifteen minutes before the test. They slipped their answers into their notebooks. As the students wrote, Holly would write gibberish such as, "We're smarter than all of you!" And when the students turned in their answers, Holly and Jimmy would turn in their pre-written answers.

Alex entered the classroom, tests in one hand and coffee cup in another. He stood in front of his students and did a little bow. "I hope you're looking forward to the test, and I hope you all do well."

A few of the students managed to lift their eyebrows; most stared straight ahead. Edward nodded vigorously. Though he had gotten all "A"'s, Edward had studied hard. He wanted to write a perfect test.

Alex felt terrific. Wayne the weight lifter must have had an expensive vitamin and steroid habit. Alex had bench-pressed his couch this morning, and then his refrigerator. He always could have, of course, but he had never before thought of it. The mastery of weight was exciting. Alex even tossed the fridge into the air several times, as a child tosses a ball into the air.

Seeing the students' anxious faces, Alex could not resist. The students needed some levity. Alex dropped to his knees and, gripping the desk corner with his teeth, lifted his desk into the air. With a jerk of his head, he tossed the desk from his mouth to his left hand. He lightly tossed the desk back and forth, from hand to hand. A few students chuckled, but most were alarmed. Edward broke the tension by applauding. With a flourish, Alex tossed the desk into the air, caught it with one hand, and gently set it back on the floor.

"You folks are too serious," Alex said. "You're about to take an exam, not be murdered."

The students stared at him, stunned, as he handed out copies of the test.

Alex worked on his manuscript while the students perspired over their tests. He occasionally looked up to gauge their progress. Several students were writing quickly, chewing their lower lips. A fat kid flexed his fleshy forehead as a body builder flexes his biceps. Some students had given up and rested their heads on folded arms.

The fourth chapter of *My Life as a Dead Man* was going well; Dr. Dave had crawled from the grave and resumed his practice. All his patients, save the elderly, had abandoned him. The elderly begged him for his secret. He shrugged. He did not have a secret, but he recommended fiber. The IRS was upset: it could not collect income tax from a dead man, yet there he was, earning income and not paying taxes. Furthermore, a liberal Democrat was courting Dr. Dave to join the party.

Alex was writing the first confrontation between Dr. Dave and his mother—she was hoping he would take over her house payments—when the first tests were turned in. Alex glanced at his watch. It was already 3:30. Only twenty more minutes.

Jimmy was among the first to turn in the test, and he waited for Holly to finish her letter to a friend. He stood outside the classroom, blowing his cigarette smoke at the "No Smoking" sign.

Jimmy got impatient and glanced into the classroom. Holly was at Alex's desk. She was performing her Coy School Girl routine: hands clasped behind her back, head lowered, one foot gracefully tracing a circle in front of the other. Coeds sure have it easy, Jimmy mused. They can blame failure on sexism. Or they can turn it all around by acting weak, and expect a favor.

Edward Shithead joined Holly and Alex. Feeling left out, Jimmy entered the room. He wanted to join in the witty banter, but he did not know what to say.

"I appreciate the consideration," Holly said.

"Not at all," Alex said. "Excellent students earn a little consideration."

"See you Saturday," Edward concluded. Alex nodded crisply and returned to his work.

"Coffee's on me," Edward announced.

"Then wipe it off," Jimmy snapped.

Claire was anxious, and she wished she had never called Edward last night. But she felt at her wit's end. She had always submitted to men's wishes: her father's, then her ex-husband's. The result was always disaster. She had just started living for her own happiness, and she would not stop now.

When she saw Edward enter the union with two other students, her anxiety rose and her resolve plummeted. How could she talk frankly in front of strangers?

Edward acted nonchalant. He waved casually at Claire and led Holly and Jimmy to Claire's table.

"Claire Sweet, this is Holly Dish and Jimmy Stubbs."

"Pleased to meet you," Claire said. She felt herself slipping into her chronic pleasantness. She would smile beautifully, listen politely, and speak courteously. And she would say nothing to Edward; he would still nurse the pathetic fantasy that she was interested in him.

Predictably, Claire charmed everyone. Even Jimmy found no fault in her—how could he? She was lovely. She listened to him as if he were worth listening to. And Holly, normally jealous toward willowy figures, found herself liking Claire. Edward reveled in his sudden importance. As the talk progressed, he became fully professorial. Words such as "context," "world view," "deconstruction," and "postcolonialism" rolled off his tongue.

Some time later, Claire found herself saying "Nice to have met you" to the departing three. She was exhausted and wanted to sleep for three days. She wanted freedom from her sickening pleasantness. She slapped her empty coffee cup from the table, and it careened off the wall. Christ, it felt good to be by herself and to hit something.

Then he was back, standing over her.

"Are you all right?"

"Yes." Her drawl was weary, as if powered by fading batteries. Please just leave, she wanted to say. Please just leave forever.

"What's wrong?" Edward placed a fresh cup of coffee in front of her.

"Thank you," she said thickly, trying to sound appreciative. She avoided his gaze, but he was persistent. She turned away, and he moved to the other side of the table to be nearer to her.

"What's wrong?"

"Please just leave me alone." She made herself look at him.

Edward's hopes increased. Could it be, he bravely wondered, that Claire was jealous of Holly? That Claire feared Edward had given her up for Holly? He pushed the idea aside even as he savored it.

"I'm sorry, but I think I've got something to do with you feeling bad." Edward remembered not to grin. It was hard—everything was working out so goddamned well!

"Sort of." How could this kid understand that he simply had a foolish crush on her? "But it's more than you. It's—" She looked away. "I need some time just to myself. I'd rather not talk about it, really."

A thrill shot through Edward's heart. She really did want him! He wanted to bring her hand to his mouth. The drama of the situation became cinematic, and Edward the aspiring movie director imagined what should come next:

Edward: "We've been hiding our attraction for a long time."

Claire: (Now resting her head on his shoulder) "A long time."

Edward: (Resting his hand on her lap) "Our lives are going in different directions, Claire. It's sad, but it's happy too."

Claire: "What should we do?"

Edward (Caressing her thigh) "I'm with Holly too, so I know you can't put up with that forever, but—"

Claire: "But?"

Edward: "We can be together for one night."

Claire: (Pushing herself against him) "Let's do it."

Edward: "You mean—"

Claire: "Spool me, Edward."

Edward fidgeted while Claire looked away.

"If you don't want to talk about it..." Edward said softly.

"Not right now." He's so goddamned dumb, Claire thought. I've dropped enough hints and he still comes sniffing around.

"Okay. I won't push it. But when you said on the phone last night that you wanted to talk to me, I thought it had something to do with us."

Claire said something, but Edward did not understand because her hand was over her mouth.

"What did you say?"

"It has a little to do with us, but it has more to do with me," she repeated listlessly.

Maybe, Edward thought, she feels inadequate. Being older but a freshman. Divorced, starting a new life—maybe she thinks I won't accept her.

"Have I done something wrong?"

"No."

"Let's try this," Edward said briskly. "How about we just put our talk on hold until Saturday?"

"Why Saturday?"

"I'm having an end of the semester party Saturday night."

Claire tried to sound interested. "Who's coming?"

Her question bothered Edward—what did it matter, as long as he was there? "It's just a small party. Those two people you just met, Jimmy and Holly. They might bring a couple friends along. Professor Resartus, too."

Claire nodded.

"Bring a friend over. At least come over and have a few beers. Let your hair down." And your pants, he thought.

She considered the invitation. The professor was interesting, and Holly was cool. What was wrong with a little beer and casual talk?

"Thanks, Edward. I'll be there."

Beer in hand, Edward spent the evening cleaning his apartment. He even tried smoking: he knew that parties featured lots of enthusiastic smoking. The cigarette was terrible, but he kept the pack for his guests.

The odds seemed good: two women (maybe more if they brought a friend) in his apartment and lots of booze. Jimmy was no competition. No, Jimmy was merely a hired hand, a guy sneaky and small enough to attach a lock to Edward's apartment in the middle of the night. Resartus—well, he was interesting, but probably not sexually attractive. Edward would be the evening's star: the guests would enjoy his hospitality, his booze, his wit.

He imagined Holly sitting on the couch. She wore shorts and a sleeveless tee. She was flush with beer and mischief—a sheen of sweat on her upper lip—and she was eyeing him. He sat beside her.

Giggling, she slapped his hand from her neck. As the party got loud and loose, she jammed two bottles of beer in her shorts, took his hand, and led him to the bedroom.

Claire was in bed, the sheet drawn lazily over her midriff.

"Don't you know a conspiracy when you see one?" Claire asked. "We got you drunk so you'd come to bed with us."

Chapter Thirty One: A Conspiracy

Just before the party was to start, Edward judged he had used too much cologne, so he took a quick shower. The air was still florid with cologne, so he took another shower and opened all the windows. A minute after the second shower, he was perspiring.

To further guard against odor, he took another shower and splashed on more cologne.

He was thinking about another shower when someone knocked on the door. "Just a moment," he called. He wiped off the excess cologne and checked the living room one more time: peanuts in bowls, two packs of Arctic Blast cigarettes near the ashtray.

Edward took the stairs in one giant step. He opened the door, welcoming his guests with a rigid grin.

Nobody was there.

His grin was wasted on a squirrel that searched the weedy yard for nuts. Edward threw a stone at the squirrel. It missed by three yards, and the squirrel did not move.

"So that's what you're servin' us. Stewed squirrel." Claire stood by the corner of the house.

"Good to see you," Edward blurted. He meant it: Christ, was she good to see. She wore her customary faded jeans and white blouse. Her wavy hair was in a bun atop her head; a pencil served as the hairpin.

Her elegance was natural. She would be lovely in a feed bag.

"While I was waitin' for you to answer the door, another guest arrived."

Holly appeared, twelve-pack in hand. "Just in case we run out," she announced. Edward nodded and remembered not to stare. Holly wore a bust-and-belly hugging white tee and baggy black shorts. Now she stood beside Claire, and the two looked related: they shared a mischievous smile, one corner of their mouths higher than the other.

"Come in, please." Edward relieved Holly of the twelve-pack, while Claire insisted on carrying in her paper sack filled with ingredients for White Russians.

"White what?" Edward asked.

"White Russians. Booze and milk."

"Huh...well, that's pretty exotic." As he followed them in, Edward allowed himself a small gesture of victory: he thrust his arms into the air like a triumphant boxer.

"When are the other folks comin'?" Claire asked.

"Any time now." He fervidly hoped nobody else would show.

Claire and Holly sat on the couch while Edward made them drinks: a gin and tonic for Holly, a screwdriver for Claire. Edward strengthened each drink by adding two fingers of vodka.

He served the drinks on a tray, and Claire nodded approvingly. "How gentlemanly."

"Wow," Holly said. "This is a strong drink." She squinted, then swallowed half in one gulp.

"Careful honey," Claire cautioned. "Edward's tryin' to get us drunk." She folded her legs beneath her, took a cigarette from the pack on the end table.

"I didn't know you smoked," Edward said.

"Only when I party. Goes down nicely with a drink."

Holly shook her head. "I used to smoke in high school, but I quit when I started running. It really cuts your wind."

Edward sipped his own drink: white wine. He wanted to be relaxed, not drunk. He figured that seduction was easier when only the seducee was trashed.

"So Kris couldn't make it?" Edward asked Holly.

"She's trying to catch up so she can turn in her stuff late. You'd think she'd learn after two years in a row of lowered grades. But she's too busy partying to study during the semester."

"When I was nineteen and twenty," Claire said, "I was working at a K Mart in Atlanta to save money for college. I didn't have the time or cash to party much." She examined her nearly empty glass. "I didn't even know how to party," she chuckled. "When I finally was able to go to school—after a marriage, after movin' to Peoria, after gettin' a divorce—after all that, I get to college and I figure, 'Great, I'll be around people who like books, who like to study, who like to learn.' You know, I'll be around real students."

"Yeah, all three of them," Edward said. Holly stuck out her tongue at Edward.

"Finally," Claire continued. "I'm learnin' how to party." She drained the rest of her glass and lit another cigarette. "I knew I'd like college."

They laughed and Edward rose to get more drinks. Standing in the kitchen, he was woozy. The wine did not cause the wooziness: the company of two attractive women caused it. Maybe Resartus and Stubbs really won't make it, he hoped, and then—who knows? Stretch the party out over the weekend.

"Come on in," Holly yelled.

Jimmy Stubbs stumbled into the apartment. He had already been drinking; he stood unsteadily beside the couch, an unlit cigarette in his mouth.

"I met you yesterday, didn't I?" he asked Claire. He tried to focus his eyes.

"You sure did." Claire lit his cigarette. "My name's Claire Sweet."

"That's right."

"You didn't bring along anybody?" Edward asked.

"Nah. The guys in the frat house are already gone for the summer. They couldn't wait to get outa this town. Can't blame 'em. Not much to do in the summer, unless you're taking classes. But that's not exactly entertainment."

Jimmy began to complain about his advisor, who had demanded Jimmy re-take two business classes this summer. "I'm sick of this place as it is. And to stick around during the summer." He snorted, and the snort turned into a ripping cough.

"Have another smoke," Claire joked.

"In a moment, thank you," he gagged.

"I should have bought more than two packs," Edward remarked.

"I brought some," Jimmy said. "And I congratulate you on your good taste. We both like the same brand." Jimmy tossed his pack of Arctic Blast menthols onto the end table.

"Whoops," Claire said. "Someone else at the door."

"Door's open," Edward said.

Alex Resartus entered. He stood politely inside the entrance, nodding hellos. He looked almost normal, dressed in a nearly-stylish charcoal jacket, white shirt, and black cotton slacks. The only odd touch was the tennis shoes: one black, the other blue.

"Good to see you could make it," Edward said. He extended his hand, then led Alex into the living room.

Alex pushed a lock of hair from his eyes. "I thought I wouldn't make it. My car has been running badly, and on the way over here it died on me. Had to push it for a bit."

"Where is it?" Edward asked.

"In the parking lot for that apartment complex down the road. I think it's called The Village."

"How far did you have to push it?" Holly asked.

"About a half mile, I guess. A few people saw me, but nobody offered to help."

"I think you need a drink," Edward said. "How about a gin and tonic?"

"I'd love one."

Jimmy frowned. He wondered if he could push a car a half mile. Then he remembered Alex's stunt in class this afternoon. "Professor Resartus—"

"Please call me 'Alex'."

"Al, how did you pick that desk up today? By the desk's, I mean with your teeth."

"When I was a kid, my parents took me to the circus. I liked the stunts: high wire walking, trapeze, lion taming, juggling, all that. I liked to imitate them. I couldn't walk a high wire, so I just started juggling things."

"So you learned to juggle furniture?"

"It's easy, really. You just get it balanced. Once it's balanced, it's light." He shrugged and sat down.

"What's this all about?" Claire asked.

While Jimmy and Holly explained Alex's stunt, Edward got more drinks.

Claire was skeptical about the story. "You tossed a desk back and forth?"

"Just like a softball," Holly asserted.

"Prove it!" Claire cheerfully challenged.

"Maybe later," Alex allowed.

After each guest had a fresh drink, Edward proposed a toast. "I'd like to make a toast to Professor Resartus, who has started writing a novel. May it sell a million copies."

Everyone but Jimmy said "Cheers" and sipped their drink. Jimmy was wondering why anyone would want to even read a novel; actually writing one was beyond stupid.

"Why does anybody write stuff anyway?" Jimmy blurted.

"To be elsewhere," Alex instantly answered.

"Far out," Claire remarked.

"It just so happens," Edward announced. "I asked Professor—"

"Call him 'Alex'," Jimmy reminded.

"—I asked Alex to bring along his manuscript. He's going to read a bit from his first chapter for us."

"How wonderful," Claire said. She had been reading *The Best Year of His Life*. She thought it was sick, yet she did enjoy it. "Let's hear some right now."

Jimmy rolled his eyes.

"A little later?" Alex asked. "There's nothing like reading and thinking to snuff out a party before it starts."

"Yeah," Jimmy agreed. "Wait until we're good and ripped. Then it'll be bearable."

Edward winced. But when everyone laughed at Jimmy's remark, Edward laughed too. He fetched more drinks for everyone—the guests had grown talkative and thirsty.

Two hours later, Jimmy was face down on the floor. "What did I say about good and ripped?" he asked the carpet.

Nobody answered.

Claire and Holly were sitting on the floor, backs against the wall. They were speaking low, but animatedly, eyes wide and hands gesturing.

Jimmy studied the women. Girl talk mystified him. He had seen women talk like that before: quiet but intent, graceful yet fervent. What the hell could they be talking about? The only time Jimmy talked to people so intently was when he hated them, or when they hated him.

"What did I say about good and ripped?" Jimmy repeated. He looked to Edward or Alex for a response.

No answer.

Edward was talking almost non-stop; he paused only to wipe spilled drink from the coffee table. Alex sat quietly, nodding, sipping his drink, smoking.

Jimmy coughed into the carpet. All the goddamned cigarette smoke. He retreated into the bathroom and forced open the dirty window. He sat on the edge of the bathtub, savoring the fresh air. After five minutes, he guessed that nobody had noticed he was missing. This party did not have a star, and it was time for a bit-player to take center stage.

Jimmy stomped into the living room, raised his arms, and yelled. "What did I say about getting good and ripped!"

The others blinked at him. Then Edward snapped his fingers. "Right! Alex was going to read from his new novel!"

Alex raised his hands in mild protest. "I don't want to bore you all."

"Yes you do!" Jimmy roared. He shook a bottle of beer, removed the cap. Foam erupted from the bottle and onto his hands and shoes. He finished the beer in four athletic swigs and dropped the bottle. "I will read the novel myself."

Edward glanced at Claire and Holly. Claire was laughing, Holly was shaking her head. Alex handed Jimmy the manuscript.

"First chapter?" Jimmy asked.

"Let's try chapter three," Alex suggested. "Let me set this up. My protagonist is a doctor, Dr. Dave. He died then came back to life, but he doesn't know how or why. Now he's going through the trials and tribulations that protagonists do—in this case, a dead protagonist who's realizing he'll never be accepted by the living."

"Far out," Claire remarked.

Jimmy squinted at the manuscript page until the words came into focus. He cleared his throat, belched, and began. As the story proceeded, Holly killed time by drinking and pretending to listen. Edward and Claire laughed several times.

At one point, Edward laughed as he was swallowing beer. The brew foamed out of his nose. Jimmy stopped reading and asked Edward what was so funny. "I'm not reading this right?" Jimmy challened.

"It's the story that's funny, not you."

Jimmy re-scanned the last few paragraphs. "I don't see any jokes here."

"They're not jokes," Claire broke in. "It's the situation." She turned to Alex. "When the kids get pissed at their Dad for being dead..." She nodded slightly, thinking. "They just want him to go away...like he's supposed to..." The liquor let her forget her polite laugh: her real laugh was a throaty cackle.

"Perhaps the fate of most fathers with young teens," Alex smiled.

Jimmy finished the chapter: Dr. Dave's patience was fraying, and he escaped his family's bewildered exasperation by lying at the bottom of the family pool for an hour. Only the family dog showed concern. She nervously paced the pool deck, and she was soon barking in alarm as Dr. Dave remained motionless on the pool's bottom.

Jimmy bowed as he put down the manuscript.

The audience applauded.

"One thing," Jimmy asked Alex. "How is it that Dr. Dave came back to life?"

"Well, he died and went to hell."

"But he's right back where he was before."

Alex nodded enthusiastically "Precisely. Dr. Dave's hell is his family, his friends, and his work." Alex paused to blow smoke rings at Jimmy. "You see, he thinks he's better than everyone else. He thinks he's so much better that he despises other people. He'd worn out his welcome when he was alive, and most people were relieved when he died. Now that he's back, no one wants him back."

"Far out," Claire whispered.

"Dave's character is established in the first chapter," Alex noted. "He lets his guard down for a moment and says to his brother, 'I'd rather be dead than stuck in this boring town with these dull, demanding, whining people.'"

"I can identify with that," Jimmy announced. "I'm stuck in an empty frat house all summer long in this dirty stinking town." Jimmy's situation angered him, and he crushed an empty beer can between his hands.

"All your frat brothers are gone already?" Alex asked.

"Everybody. It sucks doesn't it?"

"You have a brother named Dave," Edward said to Alex. His tone was nearly accusing. "And your protagonist's name is Dave."

"I don't remember mentioning—"

"In your first novel. It's dedicated to your family, and there's a special note of thanks to your brother."

"What a memory." David had forced Alex to acknowledge him. "Without me," David had exclaimed, "you'd still be the drooling kid in the closet!"

Alex stood. "I've very much enjoyed your company, but I do have to be going. Let me use your phone to call a cab?"

"I'll give you a ride back," Edward insisted.

"No, please. Stay with your guests. Besides, I'd rather have a sober driver, if I may say so." He winked at Edward.

"You haven't done your juggling act yet," Claire protested after Alex phoned a cab.

"So I haven't." Alex faced Jimmy. "May I borrow you?"

"Borrow me?"

"Thank you." Alex gripped both Jimmy's wrists and, like an adult amusing a child, began spinning around. Jimmy ran to keep up, but soon his toes were merely scraping the floor.

During the first three rotations, Jimmy alternately laughed and cursed. The fourth rotation lifted Jimmy off his feet. Soon he was parallel to the floor.

"Spin him faster," Edward urged.

"Fuck you," Jimmy howled. His stomach was queasy, and he was dizzy. The living room became a cylindrical blur; everyone's face was featureless, except for the open laughing mouths. The laughing mouths appeared momentarily, spun away, and appeared again. Soon the room evaporated, and Jimmy could see only Alex's manic grin.

"Look Ma," Alex called. "No hands." He instantly moved his grip from Jimmy's wrists to Jimmy's head. Jimmy's arms flailed uselessly.

"Spin him faster," Holly laughed.

Instead of spinning Jimmy faster, Alex raised and lowered him. Jimmy closed his eyes each time the floor rushed toward him. He heard everybody roaring. Suddenly, Jimmy's perspective was reversed: now it was the ceiling that advanced and retreated, advanced and retreated.

Jimmy heard someone say, "Cab's here." He found himself on his feet, but the room still spun. Claire put a steadying hand on his shoulder and gave him a cigarette.

"Hey thanks for the demonstration!" Edward enthused.

"My pleasure," Alex smiled. He straightened out his jacket and chuckled as Jimmy nearly fell down trying to light his cigarette.

"Yeah that was fucking fun!" Jimmy shouted.

"Hey everybody," Edward laughed, "let's take turns slapping Jimmy."

"Fuck off," Jimmy seethed. He pushed at Edward, who took a step backward.

Jimmy fell, and everyone laughed as Jimmy extended a raised middle finger at Edward. Alex noted that Jimmy looked mad enough to murder Edward.

Outside, the waiting cab sounded its horn.

"Good to see you all," Alex said. "Happy summer everyone. And Ed?"

"Yeah?"

"Happy graduation...you too Holly."

"Thanks!" Edward and Holly called together.

Everyone but Jimmy wished Alex a good night. Jimmy finished off the cigarette in thirty seconds and demanded another. Four cigarettes later, he felt steady enough to walk to the refrigerator for another beer.

"Good thing he didn't let go of you," Holly said. "You'd crash against the wall and be even shorter."

"I was hoping it would stretch me out," Jimmy retorted.

Everyone laughed. Claire pulled a fifth of Old Bushmill's from her purse, uncapped it, and passed it around. Holly did not want to drink it, but Claire playfully gripped her neck and shook her.

Holly took a swig, then two more. She stood up and began spinning round. "I'm Jimmy the Stub," she announced, "and I'm being spun by another man."

"Ha ha ha," Jimmy mocked. But he began laughing after a long pull on the bottle. He rose on confused legs and spun around with Holly. "I'm Holly Dish," he announced, "and I want to sleep with Giant Jim." Jimmy tripped over Holly's foot and they fell laughing on the couch.

Jimmy tried to kiss Holly. She slapped him. He tried to kiss her again and got his tongue in her mouth. She jerked away and wrestled him to the floor.

"What a little creep," Edward remarked to Claire.

"Shut up!" Jimmy managed to retort; he was struggling in Holly's headlock and became dizzy again. "You bitch, let me go!"

"Bitch, eh?" Holly mocked. She grabbed Jimmy's hair and pulled. Jimmy howled.

"Kick his bony ass!" Claire urged Holly.

Jimmy broke free and rolled onto his side to see several shoe tips rocket toward him. After Holly and Claire kicked Jimmy a few times, Edward decided to show his manhood. He picked up Jimmy in a bear hug and dragged him toward the door.

But Edward was nearly as drunk as Jimmy. He misjudged the stairs and fell. Edward slowly realized that Jimmy was underneath him, squirming and swearing. When Edward did not move, Jimmy punched Edward's crotch.

"You ugly pygmy!" Edward yelled. "Get the hell cut of here." He pushed Jimmy up the stairs, slapping him with each step. After a five minute wrestling match, Edward managed to force Jimmy outside. When Jimmy had his back against the car fender, Edward punched him in the nose. He kept hitting Jimmy until Holly came out. She yelled at him to stop.

Edward and Holly went inside and left Jimmy vomiting on his car hood.

Claire, Holly, and Edward laughed about Jimmy for ten minutes. Then Holly sighed. "I hope he can drive home."

"Maybe he'll kill himself," Edward hoped.

"Yeah, himself and maybe someone else," Claire said. She lit the two cigarettes in her mouth and passed one to Holly.

"Why don't you go see if he's all right?" Claire asked Edward.

"Who cares?" Edward sneered. He tried to gather his drunken wits: his plan was proceeding beyond his dreams. He had two drunken and gorgeous women in his apartment.

"The little creep's a lot of fun," Holly said. "We'll need him at more parties, just to humiliate him. Besides, he loves it."

Edward nodded, figuring that being head-locked by Holly was not half-bad. To show he was not completely heartless, he went outside, steadying himself against the wall in the stairway. He stared at his driveway, finally realized that Jimmy's car was gone, and went back inside.

He again misjudged the stairs and fell.

Edward woke on the couch. Pain sliced through his forehead, and he feared he had cut his head on the stairs. But he realized the pain was just a headache caused by too many drinks and cigarettes.

The lights were out, so he turned on the floor lamp and surveyed the room: a few dozen empty beer bottles on the table, three ashtrays filled with butts. The carpet boasted several burn spots. He stood up but could not stop the room from spinning, so he lay back down.

The silence of his apartment mocked him.

He pondered his pathetic failure. He had gotten drunk, he had gotten in a fight with a midget, he had fallen down the stairs and passed out. And the women had left. They probably laughed when they stepped over him.

"Edward the bitch," he muttered, "Edward with the cherry."

He cursed himself until he had to urinate. While gathering his strength to rise, he thought he heard his refrigerator door open and close. Then he was certain he heard light footsteps hurry into his bedroom.

Success! One of the women had crashed in his bed!

Edward stood up. Edward fell down.

He crawled to his bedroom and through the open doorway. The curtains were open, and the vapor lamp across the street illuminated the room. Edward saw two bare legs standing before him. At the top of the legs were watermelon bikini briefs.

"I knew you'd be here," Edward whispered. He gripped Holly's thigh.

Holly shrieked.

"Finally!" Edward exclaimed. "Finally we're alone!" He belched up the taste of beer.

"Oh shit," another voice said. "He woke up."

Now Edward started. He forced himself to stand and flipped on the overhead light.

Holly laughed.

Not knowing what else to do, Edward laughed too.

Claire was in bed, the sheet drawn lazily over her midriff.

"Don't you know a conspiracy when you see one?" Claire asked. "I got you drunk so you'd pass out."

Edward turned to Holly, who was peeling down her bikini briefs with drunken flamboyance.

"I'll flip a coin," Edward said. "Heads I fuck Claire first, tails I fuck Holly first."

"I think you woke Edward up when you were snooping through his refrigerator," Claire laughed.

Holly stretched out on the bed. Claire rolled atop her and licked her neck.

"Can't I please join you?"

Claire paused and turned to Edward. "Leave the room, Edward. Give us some privacy. And turn on your camera, too." She nodded at Edward's mini-cam, standing on a tripod under the window. "I'm giving Holly the most fab fuck of her life—"

Holly drew deeply on a cigar-sized joint.

"—and I want her to have a memento." Claire nibbled at Holly's collarbone.

Edward obeyed, then crawled back to the couch and tried to ignore the rustle of sheets, the laughter and whispers. When he heard Holly urge Claire to use both thumbs, he went outside. He sat on the lawn, coughed his way through seven cigarettes, and fell asleep.

The sound of a car woke him. Edward lifted his head to see Holly's car pull out of the driveway. The headlights hurt his eyes and he turned away.

Claire stood before him.

"I'm sorry we took over your place. We just got too drunk and too high and..." She shook her head and smiled. "You're a dear, Edward. But now you know why you and I can't—you know."

"...Then we're friends at least?"

"What do you mean at least? That's a lot, isn't it?"

Edward nodded.

"I put your camera back in the living room." Claire giggled. "Holly's so stoned and sweet...she wanted to watch the tape right away, but I said we really had to give you back your apartment."

Edward sighed.

"Oh, Holly thanks you for the Dylan Thomas essay—it was on your dresser. She took the original and put the photocopy in your desk."

"I'm glad she remembered." Edward frowned: he had dreamed of spooling Holly while she read the essay.

"I read some of it. The part about 'Tickled By the Rub of Love' was a turn on. It helped Holly come."

Edward lowered his head onto his folded arms. He was thinking of asking Claire to bed anyway. Just close your eyes, he imagined telling her, and pretend I'm a homely flat-chested girl.

When he looked up again, she was gone.

Chapter Thirty Two: Edward, betrayed

Edward lay on the grass for another minute or another hour: he was not sure and did not care. He rolled over. The moon was bright, and the crickets sang to it. He imitated the crickets as he walked slowly back inside.

The apartment was worse than he remembered. The air stank of cigarette smoke, and empty beer bottles were stacked like kindling wood in the middle of the room. An overturned ashtray was on the floor; cigarette butts and ashes had sprayed in all directions. A large wet spot was beside the couch. Edward wondered if Jimmy had pissed on the floor.

Edward urinated, gargled, and washed his face; he saw a new pimple was attempting a coup of his chin. He entered his bedroom. The bed was hastily made. The pillows were on the floor. Dispirited, he fell on the bed and stared at the ceiling. He kept seeing Claire, hunched down, her face between Holly's thighs. He tried to banish the image, but it grew more vivid. Now Claire was on top of Holly. Holly's legs were drawn up, her tensing feet on Claire's shoulders.

Edward was so engrossed by the image that he did not hear Alex enter the room.

Fleetingly, Edward wondered if he were turning queer — what was a man doing in the image? Then he realized that he was not dreaming.

He sat up. "Hi professor. Are you — what's wrong?"

"Nothing. Just out and about."

"That's good. Hope your car's all right." Edward felt odd sitting on his bed while a man stood over him. "Want some coffee?" Edward hurried into the kitchen and turned on the range.

"No thanks." Alex said, following Edward out.

"Excuse me, professor."

When Edward opened the refrigerator, Alex did not move. Edward had to squeeze his arm through the narrow opening to get some non-dairy creamer. "How about some tea?"

"Not yet." Alex blinked several times, then motioned with his head toward the living room. "I left something in here. Can you help me look for it?"

"Sure." Edward wondered why Alex was wearing rubber gloves. "What, did you lose a manuscript page?"

"Yes. That's right. I wonder if it got pushed under the couch." He studied Edward, as if expecting an answer.

"Hope not." Edward went into the living room, got on his hands and knees, and tried to see under the couch. "It's too dark to see anything. Let's move it away from the wall."

"Good idea."

When Edward rose, his head struck something. Must be the coffee table, Edward thought.

"Sorry old sport."

"I'm okay." But he wondered why Alex had not warned him. He rose and again hit his head. Edward groaned—the pain was intense, a white-hot line coursing down his spine. He tried to stand but fell against his mini-cam. The mini-cam teetered on its tripod, then slowly tipped over.

Edward tried to touch his head, but his hand was palsied and an unruly finger poked his eye. "Goddammit my head hurts."

Edward looked up. He wondered how he had struck the coffee table—it was across the room. Then he wondered why Alex was handing him a beer. A beer was the last thing he wanted.

"No, I'm not up for drinking a beer."

"I want you to know that I've come to like you in a manner of speaking, and to—" Alex tightened his grip on the bottle. "—to appreciate the quality of your mind."

Jimmy's right, Edward thought. Resartus is a flake. I wish he'd just bag it.

The bottle struck Edward's temple, and Edward covered his head with his hands, which were suddenly blood-streaked. The bottle—or was it a second bottle?—struck his hand, and his arm was icy-hot. Again the bottle struck his head. He tried to protect himself, but the bottle was everywhere. It hit his nose, his collarbone, his kneecap.

"You fucking maniac!" The bottle struck his mouth.

"Quiet."

Edward was enraged: Resartus had betrayed him. "Why are you—" The bottle crushed his nose.

"Sorry," Alex laughed. He was not sorry—he was gleeful. Each time he struck Edward, his elation grew. Each strike was a vindication of his patience, his persistence, his planning.

Edward's inner voice kept ranting at Resartus: you stupid bastard, you stupid crazy bastard! What's wrong with you!

Edward crawled backward but was stopped by the wall. He managed to sit up and cover his head, fearing more blows.

But the blows had stopped.

"Fuck my teeth are broken."

He felt enormous pressure on his head. He tried to resist, but his head seemed to be separating from his body. An amber explosion radiated from the center of his brain. The amber was blinding, and Edward closed his eyes. But the blinding amber was still there, and he wondered how he could see through his eyelids.

Just as Edward felt he could endure no more pressure on his head, the pressure lifted. Startled, Edward opened his eyes, but saw only blackness.

Alex was pleased. He had been careful to avoid cutting the body too much. When one bottle broke, he picked up another rather than risk cutting Edward deeply, then quickly twisted Edward's head full-circle, quickly killing him.

Edward's corpse slumped against the wall. One bloodshot eye studied the ceiling, the other studied the floor. Alex wanted to bite Edward's throat, but he had waited too long to get sloppy.

He allowed himself a little taste by licking Edward's bloody mouth. The blood was fabulous, more robust than he had expected. Alex celebrated his success with a couple Dunhills.

Now Alex drained the body: he pinned Edward upside down upon the wall--spikes driven through his hands and feet--and carefully collected Edward's blood from the slashed throat. Normally, the chore would have irritated him, but not this morning. The blood filled the jugs quickly, and he placed them in a grocery sack.

When the body was drained, Alex pulled it off the wall and dropped it in the middle of the living room. He relaxed for a while with a couple more smokes. Alex then placed the knife inside the now-empty bottle of wine cooler that Jimmy Stubbs had brought to the party.

Grocery sack in his arms, Alex locked the door and silently departed. He hurried across the yard and down the pitch-black alley: last night, he'd used a pistol bb gun to knock out the alley's few lights. In five minutes he reached his car, which last night he had parked at the unlit end of the apartment complex parking lot.

Alex hid the jugs in the spare tire well and walked across the lot. He crossed Locust, Cherry, then disappeared into the cornfield. He was home in forty-five minutes. Alex stood on his back porch and faced the east. A faint rose tinge filled the horizon, and a few morning doves pecked at the lawn.

Inside, Alex pulled a pint bottle of Edward's blood from his pocket. He drank daintily, one finger extended. Warmth coated his stomach and spread upward to his chest.

He noticed a crack had spread across the ceiling. "February of 1995," he remarked, as if regaling a guest. He laughed at the memory. Alex had tied a fat guy upside down in the attic, but the ropes around the fat guy's ankles slipped. Fatso fell to the floor, cracking the plaster. The impact had knocked out Fatso's front teeth.

"Memory!" Alex marveled. "Wonderful memory."

After another swig of blood, Alex called a garage for a tow truck and left his message at the beep: "My car, the pale yellow Chevy, license number 2324-12H, small rust hole in the rear left fender and a stain in the passenger front seat — it was coffee from Zip Quick, a sixteen ouncer! — is in the Village parking lot, far northwest corner. My name is Professor Alex Resartus. Please tow it to my address, 1403 W. 86th." Alex paused. "Please do it quickly. Cabs are expensive. Many thanks."

Holly Dish stood before her mirror and pulled her wet hair into a ponytail. The water from her fifth shower dripped to the floor and formed a puddle.

"Why," Holly asked of her reflection, "did you do it?" She crossed her arms across her breasts and closed her eyes. She had cried hard on the way home, cried hard again in the shower. Her tear ducts were dry, and her jaw and face ached.

Holly took a sixth shower. She had reduced a new bar of soap to a sliver, and now the sliver melted against her belly and thighs. She still did not feel cleansed, so she turned off the hot water and shivered under frigid water.

Worse than a woman's mouth on her mouth, or on her breasts or belly, was the memory of poor, stupid Edward: when Edward flipped on the light, Holly had laughed. The absurdity of the situation inspired Holly further, and soon she began wailing Peel's "I'm Prettier on the Inside."

But when the booze wore off and Claire was asleep, Holly began trembling. She dressed in a panic, hopping about on one leg, and ran out of the apartment. She could not fully grasp what she had done, and she could not formulate a consistent emotional response to it: she was simultaneously elated and sickened. The more she thought about it, the more alarmed she grew.

Now Holly stepped out of the shower and faced the mirror again. Her lips were blue from the cold water, but she had gained control of herself. She thought of Edward again, of how she had been a slutty party favor and laughed in his face. Holly remembered what being laughed at felt like. And she was ashamed.

Chapter Thirty Three: Elsewhere

Each time a car passed his house, Alex woke. Where in hell was the tow truck? He glanced at the clock — 9:40 a.m. — and again called the garage. The manager explained that the truck's towing cable was being repaired, but he assured Alex that the truck would tow his car by the afternoon at the latest.

Alex turned on the radio, reached for a cigarette. Last night, he forgot to bring his Dunhills to the party and had to suffer those Arctic Blasts. Now he remembered how many Dunhills remained: sixteen. A useless fact for most, but a triumph for Alex: his memory was better already. He relished his memory as a paraplegic relished the sudden use of his limbs.

He put the Dunhill in his mouth and struck a match.

The cigarette remained unlit. His eyes narrowed. The cigarettes...the party.

The murder investigation would be thorough, though Jimmy Stubbs was the obvious suspect: an established dislike of the victim and lots of drinking. Jimmy had remarked that his frat house was empty except for him. He had no alibi. And tonight, Alex would smear a bit of Edward's blood on the dashboard of Jimmy's car. The cotton gloves — blood on the fingertips — in Jimmy's car would make the herring most red indeed.

Everything pointed to Jimmy...everything except the Dunhills. This morning, Alex had smoked during and after bleeding Edward Head, and the four Dunhill butts were in the living room. The guests might recall that Alex had borrowed cigarettes all night — so where did the Dunhills come from?

"Well, bucko," Alex muttered to himself. "This is a problem that just can't wait until nightfall."

Alex was relieved that the morning had turned darkly overcast: no sunlight to contend with. He put on a fake beard and ponytail, then a hat, sunglasses, and high-collared jacket. He squeezed on a new pair of rubber gloves and stuck his hands in his pockets. For the second time this morning, he hurried through the cornfield with preternatural speed to Edward's apartment.

"Edward? Dammit Edward let me in! I have to talk with you."

Holly banged on the door again. Edward did not respond, and she swore under her breath. After more knocks and calls, she walked down the stairs. The door was locked, and she yelled at Edward to open the fucking door. Her volatile emotional state erupted, and she kicked the door repeatedly. When her right foot got sore from the kicking, she used her left, rearing back and assaulting the door like an enraged Karate master.

"Lemme in Edward!" Holly demanded, pausing to catch her breath. She resumed kicking and the doorjamb split, allowing her to walk in.

"Thanks a lot Edward!" Holly called, stepping inside. "Just make me stand out there like that. Let me apologize! I thought we were—well, I didn't think we were enemies!"

She guessed Edward was asleep, so she tiptoed inside to turn on a table lamp. Halfway to the lamp, she tripped and fell. For a moment, she thought she had tripped over a pile of clothes.

The corpse did not resemble a corpse. In the poor light, it resembled laundry twisted into bloody lumps. The purple face looked artificial, like a horror movie mask. The slash in the throat looked like a toothless horror movie shriek.

Holly wobbled to the phone and stared at the handset. Fleetingly, she forgot why she needed a phone.

The handset trembled. Holly had to grip it with both hands.

"Holly?"

She shrieked.

"It's all right," Alex said, standing in the dark doorway.

"God I didn't recognize you!" Holly ran to Alex and embraced him.

Alex kept Holly's face pressed to his chest as he scanned the room for the Dunhill butts. He saw them in the ashtray on the coffee table.

"He's so, he's so pretzeled," Holly stammered.

Alex had to work fast. He would cut Holly's throat and drop her body atop Edward's. Perhaps little Jimmy would serve two life terms.

"Who could, could do that?"

"Jimmy?" Alex asked mournfully.

"Oh God! God, they had a fight last night and, and—when did you grow the beard?"

"I don't like to shave on weekends."

Holly's stomach cart wheeled.

He pulled off the beard and fake ponytail. "Goddammit."

"--What?"

"Why did you have to show up here, at this—" Alex rolled his eyes. "Never mind. Pick up those Dunhill cigarette butts."

"You—?"

"Just pick them up." Alex pointed at the ashtray.

Holly backed to the coffee table. The ashtray was old fashioned: heavy glass, octagonal, with sharp corners.

"Quit stalling."

Holly stepped forward like a pitcher and threw the ashtray at Alex's face. The ashtray struck his nose.

"Now the butts are all over the carpet." Alex picked them up and ate them. "Which reminds me." Alex broke into a bleating laugh. "Get it? 'Which reminds me.'"

"Which reminds me," Holly repeated mechanically. She glanced at Edward's corpse and wondered how much it hurt to be murdered.

"Yes, which reminds me that I've got sixteen Dunhills left." Alex tossed one to Holly. It struck her shoulder, and fell to the floor. Alex lit his and waited for Holly to join him.

"Be a sport. Smoke with me."

Holly picked up the cigarette. "Trendy brand."

"How so?"

"That, that woman who was here last night—"

"Yes, I remember. Claire. She's quite lovely."

"—she started smoking these after she met you."

"Then why didn't she offer me some last night?" Alex asked, feigning offense.

"She forgot she had them. She got them out of her car after the party broke up. We must've smoked half the pack."

"Where are they?" Alex demanded.

"In Edward's bedroom."

"His bedroom?" Alex raised his eyebrows.

"Things got a little out of hand." Keep talking, she thought. "We had too much to drink, and then Claire asked me to rub her shoulders—"

Alex chortled. He had come over here for nothing! The cops would not have distinguished between the Dunhills in the bedroom and the Dunhills in the living room.

"—and then she slipped her hands inside my tee shirt. And then—"

Alex waved away her explanation. "I won't tell a soul," he smiled. "Sappho looks upon you with approval and gratitude from above."

"—What?"

"Sappho, the lesbian poetess and libertine." Alex guffawed. His rising sense of invincibility made him whimsical.

"Lesbian poet..." Holly faltered, wondering what to say next. Keep him talking, she again told herself, keep him...

"Now light up that cigarette, you shameless bohemian. We can dedicate your final cigarette to your final lover, Claire Sweet. And you'll die as an unknown martyr to the love that dares only whisper its name." He grinned. "That's quite a romantic death, isn't it?"

"Can I have a drink with my cigarette?"

"Of course."

She opened the refrigerator, removed a carton of milk. "Want some?" She felt absurd serving her murderer, but she could think of nothing else to do or say.

"Hell yes." Alex snapped his fingers. "Which reminds me! My brother always told me to drink milk. Thought it was good for bone growth, but we now know there's lots of fat in even part-skim milk." He bleated.

She filled two glasses with milk.

"Don't waste time trying to hit me with the glass. It doesn't hurt." To prove his point, he picked up an empty beer bottle and broke it across his forehead. "Ha!" Alex roared, patting his forehead. "No blood! Good trick huh?"

Holly dropped her glass. She squatted in the puddle of milk and broken glass. Fear numbed her, and she could not concentrate on an escape plan.

Alex looked at Holly as a doctor looks at a patient.

"How's your health?"

"Good," Holly whispered. "I've been working out for, for several years."

"I've spent the last few years trying to improve my health, too."

"Quit mocking me."

"I'm not. I try to ask all my victims about their health."

"Victims..." She nodded, glanced at Edward's corpse.

"The woman in Chicago — you know, the one I murdered during our field trip? — she was healthy, though I should've checked her out more. Her boyfriend or husband or whatever was healthy too, I think. So was the weight-lifter they'll never find."

"And Lori Lesterson?" Holly ventured.

"Very. Young ones usually are." He paused to drink his milk. "I cut off her hand."

"Why?"

"A red herring. Police and the press love it when they think they have a case of devil worship. The public can't get enough of it." He finished his milk. "My latest red herring will involve Edward's blood in Jimmy's car." He snapped his fingers. "Hey! Your blood too! Little Jimmy Stubbs better luck out with his court-appointed lawyer."

Holly tried to rouse herself from her inertia, but shock had rendered her passive. She simply stared at the floor, waiting for something to happen. Will he break the glass against my face? she wondered.

Alex's suddenly labored breathing made Holly looked up. Alex's eyes had turned glassy, and he suffered a thick coughing jag.

Animal instinct replaced human fatalism. Her muscles contracted, and she scrambled to her right. She was instantly half way across the living room, her limbs weightless with adrenaline.

Alex took two steps in pursuit and vomited a stream that turned from white to pink to red.

Holly squealed.

"That *idiot!*" Alex bellowed. He vomited again, the red darkening to black. Bloody foam erupted from his ears and nostrils. He stumbled forward and pushed Holly against a wall. He was about to twist her head from her torso, but he vomited again. Holly saw her chance and ran past Alex outside to her car.

As Holly opened her car door, Alex scrambled after her. Bloody snot spilled from his nose. As he gripped her by the neck, he tried to blink past the fluid from his suddenly runny eyes.

"He was allergic to milk!" Alex roared, spraying Holly with phlegm and blood. She futilely tried to spin away, feeling like a child restrained by an adult. "Of all the fucking things that've happened to me!"

"Let go of me!"

Alex punched at Holly, but he could not see well, and Holly ducked. The blow shattered her car's side window. He reared back for another punch.

With her fingers, she jabbed at Alex's failing eyes.

He gripped Holly's jaw and twisted her face toward his. With his free hand, he wiped at his eyes. His vision cleared enough to see Holly's tear-filled eyes shine a brilliant blue in the sunlight that escaped the morning's charcoal clouds.

Alex's neck sizzled like frying bacon. He turned and bellowed curses at the sun. Smoke rolled off his face. He shielded his eyes and waited for the searing white spots to fade from his vision.

When he could see again, Holly was gone.

The rubber gloves had melted into Alex's hands, and his shoes smoked.

He could think only of getting to his car, where he could recover with Edward's blood and escape to...somewhere.

Elsewhere.

The Village parking lot was wet from the morning's mist, and the sun's reflections in the many puddles blinded him. He ran recklessly, arms outstretched. The car would be in the corner of the lot, he knew, the blood still safe in the trunk.

His car was gone.

He turned in a circle several times, searching for his car as if it were a run-away dog. Then he saw it—a tow truck was pulling it away. Alex tried to shout at the tow truck driver, but the sun had seared his lips together.

The sun was intolerable. He felt trapped inside a furnace, and the roar of blood in his head was the roar of the furnace.

As Alex ran toward the tow truck, a car turned into the lot. The car radio was at maximum volume, and the driver was screaming along with The Knot's "Ugly Girls." He saw Alex too late.

The impact flipped Alex over three times, and he skidded several feet into the apartment's swimming pool.

The water churned and steamed.

As Alex settled to the pool's bottom, the water became cool and quiet. It's better down here, Alex thought. I'll stay here until the sun sets because it's, it's, because the sun's so goddamned hot that I'm hallucinating and I swear I just saw my ear lobes float away.

David's voice reverberated through the pool: "You're losing the center."

Alex wanted to tell David to shut up, but his lips were still sealed. He could not tear them apart because his fingers had melted together into a fleshy paddle.

The driver dove in. He kept trying to grab Alex, but Alex thought the driver was David. Alex flailed and growled, furious that David could see him in such a state, and he struggled to reach the pool's cool bottom, to a pale blue elsewhere.

Suddenly, there was no need to struggle—Alex had settled on the pool's floor. Alone in the pale cool blue, he watched David float upward to the rippling backlit surface, then realized it was his own trunk floating upward. Down on the pool's cool floor, a gentle surge of water rolled Alex's head over and for a second Alex could see drowned insects trapped in the pool drain. But only for a second.

Alex's boiled flesh separated from his bones.

Alex's trunk bobbed on the water's surface for a moment before bursting into flame. Foul black smoke, as if from burning rubber, spiraled skyward and the driver retreated to the shallow end. The rest of Alex floated to the surface and flamed.

Hysterical, the driver tried to swim back to the body, but Holly jumped into the pool and held him back.

"How was the funeral?" Holly scraped. The medication had dried her throat, and speaking was painful.

"Too long. Everybody and his brother wanted to say something good about him. But he was a creep. He murdered Edward Shithead and they act like it's—" Jimmy smirked. "—like it's the price of, uh, the cost of genius or something."

"You're kidding."

"I'm exaggerating a little, but I swear there was one guy who said that Resartus was a special man afflicted with a lousy mental condition, that the mean brother had twisted him into a mental case, and that both deaths were tragedies."

"That was Resartus's agent," Claire Sweet noted.

"When's Edward's funeral?" Holly asked.

"There isn't a funeral," Claire answered. "I talked with his mother. She was real nice and said the family didn't believe in funerals. They're going to cremate the remains without a service."

The three made small talk for a few minutes. Claire asked if Holly needed anything. Holly shook her head. She was anxious for Claire to leave; she imagined Claire was trying to see through her nightgown.

Claire patted Holly's hand. Holly closed her eyes, and Claire silently departed.

Holly opened her eyes. Jimmy was staring at her, as if trying to see through her nightgown.

"You too," she accused.

"What?"

"Nothing. I mean—" She pretended to be confused. "I'm sorry. I'm just tired."

"I'll visit you tomorrow. Want me to bring anything?"

Holly shook her head.

Jimmy was halfway out the door when Holly called him. "On second thought, I guess you can bring me something."

He nodded, trying to hide his impatience.

"Bring me a cola and candy bar."

"Okay," he agreed. "Pay me later for the stuff."

The dorm's resident assistant came in and asked if Holly wanted anything. "A little milk might help my throat."

Holly smiled wistfully—the night of the party, Edward had mentioned he was allergic to milk: it made him violently ill. Claire had consoled him because he would not be able to drink her famous White Russians. Claire had brought all the ingredients, including the milk and whipped cream. She winked at Holly and said, "All the more for us."

Around 2:00 a.m., Jimmy Stubbs broke into Edward's apartment. Except for a photocopied form from the county Sheriff—"Do Not Disturb This Property or This Property's Contents Under Threat of Criminal Prosecution"—the apartment looked the same as when he had left, three nights earlier: empty bottles, filled ashtrays, and CD's scattered along the floor.

Jimmy picked up the fallen video camera, and a red light on the camera began blinking. Jimmy removed the camera's videocassette and put it into Edward's battered VCR.

The scene was confusing. A couch rested on a wall, and a movie poster was on the ceiling. Still, the room looked familiar.

Jimmy turned and saw the movie poster behind him. He looked back at the screen and realized that the camera had been filming on its side.

There was no sound and no action. Jimmy was about to turn off the VCR it showed a person stuck on a wall.

"You're crazy. You're really crazy," Holly accused.

"No I'm not. Just watch the tape and you'll see."

"No!" Holly's eyes bugged.

"Then you can't call me crazy." Jimmy smiled and offered her a beer.

They watched the tape. Holly remained stone-faced throughout.

"You're a rock," Jimmy marveled.

"What was the name of Resartus's agent?"

"Huh?"

"His agent," Holly snapped. "What was the name of Resartus's agent?"

"Who cares?"

"Find out."

Jimmy wanted to say, "Find out yourself" but Holly's firmness surprised him.

Holly grabbed Jimmy's ear. "Find out now! He was at the funeral, so go ask the funeral director. And get his phone number, stupid. Hurry!"

Jimmy paused to retrieve the tape, but Holly bellowed at him to quit wasting time. He called an hour later with the agent's phone number, then demanded the tape's return.

Holly hung up and called Claire. Claire arrived in twenty minutes.

Claire and Holly watched the tape twice. Claire cried and had to have a drink. After the third White Russian, she asked Holly if she would turn the tape over to the police.

"Of course not."

Claire raised her eyebrows.

"This tape—" Holly held it in the air delicately—"is a gold mine."

"You're sick."

"I'm a future millionaire."

"How?"

Holly told her. Claire started crying again. She drank more, and at one point tried to get Holly back into bed.

"Help me, and I'll sleep with you. I swear."

"Liar."

"I need a ghostwriter."

"Nobody will publish it. It's beyond belief."

"Why? Lots of people are nuts enough to think they're vampires."

"I don't think a publisher would buy it."

"I talked with Resartus's agent this morning. He's interested. I told him that Resartus was a pyromaniac who killed Edward and set himself on fire. What a loon...he really thought he was a vampire or something."

"Ridiculous."

"All right." Holly took Claire's drink from her hand and swallowed half with one gulp. She returned the drink, stood, and pulled her baggy shorts up, crotch-tight. "I'll find another partner to share my money with."

Claire closed her eyes. The White Russians had done their magic, and her imagination created a collage: Holly's thighs, a check with several zeroes, Holly's belly, another check with several zeroes, Holly on her back.

"No you won't," Claire insisted. "I'm your partner."

Victorious, Holly smiled. She accepted a fresh drink from Claire and allowed Claire to demurely kiss her cheek. When Claire brushed a hand across Holly's navel piercing, Holly giggled.

That evening, Holly stopped by Jimmy's to gloat.

"You got some nerve stealing that tape," he complained as she breezed into his room.

"I'm a rich young woman, Mr. Stubbs. Congratulate me." She told him the plan.

"Sounds like I'm going to be rich too." He pulled a sheet of paper out of his desk. She tried to grab it, but he laughed and held it behind his back.

"You wouldn't dare," she shouted.

"I wouldn't dare!" Jimmy gleefully mocked.

"No!"

He kept laughing. Holly resigned herself to the inevitable. "How much of the cut is that grade sheet worth to you?"

Jimmy brought the grade sheet back into view. He scrutinized it as a museum curator scrutinizes a painting. "It looks pretty valuable."

"How much?"

Jimmy put the grade sheet back in the desk. "I'll be reasonable. Seeing as I could get you in all kinds of trouble—a potential best-selling author kicked out of school for changing a grade. That's not the publicity you want."

"But you changed your grade too!"

"I'm not the one writing a book."

"Pungent butt spray!"

"I'll take twenty five percent."

"No! I'll risk getting kicked out of school."

Jimmy pulled something else from his desk. "This is an essay written by the poor deceased Edward Head, but I'll bet that an exact copy was turned in with your name on it."

"When did you get that?"

"When I got the snuff film out of Edward's apartment."

"I'll agree to twenty percent."

"Twenty five. And if you're still unreasonable—" He shrugged. "Did I tell you what else I found?"

Holly's eyes narrowed.

"I found a second video tape in Edward's bedroom. It stars you and Claire."

Holly covered her face with both hands, silently cursing herself. She was so drunk and stoned that night, she'd forgotten to bring the tape.

"You surprise me," Jimmy smiled. "I'd have guessed you for a top, but Claire was the top, and you're her submissive little bottom."

"God you suck," Holly said through her hands.

Jimmy began picking his nose. "Notoriety is good for an author, but..." He examined his finger.

"Okay. Twenty five percent."

"Agreed."

She slapped him.

"What the hell is that for?"

"You're the most odoriferous buttspray ever."

Jimmy stopped picking his nose so he could enjoy a big laugh. "You're an odorif—uh, you're a stinking grease spot too."

www.ingramcontent.com/pod-product-compliance
Lightning Source LLC
Chambersburg PA
CBHW020607250626
47154CB00004B/1398

* 9 7 8 1 9 3 2 4 8 2 0 2 7 *